PUSHING BACK THE DESERT

OPERATION AJAX

Inspired by True Events

By

Gordon Zuckerman

Book 1 of the New Sentinels Trilogy

Gordon**Zuckerman**.com

v24-0429

Table of Contents

AUTHOR'S NOTE VI

CAST OF CHARACTERS VII

PROLOGUE IX

PART ONE "SURFACING THE PROBLEM" 13

CHAPTER ONE "THE RETREAT" 15
CHAPTER TWO "TROUBLE IN TEHRAN" 20
CHAPTER THREE "JACQUES CALLS SAM" 23
CHAPTER FOUR "DAVID TO LONDON" 25
CHAPTER FIVE "MIKE TO NEW YORK" 29
CHAPTER SIX "MIKE AND CECELIA RETURN HOME" 31
CHAPTER SEVEN "MIKE TO WASHINGTON, D.C." 35
CHAPTER EIGHT "MEETING ROGER MALONE" 38

PART TWO "PUSHING BACK THE DESERT" 43

CHAPTER NINE "IN THE BEGINNING" (50 YEARS EARLIER) 45
CHAPTER TEN "HARSHIM NARAGHI" 48
CHAPTER ELEVEN "IN PURSUIT OF KATE" 52
CHAPTER TWELVE "THE RIGHT FIRST IMPRESSION" 56
CHAPTER THIRTEEN "PLAYING ON THE BOYS' TEAM" 60

PART THREE "THE THIRD ALTERNATIVE" 63

CHAPTER FOURTEEN "THE DAVID MARCUS PROBLEM" 65
CHAPTER FIFTEEN "BIRTHING THE THIRD ALTERNATIVE" 69
CHAPTER SIXTEEN "THE ANGLO-AMERICAN CONSPIRACY" 74
CHAPTER SEVENTEEN "MAKING THEIR CASE" 77
CHAPTER EIGHTEEN "KERMIT AND THE CIA DIRECTOR" 82
CHAPTER NINETEEN "AYATOLLAH KHASANI" 84

PART FOUR "NARAGHI-ROTH" 89

CHAPTER TWENTY "MR. TOM" 91
CHAPTER TWENTY-ONE "MR. TOM RETURNS TO PARIS" 95
CHAPTER TWENTY-TWO "PIERRE TO AHVAZ" 99
CHAPTER TWENTY-THREE "CONGRATULATIONS" 102
TWENTY-FOUR "NARAGHI-ROTH" 105
CHAPTER TWENTY-FIVE "GETTING UNDERWAY" 107
CHAPTER TWENTY-SIX "THE CHRISTENING" 113

PART FIVE "THE NEXT GENERATION" 119

CHAPTER TWENTY-SEVEN "SAM NARAGHI MEETS JACQUES ROTH" 121
CHAPTER TWENTY-EIGHT "FINDING SALLY" 127
CHAPTER TWENTY-NINE "ATTACK AT BET-DEGANIA" 134
CHAPTER THIRTY "WHAT DID WE LEARN?" 137
CHAPTER THIRTY-ONE "SAM AND SALLY" 140
CHAPTER THIRTY-TWO "SAM RETURNS" 143
CHAPTER THIRTY-THREE "THE GERMAN PROBLEM" 147
CHAPTER THIRTY-FOUR "STATE OF NATION 1934" 153
CHAPTER THIRTY-FIVE "MORE PINS, MORE STRING" 156

PART SIX "CREATING THE FOUNDATION" 159

CHAPTER THIRTY-SIX "THE ALMOST WAR" 161
CHAPTER THIRTY-SEVEN "ADVANCED PREP" 164
CHAPTER THIRTY-EIGHT "N-R TRADING CO. LTD." 167
CHAPTER THIRTY-NINE "VISITING LONDON" 169
CHAPTER FORTY "CHANGE IN DIRECTION" 176
CHAPTER FORTY-ONE "DEVELOPING A MODERN TRADING COMPANY" 178
CHAPTER FORTY-TWO "UDEH –NATION MEDICAL" 180
CHAPTER FORTY-THREE "FINISHING THE JOB" (THIRTEEN YEARS LATER) 185

PART SEVEN "BIRTHING THE EFFECTIVE DETERRENT" 187

CHAPTER FORTY-FOUR "WE DON'T HAVE THE VOTES" 189
CHAPTER FORT-FIVE "THE COUP" 192
CHAPTER FORTY-SIX "THE WHITE HOUSE" 195
CHAPTER FORTY-SEVEN "TIME FOR A DO-OVER" 201
CHAPTER FORTY-EIGHT "THE DIAGNOSTIC TEST" 206
CHAPTER FORTY-NINE "THE GENERAL'S REPORT" 210
CHAPTER FIFTY "ALAN KAHNE OR DAVID MARCUS?" 214
CHAPTER FIFTY-ONE "ALAN KAHNE'S DILEMMA" 216

PART EIGHT "LET'S NOT REPEAT OUR MISTAKE" 220

CHAPTER FIFTY-TWO "RETREAT" 221
CHAPTER FIFTY-THREE "JACQUES AND MIKE TO WASHINGTON, D.C." 226
CHAPTER FIFTY-FOUR "MIKE AND JACQUES REPORT" 231
CHAPTER FIFTY-FIVE "RE-WRAP AT VERSAILLES" 237
CHAPTER FIFTY-SIX "GIVING BIRTH" 243
EPILOGUE 247

THE NEW SENTINELS TRILOGY 251

Author's Note

***Pushing Back the Desert: Operation Ajax* is dedicated to the men who brought the water: John Zuckerman, Sam Hamburg, Smohl Cantor.**

Throughout history, great concentrations of power have supported grand strategic agendas. Some have been constructive, and implemented by responsible, problem-solving leaders, and some have not. The New Sentinels is a series of three historically based thrillers written by Gordon Zuckerman, whose previous works include Fortunes of War, Crude Deception, and Voices Behind the Curtain. Each book tells a story of a conflict between corrupt people and those who oppose corruption. By describing the dramatic lives of the Sentinels within a framework of reality, the author attempts to impart some of the lessons of history entertainingly.

Cast of Characters

DR. TOM BURDICK: Professor, University of California, Berkeley, doctoral political science program

MIKE STONE: Original Sentinel, executive vice president of Stone City Bank, son of Morgan Stone, married to Cecelia Chang

CECELIA CHANG STONE: aka The Mighty Warrior of Hong Kong, Original Sentinel, born in Hong Kong, married to Mike Stone

JACQUES ROTH: Original Sentinel, vice president, Roth Bank, Paris, married to Claudine Demaureux

CLAUDINE DEMAUREUX ROTH: Original Sentinel, daughter of Henri Demaureux, wife of Jacques Roth

ANTHONY GARIBALDI: Original Sentinel, born in Florence, Italy, founder, and owner/manager of Sentinel Wines

NATALIE CUMMINS: Retired star of New York's and London's musical stage

SIR DAVID MARCUS: English duke, a classmate of Jacques Roth, petroleum investment adviser

PIERRE ROTH: Long-time chairman of Roth Bank, Jacques' father, and co-founder of the "Nation of Citizen Farmers"

FATHER ISADORE NARAGHI, Patriarch of the Naraghi Family, visionary responsible for acquiring Khuzestan desert land, purchasing underground mineral rights, and procuring Zagros Mountain drainage water rights

HARSHIM NARAGHI: Son of Isadore, responsible for introducing modern mining technology to the Ancient Construction of Quants, husband of Kate York Naraghi, co-founder of the "Nation of Citizen Farmers"

KATE YORK NARAGHI: aka The Red Queen, wife of Harshim, daughter of Tom York, responsible for introducing humanitarian considerations into the "Nation of Citizen Farmers"

TOM YORK: Highly regarded consultant on the economics of international dam construction, responsible for overseeing the construction of hydroelectric dams in irrigation districts, father of Kate York

SAM NARAGHI: Son of Harshim and Kate, responsible for organizing NR Trading, Ltd., husband of Sally Raphael

SALLY RAPHAEL NARAGHI: wife of Sam Naraghi, educational visionary, responsible for introducing "Advanced Prep" educational programs

SMOHL CANTOR: Polish hydrology engineer, inner-circle member of the early Zionist movement in the Palestinian territories, and cofounder of the "Nation of Citizen Farmers"

ROGER MALONE: Chairman of the Federal Reserve, member of the president's kitchen cabinet

HARRIET HOLLENBECK: Friend of Sally Raphael in Paris

DR. MOHAMMAD MOSSADEGH: Prime minister of Iran's populist National Front Party

AYATOLLAH KHASANI: Early leader of Islam, and a member of the Majlis, the Iranian senate

GENERAL APGAR: Commander of the Shah's Royal Military Guard

KERMIT ROBERTS: In-country CIA case officer, Ajax conspirator

GENERAL MAHEDDI: Former head of the Iranian military turned Ajax conspirator

ALAN KAHNE: Israeli petroleum consultant

DR. SUZANNE STRAUSS: Widowed Israeli professor of nuclear engineering, companion to Alan Kahne.

Prologue

It's the spring of 1952, and nine years have passed since Claudine Demaureux, in the spring of 1943, called on the members of her University of California doctoral study group, "The Six Sentinels," for assistance. She had become concerned that the same German industrialists who had supported Hitler and his National Social Workers Party (Nazi) to power were planning to smuggle their two-billion-dollar fortunes of war out of Germany before an Allied invasion of France. It was rumored that the founders of the Third Reich were anxious to protect their wealth so that it could be used to fund a Fourth Reich in furtherance of their goal of imposing Aryan supremacy over Europe and possibly beyond.

Over the next nine years, the original Six Sentinels had developed an enviable track record of opposing abusive agendas of concentrated power. Recently, they had prevented a coalition of military contractors from manipulating the congressional appropriations process for their self-interests.

The time had arrived for them to step back and analyze what they had learned and to discuss what needed to be done to perpetuate what they had accomplished.

It had become apparent to all involved that irresponsible agendas of self-interest were emerging at a faster pace. At the same time, the demands of their personal lives were making it necessary for them to engage in a longer-range planning discussion if they wished to continue their opposition to the major-power pursuit of self-serving agendas.

The weekly meeting of the Senior Loan Committee of New York's Stone City Bank was breaking up. Mike Stone, the bank's executive vice president, was still seated. He was talking to two of the most senior members when his secretary entered the executive conference room and made her way to where he was sitting. Handing him a handwritten note, she respectfully waited for his reply.

The message, penned on Jacques Roth's personal stationery, read as follows: "I'd like to discuss something. Could you join me for lunch at Frank's at 12:30?"

Jacques was already standing at Frank's hot dog stand, across the street from the entrance to the Stone City Bank Building. Engaged in an animated conversation with his old friend, Frank, he was aware of Mike's arrival at their long-time favorite lunch locale. After standing aside to allow Mike to say hello and order his usual, a footlong hot dog with sauerkraut, hot mustard, relish, and a Coke, Jacques suggested they take their lunches into the park, sit on a bench, and talk.

Mike, sensing Jacques' serious mood, was wondering, '*What could be so important that he needs to talk on such short notice outside the confines of the bank? Has some Sentinel event occurred that requires our immediate attention?*'

Wasting no time, Jacques asked, "Did you receive Tony and Natalie's invitation to attend a retreat at the Sentinel Vineyards next month?"

"I saw the envelope in my pile of unopened mail. What's so important about our holding another retreat? Don't we regularly schedule an all-hands retreat following the conclusion of our most recent Sentinel endeavor?"

Reaching into his inside coat pocket, Jacques withdrew his invitation and handed it to Mike. "I could not help but notice the invitation included both Tony's and Natalie's names. I didn't know they were seeing each other, much less that they had taken up residence in Tony's home at the Sentinel Vineyard. Having dated Marcus and you unsuccessfully, why would she be attracted to yet another Sentinel with the same driven personality? How can a successful star of London's and New York's musical stages find happiness with a man who has spent the last ten years of his life committed to birthing a national vintner of premium wines?"

"But that's not all," Mike said. "Look at the bottom of the page. Cecelia has announced she is going to present her report on the founding of the Sentinel Institute. I can assure you she has spent a lot of time thinking about where all our Sentinel efforts may be leading. She is convinced that, if we hope to attract, train, and motivate qualified people to perpetuate what we have started, we need to become serious.

To accentuate what she is preaching, she has a habit of saying, 'It will take a minimum of ten years before the institute will be able to graduate students capable of continuing our work, and another five years of our coaching. Fifteen years is a long time before we can hope to withdraw.'"

After nodding in agreement, Jacques said, "In protecting the congressional appropriations process, it's important that we appreciate that this was the first time we encountered a coalition of connected military prime contractors. By combining their resources and their influence, they have learned that they can leverage their efforts into a more formidable force, capable of managing congressional approval for their own self-interest. In thinking about our future effectiveness, don't we need to pay particular attention to this coalition of corporations?"

Part One

"Surfacing the Problem"

Chapter One
"The Retreat"

NAPA VALLEY: January, 1953

For ten years, the Six Sentinels and their colleagues had endured the strenuous and dangerous demands of opposing three separate "Power Cycles."

This year, Tony Garibaldi, along with his new significant other, Natalie Cummins, were hoping to continue the Sentinel retreat tradition. They also wanted to use the opportunity to announce their engagement.

During the first night's dinner, the frivolity that customarily occurs when old friends gather was enhanced by all the questions, answers, and sarcastic comments of old friends concerned about each other's happiness.

Mike was the first to ask a tough question. "Natalie, why do you think this self-confessed bachelor, committed to his work, will find the time to be supportive of your individuality and love you the way you deserve?"

"I am glad you asked," Natalie said, and then launched into a response that surprised her listeners for its candor. "From the first night when we met in the Algonquin Hotel's Blue Bar in New York, that has been a frequent topic of conversation. You may be surprised to learn it was the central question we needed to solve if either of us hoped to have a successful relationship.

"Better than most, we understand the demands of big, complex challenges, and the need for supportive, caring, and understanding mates. For years, each of us has had to endure the difficulties that arose when our mates were intimidated by the demands of our careers or were too preoccupied with their own lives and failed to respond in an appropriate fashion.

"What has changed? We are older, we have achieved success, and we enjoy a certain amount of freedom in our own careers. Now that I have retired from the stage, I am no longer tied to six performances each week. My work as a producer of a successful Broadway show, coupled with the able assistance of my crew, makes it possible for me to come and go when needed.

"Admittedly, Tony's work is on the West Coast and mine is one the East Coast. Geography should not be a problem when we aren't required to be on the job. For the rest of the time, long weekends and air travel will have to suffice. We have agreed that, when one of us calls, the other will come running."

Realizing it would be inappropriate for Jacques, Natalie's earlier beau, to say anything, Cecelia asked, "Tony, we all watched when you failed to pay attention to Claudine when we were graduating.

"She adored you and would have given up her banking career in Switzerland if you had invited her to remain in California and join you in your wine endeavors. What has changed? How were you able to convince Natalie that you would always be there for her?"

"Not long after Claudine returned to Geneva, I regretted my allowing someone of such importance to slip away," he said. "I have promised myself I wouldn't make the same mistake twice. After living alone for all these years, I have learned you can't wish for someone's love, care, and support if it's not a reciprocal relationship.

"I never thought I would have the chance to have a relationship with someone who is as talented, exciting, and can be as loving as Natalie. I love her and will never, knowingly, do anything to jeopardize what we share."

With their curiosity satisfied, the Sentinels devoted the next two days to discussing Sentinel business at hand.

Since the problem of multi-corporate affiliations was Jacques' principal concern, he assumed the responsibility for conducting that portion of the agenda. After several hours of discussion, it was Jacques who concluded, "When corporate coalitions combine their resources to support a common agenda of self-interest, it appears they have learned to do so without breaking laws. Maybe it's not the laws that should be of concern. Shouldn't we focus our attention on protecting the public's interest?"

"In our democratic, free-market society, somebody needs to decide whether the achievement of these self-serving agendas is in the public's best interests or at its expense. Dating back to the start of the 20th century, antitrust provisions protecting the public from monopolistic practices have been incorporated into law. Why have we learned that antitrust laws are no longer capable of defending us from all the abusive agendas of concentrated wealth and influence? What might have happened had we not focused our attention on the problems that arise when multi-corporate resources are used to manipulate the political process for self-serving purposes?

"Since we will have little if any opportunity to attack these corporate coalitions directly, we must concentrate our opposition on their agendas. Starting today, we need to start thinking about what form our opposition needs to take!"

The second day, by agreement, the agenda was devoted to Cecelia's presentation of her progress report on the pending development of the Sentinel Institute.

Addressing the subject, Cecelia said, "You have, prior to the completion of our last plan of action, found it necessary for us to finalize our commitment to proceed with the development of the institute. Once we developed an actual plan, we have concentrated our attention on initiating the acquisition of a suitable site, organizing our proposed curriculum, designing the campus, completing the funding, and starting construction.

"Fellow Sentinels and honored guests, I am here to inform you that we have completed our plan for the institute, established a preliminary budget, and identified a potential site. In short, we have proceeded to the point where we require your approval before we can proceed.

"Now if you will join me in the next room, I have something I would like to show you."

As they entered the room, they saw a big table covered in a sheet. Curious about what lay beneath the sheet, they stood quietly around the table patiently waiting while Cecelia and Mike carefully removed the covering to reveal a precisely prepared topographical model, depicting the park-like setting of the campus. The view of the buildings, the driveways, space for future expansion, model cars, replicas of students walking, sitting, standing in small groups, and the proximity to the Monterey Bay caught everybody by surprise. Labels had been attached to the roof of each building designating its anticipated purpose. What had previously been a theoretical idea had just become a real-life project.

Jacques was the first to speak. "I had been wondering what a Sentinel Institute was supposed to be like. Never in my wildest imagination did I think it would take so many buildings to house all the different curricula and students we hope to introduce to the institute."

Continuing her presentation, a serious Cecelia said, "If you look very closely, you will see that we have only half of the available land for our present needs. It's important for us to realize that each time we commence a new endeavor, our opposition requires us to develop a new set of tools. If we are to think of the institute as our toolbox, we need to make room for more tools."

It had been a long day. Tony and Natalie, hoping to make that night's dinner special, decided to treat their guests to the same experience they offered their most important wine buyers. Arrangements for their final night's dinner had been made to have the dinner to be presented near the mouth of the large, tunneled storage area where the big vats used for aging the wine were located. During the cocktail portion of the evening five of, the Sentinels and their guests were encouraged to walk among the big oak casks, experience the rich aromas, and learn of the variety of wine by reading the labels.

Standing near the mouth of the big cave, they could see the setting sun painting a full range of pastel colors on the oak-studded hills surrounding the Napa Valley. Standing in groups of two and three, they were all busily engaged in conversation.

Several waiters carrying trays of long-stemmed, large, white, and red wine glasses were mingling among them. Other waiters were carrying trays piled high with smoked salmon, translucent caviar sorted to Beluga standards, New England, Blue Point oysters, pâté de foie gras, and toast points.

Five of the Sentinels' best wines, red and white, had been selected. Each of the five guest chefs had been employed to prepare their course to amplify the unique qualities of the different wines.

No expense had been spared with the setting of the white linen-covered, oak-planked table. Ornamental gas lights ran the length of the table. Each place setting included five wine glasses, five forks, four spoons, and three knives, all of them carefully arranged. At regular intervals along the length of the table sat vases filled with an assortment of flowers native to the region.

Dinner was soon in full swing. Encouraged by the elegant setting, the promise of a unique dinner, and the opportunity to sample the Sentinels' latest wines, one by one, each of the Sentinels and their guests stood up and expressed what they were feeling.

The noisy, wine-influenced atmosphere made it difficult for the guests to hear what was being said. They were never certain if a toast was being made as an expression of appreciation for the previous three days, as a celebration of the successful conclusion of their most recent victory, or simply as a way to speculate how long it would be before the next concentrated power's abusive agenda would emerge.

The euphoria of the moment was suddenly interrupted when the waiter-captain announced that Jacques and Mike's presence was urgently requested in the headquarters office. David Marcus, who was calling from Tehran, Iran, was waiting to speak with them.

Chapter Two
"Trouble in Tehran"

NAPA VALLEY: February, 1953

Once the transatlantic operator announced that Jacques and Mike were on the line, David came right to the point. "After two years of unsuccessful oil negotiations, the Iranian people have become aware of the British unwillingness to increase the rate of royalty payments on Iranian oil production from twenty percent to the prevailing Middle Eastern market rate of fifty percent. The thirty percentage point difference would provide the Iranian government with the billions in funds that they could use to transform a nineteenth century agrarian country into a twentieth century developing nation.

"Prime Minister Mossadegh and his constitutional government have become convinced the British are refusing to negotiate in good faith. Left with no viable alternative, the Iranian Senate, and the Majlis, voted to nationalize the country's oil industry. No one knows how the British may choose to retaliate."

Jacques, familiar with the contemporary history of the Middle Eastern oil industry, asked, "What makes Iran so different from its oil-rich neighbors whose royalty fees have already been raised from twenty percent to fifty percent?"

Ready for the question, David quickly responded. "In 1949, voting control of the Majlis shifted from the authoritarian rule of the British-controlled Shah government and his Royalist Party to the popularly elected National Front Party. It is believed the combination of reduced political control coupled with the renegotiation of its 1941 oil-production agreement has convinced the British they need to secure a tighter grip over their historical source of oil."

Jacques asked, "If that is the case, wouldn't the British use Iran's nationalization of its oil to justify taking over the country?"

David replied, "That is the purpose of my call. To make matters worse, I have received reports from Iran's government that agents of the American CIA and the British MI-6 have been observed arriving in Tehran. Could it be that we are already witnessing the initial phase of

Instagram:
-theghettolibrarian

an Anglo-American covert effort to take control of the Iranian government and the country's oil production?"

"Duly noted," Jacques said before asking, "David, if I could change topics for a minute, I am curious to learn if, in your travels around Iran and elsewhere in the Middle East, you have heard the name Sam Naraghi mentioned?"

"Who hasn't? You cannot be in Iran and not hear the Naraghi name frequently discussed. Naraghi is a well-known and highly respected family name. I have heard they have succeeded in converting four hundred thousand acres of arid desert land into intensively cultivated, irrigated farms. Frequently, they are referred to as the family that "pushes back the desert." With the introduction of their imaginative "lease-to-own" contract, they transferred title of each of the twenty-acre parcels that comprise the four hundred thousand total to the families who farm the land. It appears their reclamation efforts have made it possible for twenty thousand refugee farming families to enjoy the benefits of private land ownership, safe, modern homes, and dignified employment. The vertically integrated operations are referred to as "the nation of citizen farmers."

Jacques added, "Sam Naraghi is an old friend. Perhaps I need to speak with him. As the current Naraghi family leader, he should have a pretty good idea of what is happening."

Mike then interjected, "It has been my experience that funding covert operations requires a great deal of financial support. Someone in London, on Wall Street or in Washington, must be aware of what is being organized. Perhaps we need to dig a little farther?"

In a halting voice, David suggested, "I must still have some old friends in London who might know what is being planned. I think it is important I return to London and try to discover what the British oil companies and government are hoping to achieve. It may take some time, but if I dig deep enough and long enough, I should be able to obtain a fairly good idea of what is being planned."

Concentrating on their conversation, both Mike and Jacques failed to notice Jacques' wife, Claudine, quietly entering the room. Following a break in their discussion, she moved forward and said, "Tony is concerned your absence is becoming uncomfortably apparent. He is afraid it might disturb the wonderful synergy of the evening he has tried so hard to create."

Refocusing his attention on the phone call, Jacques said, "David, we understand your concerns. It's obvious that we need to learn a lot more about what is going on before we can determine if this is a power cycle type of threat requiring our attention. From what you have said, time must be of the essence. After we have talked to our respective sources, why don't we plan to meet in New York and discuss our findings with the other Sentinels?"

After a quick goodbye to David, they reentered the main dining room. Jacques immediately noticed all the inquisitive looks. After flashing his trademark charismatic grin, he asked everyone present, "Which one of you smartasses was speculating about how long it would take before the next power cycle threat appears?

"David, our missing colleague, has reported from Iran. The British government and their oil companies may be planning on restoring the shah's despotic puppet government to power, and in the process, seize complete control over Iran's oil production.

"If what David has suggested is accurate, we may be facing a serious problem of British imperialism. According to David, we don't have much time to get up to speed and develop a suitable plan of opposition. Knowing how difficult it is for all of us to be in the same place at the same time, why don't we adjourn tonight, extend our stay for one more day, and plan to reconvene tomorrow morning?"

Before a discussion of the Tehran problem could start, Cecelia asked, "If we become involved with this Iranian problem, how are we going to devote the time and energies the development of the institute will undoubtedly require? Should we choose to engage, I hope we can find time to pursue both objectives."

Chapter Three
"Jacques Calls Sam"

AHVAZ, KHUZESTAN PROVINCE: February, 1953

Jacques' call to Sam was both welcome and not a surprise.

Jacques was carefully listening to his longtime friend and his family's Nation of Citizen Farmers' investment partner express the same concerns David had raised.

"Jacques, you have undoubtedly heard something about our difficulties. A regime change could threaten more than the future of Iran and its oil industry; it could place Nation in great jeopardy.

"It's important you understand the urgency of the situation. On the surface, everything appears to be normal, peaceful, and serene. Crops are being cultivated, fields are being irrigated, harvesting is proceeding, foodstuffs are being processed and loaded onto trucks, into rail cars, and aboard ships.

"But at the same time, there are reports of unfamiliar people seen taking pictures, writing down license plate numbers, and recording the dates, times, locations, and the names of some of our more prominent local leaders as they move from one place to another. There are rumors suggesting our phones are being tapped. We have suspicions that our mail is being opened. It is getting to be a question of whom and what you can trust."

Five minutes later, after Jacques had asked more questions than Sam could answer, Sam said, "Jacques, I think you need to come to Iran as part of a regularly scheduled Roth Bank review. While you are here, you could inspect the emerging situation, talk to my friends, and form your own conclusions. If the situation appears as we expect it will, the Naraghis, Prime Minister Mossadegh, Iran's constitutional government and our Nation of Citizen Farmers would appreciate any assistance you and your Sentinel friends might be willing to provide."

After hanging up, Sam sat quietly and thought. He was recalling the events that had led to his friendship with Jacques. His mind drifted back to that day, nineteen years before, when he first met the celebrated French soccer captain beneath the stands of the big Paris stadium. "*We couldn't have been more than twenty-three years old. Our respective teams were playing for the European championship. You would have thought both of us, born into families that had worked closely together for more than twenty years, would have already met.*

"The hotly contested soccer game was won in overtime by the French National team when its captain, Jacques Roth, successfully used one of his patented over-the-head soccer kicks to redirect a corner kick past our goalie. When the game ended, members of the press delayed the French team's captain from leaving the field.

"I remember patiently standing beneath the stands, waiting for him to leave the field. For some unknown reason, I suspected he might have been as interested in meeting me as I was to make his acquaintance. I watched Jacques excuse himself from the reporters and, without hesitation, make his way to where I was standing.

'Talk about two different people! Jacques was reported to be both the heir to the Roth Family banking empire and a frequenter of Paris's best bars, restaurants, nightclubs, and exclusive men's associations. I was the farm boy from Iran who had spent the last four years studying mining and engineering at a coal-belt university in rural England.

"I was surprised when, after no more than ten minutes of polite conversation, he asked me to join him for a 'captains only' tour of night-time Paris. I will never forget the events of the evening. Jacques insisted on leading me along the well-worn paths he was reputed to have blazed through the late-night mystical charms of Paris's Latin Quarter.

"Since that night, I have often wondered if we were just having drinks, meeting interesting people, and attractive young women, or if we were also taking advantage of our shared adventure to become better acquainted.

"Even if we had not met Sally that night and ended up chasing her all the way to her kibbutz in Palestine, I would like to believe we used the opportunity to become friends.

"Wouldn't it be ironic if our relationship turns out to be the driving force that enables the Nation of Citizen Farmers to defend itself from the pending British imperialist threat?"

Chapter Four
"David to London"

LONDON, ENGLAND: February, 1953

After the call ended, David sat back in his chair, mentally reviewing their conversation. 'If Jacques is planning on talking with Sam in Iran, and Mike is returning to New York to meet with his financial friends, they must have understood the seriousness of the problem and the urgency of my call.'

Unfortunately, David and his two Sentinel colleagues were not the only people who had been listening in on his call to Napa. Aware of David Marcus's ongoing association with the Six Sentinels and with each of the oil-rich government leaders in the Middle East, MI-6 agents had tapped into David's hotel telephone line. They were transcribing the discussion with the intention of passing it to higher authorities within their respective intelligence agencies on both sides of the Atlantic.

David was not looking forward to returning to London, the city of his birth and of his many years of employment in the British oil industry. For more than two years following his abrupt resignation as a senior executive at English Oil, Ltd., his fellow executives had been confused by his decision. They failed to understand, and were openly critical of, his decision to create his own oil investment consulting company to attract the cooperation of the Middle Eastern oil-rich nations. Why had he chosen to pursue a career designed to assist the same sovereign countries that had been the targets of opportunity for British government and their oil companies?

David would wonder, 'Why have they found it so difficult to appreciate why I hope to better serve the future of the world oil industry? Don't they realize these sovereign leaders of oil-rich Middle Eastern countries will control more than forty percent of the world's future oil supply?'

David had no way of knowing the frustrations some of his English oil industry friends were experiencing over British Oil's refusal to renegotiate royalty payment fees with the Iranian government. Pausing to think about the problem, he found himself wondering, "Could it be possible the oil community is dividing itself into two camps? The leaders of one camp are questioning why it is necessary for Great Britain to imperialistically impose its need for increased control over a friendly, long-term allied country and the Middle East's first constitutional monarchy? Why would the British oil companies be willing to risk their control over such a strategically important resource? How could the economic savings associated with their refusal to recognize prevailing royalty rates justify jeopardizing their control over so much oil?'

Members of the opposition camp were expressing their concerns over Britain's diminished control over its historical source of oil, needed to support its economy and its Royal Navy. They were arguing that taking charge of Iran was Britain's only way to tighten its grip over Iran's petroleum.

David's requests to meet were immediately granted. Aware of David's relationship with the leaders of the Middle Eastern nations, his former colleagues were anxious to gain any additional insights David might be able to provide.

From the outset of the first meeting, David realized how concerned his colleagues were about the topic. Before the conclusion of each meeting, they asked him to return for additional talks. Three days of first-time meetings were expanded to five days. Five days turned into two weeks.

Each night, following the day's last meeting, David would return to his old and lonely London flat, pour himself a cup of tea, and sit down at his well-worn desk. He would spend the first two hours writing down what he could recall of the day's comments. Next, he would add his own interpretations of what was said. After reviewing his notes, he would seek to connect the dots and write down any tentative conclusions that might be drawn.

By the second week, David thought he had figured out what was going on: He was cautiously beginning to conclude, 'Might it be that the higher cost of the requested royalty payments isn't the central problem? Are the British trying to provoke the Iranians into nationalizing their oil to provide them with the justification they would need to preemptively take over Iran and consolidate their interest in its oil industry?'

David did not like the conclusions he was drawing. 'Before leaving England, I need to discuss my hypothesis with a knowledgeable expert, someone whom I can trust.'

After considerable thought, he called his father, Sir Colin Marcus, the third-generation member of the Marcus family who had been president and chairman of English Oil, Ltd. 'Recently retired, Father should still be conversant with current developments in Britain's oil world.'

It was after MI-6 agents intercepted David's call to his father that they concluded David was developing a threatening insight into what indeed was being secretly planned. They were concerned, 'What if he finds some way of obtaining confirmation from his father? We have to stop him!'

David instructed his cab driver to deliver him to the service entrance of his father's country estate to avoid any interruptions. Colin met his son at the entrance and led him to his study. After explaining his concerns, David began asking his father questions.

Colin, amazed by the questions, finally suggested, "To respect the confidentiality agreements I have been required to sign, why don't you ask the questions and provide what you suspect the answers might be. If I disagree, I will tell you and explain why. Otherwise, if I agree, I will remain unresponsive."

On more than one occasion, Sir Colin would ask, "How were you able to develop the foundation you would need to ask that particular question?" Later, before concluding their conversation, Sir Colin warned his son, "David, there are a lot of people on both sides of the Atlantic who would feel threatened if they knew what you suspect. While I know you and your friends have ways of protecting yourselves, in this instance, I would be particularly careful!"

Before leaving, David took advantage of his father's offer to allow him to use his confidential cable-gram system to communicate what he had learned or suspected with his fellow Sentinel colleagues.

Sitting in the back of the taxi that was taking him to Southampton Port, he was replaying the events of the last hour in his mind. Preoccupied with his thoughts, he failed to react quickly when a large transport truck emerged from an alley, blocking the path of the cab. Simultaneously, a second van pulled up behind them and blocked any chance to retreat. What looked like a grocery delivery van had pulled alongside. Before he could comprehend what was happening, two men had pulled open the cab's door, grabbed him, and propelled him into the rear of the van. The trucks withdrew and the van disappeared into traffic. David Marcus had disappeared.

Jacques Roth, recently returned to France, was standing at the gate at Pas-de-Calais where the passengers on the Southampton ferry were scheduled to disembark. He was impatient. He stared at each of the passengers, anxious to spot his old friend. When David failed to appear, Jacques was more confused than worried. 'David must have missed the ferry. Had he given me the wrong information? There must be some mistake.'

When the second ferry arrived and David again failed to appear, bells in Jacques' mind were signaling danger. 'If someone is so threatened by David and his questions, might they have found it necessary to have him captured or possibly killed? If they know about David, they must be aware of his Sentinel colleagues. Is there someone standing outside the terminal waiting for me to exit? Am I in danger? Do I need to warn the others?'

Chapter Five
"Mike to New York"

NEW YORK CITY: March, 1953

After the others had left Sentinel Wines, Mike and Cecelia Stone accepted Natalie and Tony's invitation to remain for a few extra days. The four old friends were anxious to spend some quiet time together. Although they had known each other individually, they wanted to have some time to become better acquainted with them as a couples.

Mike couldn't help but think how different their situation was to Cecelia's and my relationship. *'Cecelia and I fell in love at first sight that afternoon when we were introduced to each other at the I House on the Berkeley Campus in September of 1935. Since then, I can't remember a time when we weren't devoted to each other. Having led independent and full lives for the last eighteen years, won't it be interesting to learn more about what Tony and Natalie are experiencing?'*

The four friends were enjoying lunch on the sunlit veranda overlooking the Sentinels' first vineyard; Tony and Natalie were asking most of the questions.

Tony, "Mike, you asked about our ability to create a successful relationship amid so many challenges. Might I ask how *you two* were able to overcome the obvious problems created by such different heritages, coast-to-coast separation, and parental prejudices?"

"What a good question," Mike responded. "Before Cecelia answers, I would like to explain. As different as our two cultures might have been, we shared the need to establish and pursue our own goals, independent from what our fathers and the world had planned for us. Because our feelings for each other were so strong, we concluded that we needed to do whatever was necessary to preserve our relationship. And then, something else happened. When people understood the strength of our personal feelings, they stopped trying to separate us and began to show a greater interest in what we were all about. They had to make a decision: either they could be supportive and caring or they could leave us alone. Pleasing those who didn't understand was never an acceptable conclusion."

Cecelia responded differently. "You have to appreciate what it is like, as a young girl, to grow up in a prestigious, formally structured Chinese family under the influence of such a powerful and domineering father, the Tai-Pan of the Chang Family Dynasty. You went to private schools; you were educated to become the wife in an arranged marriage to the son of a family perceived to be of economic or political consequence. If you weren't there, you would have had a hard time understanding my frustration over being restricted to a life defined by the traditional customs of the Middle Kingdom for women of advantage.

"I spent so many years sitting around the family dinner table listening to my father and his important friends discussing worldly, important, and interesting problems and being prevented from learning about the world beyond the Middle Kingdom. It was becoming a great and growing problem. There wasn't a night when I didn't think about what my future might be if I were to marry someone I didn't love and go on to fulfill the duties of the wife of the head of the family.

"When presented with the opportunity to attend Dr. Tom's doctoral studies course, I thought and still believe I had been released from my personal prison. I was free to pursue my intellectual interests and look forward to marriage with a loving man whom I adore.

"Meeting Mike and being exposed to the Sentinel world is more than I could ever have expected. There isn't a day when I don't think about what I should do to preserve and enhance our world."

Natalie was quick to respond, "Aren't both of you saying the same thing? When you are fortunate to become part of a fulfilling world and to connect with the right companion to share it with, then you must appreciate each other and do what is necessary to make it work?"

Their serenity was disturbed by the noise and plumes of dust kicked up by a fast-approaching motorcycle. After pulling to a hasty stop and parking his vehicle, a Western Union messenger made his way up to the veranda and delivered a transatlantic cablegram marked "Urgent."

Mike, after carefully reading David's summary explanation twice, knew it was important he return to New York as quickly as possible. *'If David is right, the much-publicized efforts of the British to warn the American public about the need to protect Iranian oil from the Russians needs to be exposed as a British fabrication. If the Russian threat does not exist, it makes you wonder what the British are trying to achieve. Could it be that the British have more sinister motives?'*

Chapter Six
"Mike and Cecelia Return Home"

NEW YORK: March, 1953

Mike was thinking about David's cablegram when their plane started to descend for its final approach to New York's LaGuardia Airport. Letting his mind wander, he was speculating, *'If true, might the British plan include the cooperation of the United States? Could we be talking about some kind of Anglo-American conspiracy to take control of Iran?'*

His thoughts were interrupted when the pilot announced, "Ladies and Gentlemen, may I have your attention. When we land, please remain in your seats. There is a security detachment waiting to escort two of our passengers off the plane."

When the first uniformed officer entered the plane, Mike recognized him as Officer Harry, the head of Stone City Bank's security force. *'Why would it be necessary for him to escort us off the plane?'*

From experience, Mike knew to remain quiet, to follow instructions, and to wait patiently for the explanation. After descending the stairway, they found themselves being escorted toward the rear-most car of a three-vehicle caravan of black limousines parked on the tarmac near the plane. His father, Morgan Stone, chairman of Stone City Bank, was sitting in the far corner of the rear seat. Mike, after making sure Cecelia was comfortably seated in the back seat, climbed in and seated himself on the jump seat opposite his father.

He was thinking, *'As pleased as I am to see Father, why has he found it necessary to have us escorted off the plane and to meet us personally at the airport?'* Before Mike could say anything, his father handed him a cablegram, and said, "I think you need to read this."

After studying its content, Mike recognized it was a personal communiqué that had circulated among Morgan Stone, Harshim Naraghi, Pierre Roth, Henri Demaureux, and Smohl Cantor. The cablegram indicated that David Marcus had mysteriously disappeared, somewhere on the route from his family's estate to the Southampton Ferry. Smohl went on to write, "I think we should interpret his abduction to mean the British government investigative agencies are now threatened by what David has learned. If they know of David's involvement, they must suspect the rest of the Sentinels could be involved. Their personal safety could be in jeopardy."

Morgan continued, "Mike, there is something I need to explain. For a very long time, Pierre, Harshim, Smohl, Henri, and I have been meeting. Following the First World War and the breakup of the Ottoman Empire, several matters regarding the organization and enhancement of Nation have required our attention. It's entirely possible our efforts to support Nation during its early stages are not so different from the power cycle threats you and your Sentinel colleagues have been encountering over the last ten years.

"I have taken the liberty of alerting the Roth Bank, in Paris, and the Stone City Bank security teams of our concerns. Security detachments have already been organized for your protection. But there is a problem. Roth and Stone City Banks' security agencies' skills and resources are limited to domestic situations, and they cannot provide you with their protection should you travel outside the United States or France. Accordingly, Pierre, Harshim, Henri and I have appealed to Smohl Cantor and the Israeli Mossad for additional assistance."

Not certain how to react, Mike sat back in the jump seat of the luxurious limousine. He needed time to think. It was only when Morgan asked, "Son, tell me your plans. I might be able to help" that he was able to formulate a response.

"Father, it's really quite simple. My friends and I believe that if there really is a covert plan being prepared to overthrow the Iranian government, it will require a great deal of money. If we can identify the source of financing, we might be able to work backwards and develop the proof we will need to prove there is a covert Anglo-American plot in the making.

"David agreed to go to London. Jacques is headed to Iran to meet with Sam Naraghi, and I intend to speak with our friends in New York and Washington. Once we have completed our investigations, we plan to meet and try to fit the pieces of the puzzle together. Hopefully, once we have achieved a better understanding of what is involved, we should be able to formulate a plan of action to oppose the implementation of any Anglo-American plan."

The limousine was pulling to a stop in front of the high-rise co-op apartment building on New York's Upper East Side, where Cecelia and Mike lived. Morgan put his hand on Mike's arm and looked him in the eyes. "Mike, if what you and your Sentinel friends suspect is really happening, you will be opposing serious, powerful, and dangerous adversaries. The Stone City Bank security teams are already in place. Most likely, you will never see them, but they will be there. Good luck and watch your step!"

When the elevator door opened on the thirteenth floor of their building, Cecelia and Mike noticed three men whom they did not recognize. Two were stationed at opposite ends of the corridor next to the exits. The third agent was standing next to the elevator entrance. Immediately, he presented identification to the couple and explained that they were Stone City Bank security officers assigned to them for their protection.

By noon the next day, Mike was learning that arranging meetings with each of the people named on his New York short list was taking more time than he had expected. Normally, calls made on the personal lines between senior banking executive officers were readily accepted as a matter of professional courtesy.

Mike was surprised when his friends responded, "Believe me, this is the first time I have heard about what you are asking. You must understand the sensitivity of the matter. I need to call you back."

Rather than becoming upset by the strange responses, Mike smiled and thought to himself, *'I must be pressing some extremely sensitive buttons. Ultimately, my friends will have to agree to meet. Although it may be a bit more difficult for me to learn anything of importance.'*

After three days marked by a series of frustrating and uninformative meetings, Mike concluded that his friends were either unaware of any Anglo-American plan or had been instructed to remain unresponsive. *'If I am not going to find the answers I have been looking for in New York, it's time for me to move on to Washington.'*

Sitting on the balcony of their apartment overlooking the East River, Mike and Cecelia were enjoying the warm summer breezes, their nightly martini, and discussing Mike's dilemma. He was curious to learn what his enchanting, highly intelligent and insightful wife might say.

It didn't take long before the Mighty Warrior from Hong Kong, as Cecelia was known, responded. "If an American oil company is involved, wouldn't they be expected to make a significant capital contribution? Investments of that magnitude require renegotiation of bank credit agreements, the sale of stock, or the issuance of additional bonds, all of which require the approval of at least one federal government regulatory agency.

"When you go down to Washington, maybe you should talk to some of your friends who regularly deal with the agencies. Perhaps someone is aware of a pending application that might reveal what you are trying to learn."

Mike, never surprised by Cecelia's ability to see behind the curtain, spent the next two days arranging his Washington schedule. Not certain what kind of reaction he would receive, he was surprised by the lawyers, lobbyists, and loyal elected representatives' reactions to his requests for a meeting. To a person, they were willing to rearrange their calendars to meet with him.

Chapter Seven
"Mike to Washington, D.C."

WASHINGTON, D.C.: March, 1953

It was during the second day, when Mike asked a particularly close friend why he was receiving such a favorable reaction to his requests for meetings, that his friend said, "Mike, do you think you work in some sort of a vacuum chamber? After you started asking questions in New York, and David Marcus was reportedly asking similar questions in London, the bells started ringing in Washington.

"Your friends here have become interested. Why wouldn't you think that we are as curious as you and your friends are to discover what you are trying to determine and possibly be of assistance?

"A word of caution. If whatever you are trying to learn is so well hidden, it must mean powerful people are involved, and they will want to make sure that their secret remains undiscovered. After all that you and your Sentinel friends have been through, you must be aware of what can happen when powerful people become threatened and decide to protect themselves."

Mike did not need to be reminded. More than ten days had passed since they had received word of David's disappearance. Equally disturbing was the fact that no law enforcement agency on either side of the Atlantic had produced even a hint of David's whereabouts.

Before leaving for the airport, Mike called his old friend and fellow Sentinel colleague, Don Cerreta, an acclaimed federal prosecutor. Don answered his private line after the second ring. Mike, speaking in code, immediately asked, "I just needed to check and make certain you have not forgotten about our dinner engagement tonight. I hope you have made a reservation for our accustomed time of meeting at the same great restaurant where we ate the last time I was in Washington?"

Unprepared for Mike's unexpected call or his use of coded language, Don quickly surmised something of a serious nature must be involved. '*This isn't a social call!*' Don quickly agreed that he would make the reservation and hung up the phone.

Arriving a few minutes late, Mike noticed Don sitting at the same table they had previously occupied. Don was enjoying what looked like a chilled martini served up in a long-stemmed and well-frosted glass.

Before proceeding to the table, Mike casually scanned the room. Not seeing anyone of interest, he moved in the direction of the bar, engaging his old bartender friend in sociable conversation. After making sure Don was aware of his presence, he slowly proceeded to the men's room. Five minutes later, when he emerged, he looked at the bartender and Don for confirmation he had not been followed and quickly moved to the table.

Coming right to the point, Mike said, "Before you say anything, I need to explain what has happened since our last meeting in Napa." Concluding his remarks, Mike said, "Something is fishy! When I checked with my friends in New York, I learned that there are several big oil issues that have entered the Wall Street funding queue, but nothing that included new offshore oil production. When I asked if they had noticed anything that might be strange or unusual, all I got were blank looks and nothing answers.

"If the British and American oil companies are planning to assume control of the Iranian oil, Cecelia believes there has to be a demand for a sizeable raise of fresh capital. You would think somebody would be aware of it. I hope you, and possibly some of your friends at Justice who monitor the actions of the regulatory agencies, might be able to help me."

Responding, Don said, "Why don't you order dinner and a good bottle of wine while I make a couple of calls? I recommend the breaded veal cutlet and a good pinot noir from Bourgogne."

By the time Don returned, the wine had been served and a platter of antipasti had been placed on their table. After sitting down, removing his napkin, and sampling the wine, Don said, "It seems we are in luck. We are expected to appear at the office of the director of the Securities and Exchange Commission at 8 a.m. sharp tomorrow. The director will have somebody waiting at the side entrance to escort us into the back elevators and up to his private office."

Meeting with the director of the Securities and Exchange Commission (SEC) would be a new experience for Mike. While his relationship with Roger Malone, chairman of the Federal Reserve, dated back more than seven years, nothing he had previously worked on had prepared him for a meeting with the SEC director.

The meeting started well enough. At least until the director announced, "In preparation for this meeting, I called our mutual friend at the Fed, Roger Malone. At first, he seemed confused by my call. When I told him you were inquiring about possible funding of an offshore oil production project, he seemed shocked and curious. The chairman asked if I would learn as much as I can and provide you with our best assistance.

"The direct answer to your question is that I am not aware of any plan to raise capital for an offshore oil development project. But there was a strange occurrence that caught my attention. Several days ago, I received a call from our White House liaison staff member. He was inquiring about the possibility of our fast-tracking the approval of a large oil capital raise of the highest credit rating. When the caller refused to answer any of my questions, I am afraid I lost my temper and said, 'Not only do I resent receiving this kind of informal inquiry, but I am even more upset when I am not being fully informed.'"

Following Mike and Don's departure from the meeting that had never happened, Mike didn't trust himself to think about the director's suspicion. How could a major investment be organized and remain a carefully guarded secret? Out of force of habit, Mike turned to look out the rear window of their taxi. That was when he spotted a nondescript car pull away from the curb. His driver must have seen the same thing. A sudden hard right turn of the cab into an alley succeeded in capturing Mike and Don's undivided attention.

The cab sped down the alley. Another hard right, followed by two left turns delivered them into the entrance of a large public parking garage. Their confusion was compounded when the cabby suddenly announced, "Mr. Stone, Mr. Cerreta, once we enter the garage, you will need to be prepared to quickly exit this cab and enter a second cab that will be waiting alongside. After I exit the entrance on the other side of the building, the driver of the other cab will deliver you to the side entrance of the Federal Reserve Building. The chairman is waiting inside to meet with you."

Chapter Eight
"Meeting Roger Malone"

WASHINGTON, D.C.: March, 1953

Within ten minutes of entering the second cab, Don and Mike found themselves standing in the chairman's private conference room. They were not alone. In addition to the chairman, several high-ranking U.S. elected government and appointed officials were standing around the conference table. They were waiting to greet Mike Stone, their old friend and the much-respected co-leader of the Sentinels.

For more than seven years, some combination of these men had watched, with curiosity and admiration, each time the Sentinels sought to oppose the self-serving agendas of concentrated power. Proud of their earlier efforts to assist the Sentinels in keeping bad things from happening, to a person, they were curious to learn what had caught the Sentinels' attention this time.

These officials were also shocked by the realization that the Sentinels had been asking about a highly secret plan code-named Ajax. From experience, they knew that the Sentinels wouldn't be asking questions of so many highly placed people if they weren't acting on reliable information.

As the presiding member of the group, Roger Malone was faced with a sensitive dilemma. '*How much information should we divulge about Ajax and the growing problem it is creating for Dwight David Eisenhower, the newly elected president? Maybe it would be best if we first learn what the Sentinels have discovered?*'

Hoping to continue the meeting in a congenial manner, Roger Malone asked, "Mike, before we get started, perhaps you wouldn't mind helping us understand how you became interested in this Iranian oil problem?"

For the next ten minutes, Mike explained the strange set of circumstances that had led to his investigative visit to Washington. "Roger, you remember our colleague, David Marcus? He called from Tehran to warn us something very strange may be taking place. Later, we received his confirming cable alerting us to the strong possibility that our worst fears may be realized.

"Based on our preliminary analysis, we concluded that the United States and Great Britain may be seriously considering overthrowing the Iranian government and seizing control of the world's fourth-largest supply of oil. We realize it is early in the process, but we are trying to confirm our preliminary thesis.

"If what we suspect is true, we are concerned that a regime change in Iran could jeopardize the twenty thousand-family-strong Nation of Citizen Farmers that three generations of Roth and Naraghi families have worked so hard to achieve.

"A battle over oil is not our main concern. It's the preservation of Nation that has caught our attention. We are convinced that removal of Iran's constitutional government would eliminate safeguards needed to protect the Nation of Citizen Farmers. Consequently, we are left with no alternative but to conclude that an attack against Iran would be an attack against Nation and would require the Sentinels to become involved.

"Roger, what has us confused is how the United States became engaged in Britain's mess. Why would the previous president condone a covert imperialistic operation that contradicts a longstanding foundation of American foreign policy?"

Impressed by Mike's revelations, Malone paused to think. *'When viewed through Sentinel eyes, I can appreciate their concern. How do I explain that, despite what has been tentatively planned, the current president is seeking a different alternative to avoid his approving the final stages of Ajax, a plan that he can secretly support? If word of his seeking an alternative plan to oppose Ajax were to become known, all hell could break loose. I can't imagine what the Anglo-American oil cartel's reaction might be.'*

Malone continued, "There is one more question I need to ask. Assuming you confirm your theory, what are the Sentinels planning to do? We've seen you Sentinels do some amazing things. If you are considering opposing the American and British oil companies and their governments, what makes you conclude you would have a realistic chance of succeeding?"

Mike was prepared for the question. "Roger, have you forgotten in 1946, less than seven years ago, we were faced with a similar problem in Indonesia?" he asked. "The central issue we had to deal with was that of how to separate government control of its oil industry from the responsibility of managing the oil production. Had we failed to introduce competitive bidding between Royal Dutch Shell and a coalition of Western independent oil companies, we would have had no viable alternative but to support the restoration of the Dutch colonial government.

"Aren't the British suggesting that an Anglo-American-sponsored regime change is required if we are to preserve control over Iranian oil? Different times, different players, different geography, but the same problem. What is there to prevent us from offering to assist the existing Iranian government to implement a competitive bidding arrangement for its oil production? We understand Prime Minister Mossadegh has solicited offers from the other Big Oil companies, and they all refused to compete with the interests of fellow Oil Club members.

"Let us not forget the Sentinels continue to enjoy a positive working relationship with what has become the Independent Oil company. For the last six years, it has been satisfactorily performing all the duties normally associated with each of the seven members of the Oil Club. Independent Oil still enjoys access to the International Energy Development Fund (IEDF) and could choose to competitively bid against the British and American oil companies."

Appreciating Mike's candor, Roger decided to place his trust in Mike and the other Sentinels. "Mike, the situation has become even more complicated. The president is caught in a precarious position. He now realizes the much-publicized threat of a Russian intrusion in Iranian oil is no longer an important consideration. Even worse, he has received reliable information that the 'Russian Threat' was a British publicity fabrication. They were hoping to capitalize on America's fears of Russian interference to encourage the former president to support Ajax.

"It's important that you appreciate the gravity of the situation. To encourage America's involvement, British Oil offered its American oil company cousins half of their eighty percent royalty revenues in exchange for their active participation. Their offer is contingent upon obtaining the cooperation of the United States government."

Mike, Don, I think we need to have a confidential 'all-cards-face-up-on-the-table' conversation. The president might be receptive, at this stage of the game, to an alternative course of action, provided he is handed a viable *'done deal'* plan of action, a 'Third Alternative'.

Don asked, "Might the introduction of Independent Oil Companies' (IOC) competitive bidding force Britain's hand? What do you suppose might happen if the Anglo-Iranian Oil Company (AIOC), were forced to outbid the Independent Oil Company? Either way, Iran retains control over its oil and will achieve its objective of raising its royalty fees from twenty percent to fifty percent. And, at the same time, preserve its constitutional government."

"If our plan to introduce competitive bidding succeeds, why wouldn't the president conclude he has been handed a viable done deal?

Chairman Malone, "Gentlemen as usual you have succeeded in making your point. Why don't you give me some time to discuss your proposal with the president?"

Pleased with the outcome of their meeting, Mike and Don suggested to Jacques that a meeting be convened be convened at the Roth Chateau at the earliest possible time.

After reading David's and listening to Jacques' and Mike's report, the senior Roth found it necessary to intervene. "I am prepared to accept the logic of your suggestion, but with one significant exception. Don't we need to consider what we have to do, should our Third Alternative plan fail? It seems to me we will need to develop a backup plan to protect Nation before we can consider becoming a party to your Third Alternative proposal."

Standing, Smohl said, "For some time, we have been thinking about the threat to Nation created by foreign country interest in its undeveloped oil potential. For years, we have considered its economic potential as a target for third-party intrusion. Maybe we should think about what could happen if we were able to implement a different kind of arrangement. What might change if we were to contract our oil reserves with the same independent American Oil Company the Sentinels introduced in Indonesia in 1946?

"If the active operation of an American–based oil company were to qualify as an American foreign investment interest, wouldn't it be deserving of American military protection? How could the United States fail to protect one of its designated foreign investment interests without jeopardizing the security of all its other foreign investment interests? I can't even begin to imagine what event would force the United States to abandon a keystone of its foreign policy of long-standing. If we were to succeed, wouldn't we have developed the 'Reliable Deterrent' we need to protect Nation and its oil reserves from possible Anglo-American ambitions?"

Not certain of how to answer Smohl' s question, Harshim asked, "Old friend and valued partner, do I need to remind you that, for as long as I can remember, we have been evaluating different oil company proposals? A long time ago, we concluded that the execution of a development and production contract would adversely affect the surface agricultural operations of our Nation of Citizen Farmers."

Jacques, who had been waiting to respond, finally suggested, "Maybe we need to extend our thinking a bit further? If we were to negotiate with a friendly party, why couldn't we retain control over enough of the future surface activities and avoid disturbing Nation's farming operations?"

Smohl said, "Clearly, we are going to require the motivated cooperation of Independent Oil, the American government, and the present Iranian government. Aren't we talking about a very tall order? Even if we succeed in achieving the cooperation of each, we still will be faced with the problem of demonstrating that Independent's oil operation satisfies all the requirements of the American Foreign Investment Act. That will necessitate exploration, drilling of wells, and delivering the oil to legitimate purchasers in a very short time."

Sam and Harshim sensed that they were on the verge of being asked to make an especially important and defining decision, one that could affect their lives' work and their futures for a long time. They needed time to think.

Snifters were refilled, new cigars were lit. Everyone was trying to discover some reason why Smohl's idea wouldn't work. The sun was beginning to illuminate the eastern sky. As they were filing out of his library, Pierre pulled Smohl aside and asked, "Is there anything we can do about David Marcus's situation?"

Part Two
"Pushing Back the Desert"

Chapter Nine
"In the Beginning"
(50 Years Earlier)

AHVAZ, KHUZESTAN PROVENCE, IRAN: August, 1902

By 1902, Harshim Naraghi, the 18-year-old first-born son of Isadore and Ruth Naraghi, stood six-feet, three-inches. He was a gangly youth with broad, square shoulders. Blessed with long, sinewy muscles developed through years of hard agricultural work, he possessed unusual strength, athletic agility, and the ability to run long distances. At school, when his classmates chose soccer sides, he was always the first to be selected.

Serious about his chores, his schoolwork, and learning all he could about his family's dream of transporting water to the desert, Harshim always took advantage of the nightly conversations around the family dinner table to ask Father Isadore to talk of earlier times. On more than one occasion, Father Isadore would explain how each succeeding generation of the Naraghi family had managed to acquire ownership of additional desert grazing lands on the western slope of the Zagros mountains and the rights to use the Western Zagros drainage water for agricultural purposes.

Amused by Harshim's interest, the elder Naraghi was quick to respond. "While our principal use of the land is for grazing purposes, for as long as we have been pushing back the boundaries of the desert, our family, every five years, would dig another quant, an underground aqueduct, to transport additional runoff waters, make more of the desert bloom and push out its boundaries a little.

"The practice of hand digging and lining the quants with tile made for slow going. Over time, the irrigated acreage and the people needed to farm the land began to add up. By the time my generation came along, it had become apparent that pushing back the desert made a lot of sense.

"I am not certain when the idea of applying modern mining techniques to the excavation of quants first occurred to me. For as long as I can remember, I have had this dream of utilizing all the runoff waters to make the desert bloom."

Father Isadore continued, "The recent development of new mining extraction techniques, if applied to the excavation of quants, might allow us to extend the boundaries of irrigated land much further out into the arid deserts."

One night, over the family dinner table, Harshim unexpectedly announced, "Depending on the accuracy of my calculations and assumptions regarding the size and length of the proposed 'Super Quant,' I have concluded we could expand the area of service of a drainage system from four hundred acres to two thousand acres, or by a factor of five.

"In addition, new mining techniques might reduce construction time from five years to less than three years and improve our ability to convert more desert to irrigated farmland. When measured over a ten-year period, the introduction of modern mining equipment might make it possible for us to introduce four more quants and create eight thousand acres of irrigated and cultivatable farmland. Here are my supporting calculations."

Obviously pleased by his fifteen-year-old son's ability, Father Isadore, the stern taskmaster, announced, "Now it's time for us to consider how much more acreage we could add if we were to build dams and utilize one hundred percent of the available runoff water of a particular drainage basin."

Harshim could still remember, for the next three winters, following his father on his weekend hiking expeditions to the snow-covered, high-altitude Zagros Mountains. Each day, using snowshoes, they would carry all the tools they would need to measure the volume of the larger snowfields. After measuring their area and depth, they would enter their measurements and calculations in one of their coded notebooks.

In the summers, they would visit the running streams and measure the volume of the total water each drainage basin was releasing and record the number of days it would continue. Once they were able to calculate the total runoff volume of a particular drainage basin, they were able to determine how many acres the water would irrigate. To their amazement, they concluded that it was capable of servicing twenty-thousand acres. That was the day when Father Isadore decided to find a way to install hydro-electric dams.

The time had arrived for the tall, quiet, gangly young man with a burning sense of purpose to board the train leaving Ahvaz on the first leg of his journey to the Birmingham School of Mines, located in the heart of England's coal mining country.

Chapter Ten
"Harshim Naraghi"

MARITIME ALPS, FRANCE: June, 1907

In the summer of 1907, after four strenuous years of concentrated study in England and dedicated playing of team soccer, an older, more physically developed, and even more-driven Harshim Naraghi was exiting the school's front entrance for the last time. He was no longer the gangly, introverted kid he had been when he left home. The soccer play, disciplined workouts, and hard work required by his summer mining jobs had changed him into a big and powerful man, blessed with boundless stores of energy. Despite the changes in his appearance, Harshim remained the same kind and gentle man who had departed Ahvaz four years earlier.

The demands of his studies and the soccer field and the limitations of his budget prevented him from participating in the frivolous activities common among undergraduate students. Rarely was he able to meet young women or join his classmates for a pint of beer at their favorite tavern.

Summer vacations and travel were not an option. On the Monday following the last day of school, Harshim could be found working in a mine. The work meant he was obtaining practical, on-the-job training in modern mining. Harshim was being exposed to all the problems that could be encountered in mines that used state-of-the-art practices and modern equipment.

In the summer of 1907, aware of the challenges that would be awaiting him at home, Harshim decided to travel to the Maritime Alps separating France from Italy. He was curious to learn more about the 1865 digging of the Mt. Cenis Tunnel. Constructed in a remote, high-altitude location, the tunnel made rail traffic possible between Italy and France. The introduction of a trans-European rail transport system made it possible to cut weeks off delivery times, reduce transportation costs, and increase load capacities.

The eight-mile tunnel had been constructed without the use of electrical or diesel-generated power. For four years, Harshim had been studying how mining engineers had learned to trap the water from high mountain streams and direct it into tall metal cylinders filled with trapped air. The weight of the stored water compressed the encapsulated air and, with the assistance of specially designed, copper-reinforced, rubber pneumatic hoses, powered a generator. In turn, the generator powered the mining equipment required to drill a tunnel twenty-four feet in diameter through solid granite -- large enough to accommodate a freight train.

Forty years after its completion, the tunnel was still considered a marvel of modern engineering. Unwilling to limit his knowledge to the content of his academic study, Harshim decided to delay his return home by a few days so that he could inspect the tunnel in person.

After arriving on site, Harshim devoted his days to long hikes up the railroad beds to the high-altitude tunnel. After removing years of overgrown grass and bushes and searching, he began to discover the remains of the corroded hydraulic equipment that had been discarded there forty years before.

Aided by a wire brush and elbow grease, he removed the rust and corrosion from the name plates. Taking note of the different manufacturers and their listed locations, he began to think about visiting those engineers who might still be involved in the design, manufacture, and operation of more contemporary equipment.

When he discovered discarded drilling tools with their rotary bits, he knew they didn't resemble the drills that had been used in the mines where he had worked. A quick check with the Birmingham School of Mines revealed that this particular bit design had been developed in the American Southwest for use by wildcat oil well drillers. They had developed the special kind of bit needed to cut through the granite and other deep glaciated plates they encountered in drilling down to the depths where they expected to find oil.

The descriptions of the American wildcatters captured his attention. Harshim was impressed by their self-confidence, their bold efforts to find oil, and their ability to solve all the problems that arose in drilling deep wells. More notes, more time, more road trips, and more delays returning home.

The University of Grenoble, located fewer than twenty miles from the western entrance to the Mont Cenis Tunnel on the western slope of the Maritime Alps, was developing a reputation for its Alpine technical engineering department, its proximity to great skiing, and its popularity among foreign students. The school library contained one of the finest collections of literature describing the step-by-step process involved in the construction of the tunnel. Frequently, Harshim could be found at the school library, looking for and studying materials not included in the standard curriculum at Birmingham.

Never comfortable about eating dinner and spending nights alone in strange hotel rooms, Harshim quickly learned to locate the pubs where locals would gather for nightly glasses of beer while they wagered on a good game of darts. On many a night, while waiting for his turn at darts, he would sit at the bar, engrossed in conversation with strangers.

One night, while concentrating on a particularly close, high-stakes dart game with his new Parisian friend, Pierre, Harshim was startled when the tavern's two swinging doors opened suddenly. A group of what appeared to be old friends burst into the pub.

Annoyed by the interruption, Harshim looked up. His attention was immediately drawn to a tall girl with flaming red hair. Even from across the crowded, smoke-filled room, he was struck by her beauty, her height, and her hearty laughter. Temporarily forgetting his dart game, he followed her with his eyes as she and her friends made their way to the far end of the bar. Having never had much of an opportunity to be around interesting women, he realized she was one of the first women whom he looked forward to meeting.

After losing the dart game, he looked around the room to find that she was no longer at the bar. Gone! He knew he had missed an opportunity to meet an unusual woman.

Harshim would never know if it was some instinct or the unusual look in Pierre's eyes that caused him to look around. The red-haired woman was standing quietly to one side, waiting to be noticed. He was even more surprised when he stood up - he had to stand on his toes if he hoped to see over her head!

The big, gentle, but socially awkward engineer was trying to think of something clever to say, when she asked, "Would you like me to help you win back the money I have watched you lose?"

What does a woman say when she notices the look of confusion in the eyes of a really big and powerful man to whom she is attracted? Here's what the red-haired beauty said: "I was raised in Ireland's County Cork with three older brothers. Believe me when I tell you how quickly I learned about the consequences of not being able to hold my own with the boys, which included in games of darts. Don't you think we need to determine how much these men are prepared to wager to prove they can beat a woman?"

Any doubts Harshim might have been harboring about her dart-tossing abilities disappeared after they won their first three matches. Together, they had won more than enough money to offset his earlier losses. But his immediate concern was not about the wagers. Standing next to this striking, strong-willed woman, he was experiencing a strange sensation. *'Am I attracted to her for her beauty, her size, or her game nature? Or is this my first experience of being with a truly exciting woman?'*

Other bar patrons were choosing partners and patiently waiting for their turns to challenge. The atmosphere in the quaint and normally quiet pub was coming alive. The size of the wagers was increasing. The volume of the side bets was growing. Cheering for one team or the other filled the air. The normal closing hour had long since passed.

Two hours later, Harshim and his partner were standing outside on the wood-planked sidewalk counting their winnings when the tavern doors again swung open. Her friends were leaving, and they were loudly insisting she accompany them. Harshim, his hands full of small bills, was disappointed. All he could think to say was, "I was hoping we could become better acquainted. I don't even know your name."

He would never know what surprised him more -- the sudden presence of her friends or her response to his comment: she reached forward, flung her arms around his neck, and kissed him squarely on his lips. After disengaging, she said, "My friends call me Kate, Kate York. I will be leaving town tomorrow morning with my father, Tom York. We are traveling to Torino. I will leave our forwarding address with the concierge. Why don't you follow? I think we still have a lot to discuss!"

Chapter Eleven
"In Pursuit of Kate"

GRENOBLE, FRANCE: July, 1907

Harshim was confused. He had spent little time talking with young women, certainly no one like Kate. All he knew was he had never been so attracted to any other woman. Without really understanding why, he knew, 'If I don't find her, I will never know if I have allowed something valuable to slip away.'

Checking at the hotel where she and her father had been staying, he learned that Mr. Tom York and his daughter had left a forwarding address of a hotel in Torino, Italy. It was familiar to Harshim, who had stayed there during one of his earlier field trips. He had been studying the melted-snow runoff of the Riparia River, which flowed eastward out of the Maritime Alps toward Torino and its rich agricultural lands. His research project reminded him of similar studies he had performed years earlier with his father on the western approaches of Iran's Zagros Mountains.

Arriving at the hotel late in the afternoon, Harshim selected a prominent seat in the lobby and waited for Kate and her father to return from their day's work. He was rereading his paper describing the hydrological potential of the Maritime-Alpine Alps when he looked up, startled by the presence of Kate and her father standing directly in front of him. "Father, this is the man I have been telling you about," he heard Kate say.

Scrambling to his feet, Harshim was uncertain as to what he should do next. He needn't have worried. In one quick movement, Kate embraced him and again kissed him squarely on his lips, before turning toward her father and saying, "I would like you to meet the man who I hope has come to rescue me from your world of travel, designing new dams, and all those boring engineers."

Sitting at dinner that night, Kate could not have been more pleased. Harshim was drawing on his knowledge of the area's hydrology to encourage Kate and her father to describe, in considerable detail, their current consulting assignment.

Unfortunately for Harshim, the longer the conversation progressed, the more he began to believe, '*Obviously this father-daughter team has been traveling all over the world, consulting on the design and construction of some very impressive dams.*

'Judging from what her father has mentioned about her work, Kate is accustomed to playing a role far more important than that of a personal assistant. When he talks about how they divide up the different segments of his assignment, it sounds as if she has learned to complete many of the same technical tasks her father had been retained to perform. Obviously, she is talented, comfortable working in an all-male environment, and talking about technical problems.

'Not only is her technical experience far more advanced than mine, but Kate must be at least three years older. Aside from her obvious beauty, her quick wit, and her boldness, she is so much more mature and worldly than I. How could such an unusual woman be attracted to someone like me?'

It was over the second bottle of wine that the conversation switched to Harshim. He described his family and their historical efforts to harness the Zagros Mountain runoff water, transport it to the Western plains of the Khuzestan desert, and make the fertile and arid land bloom. "When I return, I am expecting to start work on our first Super Quant. With the installation of each Super Quant, we hope to increase the irrigated acreage from 500 to 5,000 acres for each district we develop."

At first, neither Tom nor Kate understood the scale of the project Harshim's family was expecting him to develop. But they began to understand when Harshim casually mentioned, "The subject drainage basin is the first of the twenty we control. Someday, we hope to use all of them to transport water to the desert."

Impressed by the magnitude of the Naraghi family dreams, Tom asked, "I can understand how you might apply your familiarity with modern mining techniques to the construction of a modern quant system, but do your calculations include the installation of modern hydroelectric dams?"

"Good question. That is a problem we still need to resolve. To our knowledge, the professional skills required to design and construct an appropriately sized dam are not available in Iran or in the immediate region. Even if they were, we couldn't afford the cost."

When Tom started to ask questions, Kate's mind began to wander. *'How can such a large, strong, ruggedly handsome, and gentle man appear to be so shy when he is in the company of an adventurous woman? When he talks about his dreams, his personality seems to change. Short sentences are replaced by long sentences, which, when joined together, tell a story of considerable interest. The more I listen to him describe his life, the better I can understand why I am so attracted to him. Kate, ol' girl, when have you ever encountered a man quite like him? A life with him could be one hell of an adventure; you better start paying attention!'*

After refocusing her attention on the conversation, she heard her father say, "Harshim, I am interested in what you and your family are planning. Please keep me informed. It has been a pleasure meeting you, but I do have one suggestion. Do not underestimate Kate's comment about you rescuing her! She can be an incredibly determined woman! I have spent much of my lifetime watching Kate pursue her dreams. If I were you, I would ask her why she is frequently referred to as the Red Queen. Remember, you have been warned. That said, I think it's time for me to retire. I hope you and Kate will have a pleasant evening. I look forward to our next meeting."

Following Tom's departure, Harshim began to think, *'For the first time in my life, I find myself totally attracted to a woman. How do you suppose she would respond to my asking her to visit me in Grenoble and to accompany me on my weekend field trips?'*

During the week, back at his meager flat in Grenoble, he would work non-stop on his research. He had a difficult time waiting for Thursday night and Kate's arrival. Early Friday mornings, they would embark on that week's planned field trip. '*Strange,*' he thought. *'Kate never complains about the difficult physical work. She seems to enjoy spending time with me.'*

On Saturday nights, tired from their days of hard work, they would find themselves in another strange town, searching for that perfect hole-in-the-wall restaurant. The selection process had become an exciting game. With their little game complete, sitting at a candle-lit table, Kate would encourage Harshim to talk of the world that was waiting for him in Iran. She never tired of listening to her man talk about making the desert bloom, pushing back the boundaries of the desert, and extending the living barriers of the deserving people who perform the work.

Impressed by his interest in the human and social needs of his farmers, Kate said, "In Ireland, we have two kinds of farms. The big estates, owned by wealthy families, are typically broken up into economic-sized parcels and leased to local farming families. We call these people tenant-farmers. Then there are the farms owned by the people who work their own land. We call them owner-farmers. I'll bet you can't describe what distinguishes one from the other?

"Pride. The productivity of the owner-farmers exceeds that of the tenant farmers by as much as thirty-five percent. You talk about wanting to increase production by adding new tracts of land. Have you ever stopped to consider what might happen if you were to discover some way of converting your tenant farmers into more prideful land-owning citizens?"

"What an interesting idea. Kate, you never cease to amaze me. Equally important, with the transfer of title to land-owning citizens, what promises to be a family-owned, grand agribusiness experiment could evolve into a great humanitarian effort!"

After pouring each of them another glass of wine, Harshim sat back. "Kate, in addition to learning how to convert our tenants into citizen farmers, you are asking a second question," he said. "With the attention of the members of my family so focused on developing the next irrigation district, who is going to be responsible for figuring out how to implement the transfer of title you have been discussing?"

"Harshim, are you suggesting I accompany you when you return home?"

Caught off-guard, he paused, stared into space, rubbed his forehead, and then finally said, "All I know is I don't want to lose you."

From that point on, their weekends took on an entirely new meaning. Kate, hoping to demonstrate what a problem solver she could be, was no longer willing to limit her duties to lugging around heavy measuring devices, cleaning rusted manufacturer plates, and listening to Harshim thinking out loud about the significance of what they were discovering. She wanted to talk about what kind of professional role she might expect to fill.

Harshim was experiencing problems of his own. Knowing the family environment that awaited him, he was having difficulty imagining how Kate could fit into the role of a traditional Iranian family woman. If she were to accompany him to Iran and marry him, she would be expected to take care of domestic chores, bear children, and keep her husband happy.

Kate and Harshim were becoming increasingly aware of their growing physical attraction to one another. One night over dinner, after listening to Harshim awkwardly hint about the possibility of allowing their relationship to ascend to the next level, Kate concluded that she could not rely on Harshim to take charge.

She extended her hand toward Harshim and said, "Hey, cowboy, don't you think it's time for you to escort a lady to her room?"

Chapter Twelve
"The Right First Impression"

AHVAZ, IRAN: September, 1907

Each week, Harshim wrote a long and descriptive letter to his family in Ahvaz, Iran, nearly 350 miles south of Tehran. Each time a letter arrived, Father Isadore would insist on reading it, out loud, over the family dinner table. The family's reactions to Harshim's letters were mixed. Their growing frustration over his delayed return was somewhat offset by his reports of the technological breakthroughs he was witnessing.

Everyone at the table was hoping his letters might provide some clue as to how four years had changed the tall, shy young man. His mother, Ruth, anxious to see her son, was trying to develop a better understanding of him by listening to the tone of his letters. When his letters began to say *'we'* instead of *'I'*, she concluded that a woman had entered his life. On more than one occasion she would say, "What kind of woman would travel around with a strange man? I just hope he is not bringing some *ambitious woman* back with him."

In October 1907, Kate and Harshim set sail from Marseilles on a freighter bound for Abadan, Iran's principal access to the Persian Gulf. Ten days away from the press of work gave them ample opportunity to spend quiet time together and talk of many things. Kate would ask, "How is your family going to react? What kind of a first impression do you want me to make? How should I be dressed when I meet your family and friends at the train station?"

Kate was not the only person concerned about the impression she would make upon arrival. So too was Harshim. *'If we seriously contemplate expanding the irrigated land serviced by each drainage basin from five hundred to five thousand to twenty thousand acres, we will need to revise centuries of thinking and doing. If I am to accomplish what I hope to achieve, I will need to be viewed as a man of vision, action, and change.'*

Still impressed by the spirit he had observed from his study of Southwest wildcat oil drillers, Harshim decided to dress in the same fashion as his role models of change.

Aware of Harshim's wish to create the impression of a Southwestern American wildcatter, Kate considered, *'Why can't I dress in my best Irish riding habit? After all, I have always felt comfortable wearing my well-shined, tall, English riding boots. Carefully tailored riding pants are designed to show off a tall woman's legs. If I choose to wear my bell-shaped, dark-blue blazer with the large brass buttons, I could wear my favorite high-collared, pleated, silk blouse, and tie my favorite royal-blue scarf around my neck. Finally, I could arrange my red hair into twin pigtails fastened by red-and-white ribbons that will stick out from by blue riding helmet. Hopefully, they will want to learn who the interesting woman underneath the strange clothes might be.'*

On the appointed day, parents, relatives, friends, old schoolmates, and local businesspeople started arriving on the train station platform as early as two p.m., an hour before the scheduled arrival. Not wishing to miss seeing Harshim step from the train, they were patiently standing around, speculating how four years might have changed the future leader of the Naraghi family. *'What new ideas would he be bringing home? Is he still so tall and skinny? Is he still a kind and gentle man? Will he wish to continue to develop more land and make room for us to grow? Will he be a good leader?'*

Everybody was anxiously waiting to see who would be stepping from the train. They watched as the other passengers disembarked. Not seeing anyone who remotely resembled the tall, skinny kid they had watched leave more than four years ago, they began to worry. *'Had Harshim missed the train?'*

Harshim's mother, Ruth, was the first to notice a big, powerfully built man dressed in faded denim blue jeans, a bright blue-and-white checkered shirt, a thigh-length leather coat, American cowboy boots with two-inch heels, big dark glasses, and a wide-brimmed, beaver skin hat, step from the last car. *'He seems so much bigger and more muscular! Clearly, he is not the same youth who departed four years ago. Why is he wearing such strange clothes? What kind of a first impression is he trying to convey?'*

Ruth may have been surprised at the sight of her son, but she was wholly unprepared for the sight of the tall, full-bodied, strikingly beautiful, red-haired woman dressed in Irish riding clothes who stepped from the train behind him.

Ruth's first thought was, *'This is not some ordinary woman who has come to Iran to become part of our traditional family world. Whoever she may be, I think we better get used to thinking of them as two powerful people who have returned to make big things happen!'*

Quietly standing together at the far end of the platform, Harshim and Kate embodied youth, vigor, and individualistic character. With one glance, the other people on the platform concluded that these two beautiful people, whoever they were, had not arrived to fulfill traditional roles.

Father Isadore was both concerned and confused. *'How did Harshim manage to meet such a beautiful woman and persuade her to follow him all the way to Iran? This is one story I am going to enjoy. I hope her presence won't conflict with our efforts to push back the desert.'*

Ruth, Harshim's mother, was wondering, *'What is Harshim thinking? How could he expect such a lovely and seemingly refined woman to be happy living the life of a traditional Iranian wife? She doesn't even speak our language. Somebody has some explaining to do!'*

Kate extended her hand and offered a warm, firm, and friendly handshake. She focused her attention on Harshim's mother. She was trying to get a sense for what Ruth was thinking. It didn't take her long to find out. When Ruth smiled, opened her arms, engaged Kate in a hug, and said in broken English, "Welcome to our home," the dart thrower from County Cork began to relax.

Harshim's father's reaction was different. "Miss York, Harshim, in his letters, has described you as a person who graduated from college with an engineering degree. For the last three years you have accompanied your father all over the world assisting him with his dam construction consulting assignments. I look forward to learning more about what you have learned and what you hope to accomplish while you are here in Ahvaz."

Understanding the importance of introducing Kate to everyone who was waiting on the station platform, Harshim said hello to his old friends, members of his family, and business and professional associates. He asked each of them simple questions about what had happened in their lives since he left. To ensure they understood that Kate was special, he briefly told of her early years working with horses to support her college education; her four years of engineering study; and her three years of helping her father design and build major hydroelectric dams in exotic foreign locations.

For many of the people gathered there that day, meeting such an attractive, Western, college-educated, and well-traveled woman could have been an intimidating experience. Those who spoke English directed their questions to Kate. The others talked to Harshim and waited for him to translate. To a person, they were pleased by the interest Kate showed when she talked to them.

Father Isadore and Ruth proudly watched as Kate and Harshim slowly made their way from group to group. Judging by what was said, and seeing everybody's reactions, Father Isadore and Ruth concluded that Harshim and this remarkable woman were a sensitive and caring couple interested in learning more about the people they were meeting.

Chapter Thirteen
"Playing on the Boys' Team"

AHVAZ: October, 1907

Two weeks following their arrival in Iran, Harshim was becoming concerned about Kate. During the days, she was left with the women and was expected to perform her share of the household chores. Her attempts at conversation with the other women proved useless. At nights, at the family dinner table, she was expected to remain silent and listen to the men talk about the problems they had encountered. For days, they had been trying to devise a way to transmit the compressed air needed to drive the big excavating equipment along the length of the contemplated route.

Seated in her customary place next to Harshim, Kate was left with no choice but to watch and listen in silence as the men agonized over the problem. After a time, when it appeared no practical suggestions would be forthcoming, Kate broke her imposed protocol of silence. "If you were to use compressed air to power electric power generators, why couldn't you use copper wiring to transport electrical power over the greater distances?" she asked.

Confused by Kate's unexpected comments, the men focused their attention on Harshim, expecting some sort of an explanation as to why his lady friend was allowed to speak. After taking time to consider his answer, Harshim addressed the others at the table. "I think we need to pay attention to what Kate is suggesting," he said. "For more than three years, Kate and her father, Tom York, have been consulting on some of the great dams that have been constructed in different parts of the world. If any of you doubt her competency to speak on this subject, I would suggest you address your questions to Kate."

Strained silence was the only reaction.

Later that night, when they were finally alone, Kate announced, "From the moment when you leave in the morning until after dinner, I live in a world of solitary confinement! As hard as I have tried to fit in, the women could not be any more resentful. We don't speak a common language. I am prevented from understanding anything they may be asking or developing. It's difficult for me to develop any kind of a personal attachment!

"Tonight, I could sense the men's resentment when I interrupted the conversation. I feel trapped! When I agreed to accompany you home, I distinctly remember making myself quite clear. Any thoughts of my remaining or asking you to marry me depended upon my becoming professionally engaged in what you are hoping to accomplish. Without that opportunity, I am concerned about whether I could be happy here!"

No one needed to tell Harshim that the next words he uttered could affect the rest of his life. Wanting to be careful, he was still thinking about how he should respond when, unexpectedly, Kate got out of bed. She went over to a corner of their room and withdrew, from the large desk there, some of the old maps and diaries that he and his father had compiled during their early surveys.

Surprised she knew of their existence; he was unprepared for what she said next. "When I looked at the map displaying the land you hope to bring under irrigated cultivation, I failed to understand why you are going to all the trouble of installing the new quants, when you are only planning to utilize less than twenty-five percent of the available water. Not only would the installation of a hydroelectric dam increase, by a factor of four, the land you could bring under irrigation; it would also provide the electric power needed by your big machines and, over time, create substantial revenues from the sale of the excess electric power."

A week later, as they were sitting down to dinner, Harshim announced, "Kate wishes to make a presentation. She has done her homework and developed a plan for introducing a hydroelectric dam into each of our new irrigation districts. According to her calculations, the dams would allow us to increase the acreage serviced by each drainage basin from five thousand to twenty thousand acres."

Kate, having watched her father make similar presentations, was prepared to make the case. "Working from Harshim and Father Isadore's earlier calculations, from other studies, I have learned that the generated electric revenues can easily amortize the cost of a new dam. Adding dams to your plan will pay for itself, allow you to spread the cost of operating your quants over a much larger area and, most importantly, provide resources for so many more needy people."

Mesmerized by the scale of what she was suggesting, the men of the Naraghi family started to ask questions. Taking her time to answer, Kate was watching as the faces around the table began to register interest in what she was saying.

Father Isadore, the ever-protective patriarch, finally asked, "Before we have the benefit of the resultant revenues, where do you expect us to find the money we will need to fund the construction of each new dam? The costs of installing a 'Super Quant' will stretch our family resources to the limit. While I can understand the merit of installing hydroelectric dams, we just don't possess the financial resources to make it happen."

Kate, prepared for the statement, answered, "I think the problem can be better addressed once we have the results of an engineering study. For three years, I have helped my father, Tom York, make similar presentations to major banks. My father understands dam construction economics better than anyone. The big international banks consistently retain him to perform their economic-feasibility studies."

It had been a long time since the diners had seen Father Isadore appear so interested in a new idea. "Kate, how are we going to find qualified people to develop your idea and convince some international banker of the viability of what we will be proposing?"

Kate responded, "Father Isadore, perhaps I should remind you, enough time has passed to permit the comparison of my father's economic forecasts with the actual results. The proven accuracy of his work has been recognized. Why couldn't a report by my father of our intentions accompany our application to the same banks already familiar with his work?"

Later that night, after Kate and Harshim had retired to the privacy of their bedroom, Kate was still excited. After crawling into bed and placing her arms around Harshim's big back, she bent forward to whisper in his ear "Harshim, have you ever stopped to consider where all this is leading? How are you prepared to react to a truly happy woman?"

Part Three
"The Third Alternative"

Chapter Fourteen
"The David Marcus Problem"

TEL AVIV, ISRAEL: April, 1953

Smohl was sitting at a sidewalk table outside his favorite Tel Aviv coffee shop enjoying a cup of his preferred blend of Egyptian and Moroccan coffees. An old friend who was both a former WWII colleague and the current director of the Mossad was sitting at an adjacent table. Anyone watching would have seen two men engaging in the type of casual, friendly conversation that strangers commonly use to entertain themselves.

But there was nothing casual or of a friendly nature being discussed. Smohl was receiving the Mossad report on David Marcus. "Your friend is being held in an MI-6 safehouse in London under high-priority protection. He is not charged with a crime, nor is he suspected of colluding with a foreign government. The circumstances surrounding his detainment appear to be a result of British concern over his divulging information that might complicate their covert operation.

"My people have advised me, if you hope to obtain his release, you need to call your old friend, Walter Parameter at Whitehall. Given your longtime relationship, only you can explain the extenuating circumstances involving your friend. Rather than risk the public disclosure of Operation Ajax, they may choose to negotiate his release."

A sly smile began to appear on Smohl's otherwise pensive face. '*It's been more than five years since "Ol' Walt" and I worked together to prevent the seven-member "Oil Club" from consolidating their control over ninety percent of the world's oil production. I would be surprised to learn we don't still share the same mistrust of the big oil companies.*'

"Thanks for the report. This is one request I plan to make in person. Let's hope Ol' Walt will appreciate why it's important to prevent his own government from pursuing the imperialistic takeover of a friendly, loyal nation or the embarrassment of holding the son of a royal duke hostage."

A few minutes later, Smohl, lost in thought, failed to notice when his friend unceremoniously asked for his check and departed.

Allowing his mind to wander, Smohl was considering a new alternative. '*Why couldn't we reinvent David Marcus as an Israeli oil consultant? With proper training, and exposure, what is there to stop us from introducing Marcus as the Mossad mole we need to insert into the inner circle of the Anglo-American planning for Iran? I can't imagine the Anglo-American oil companies would pass up an opportunity to develop a more complete understanding of the quantity of oil they hope to control. Marcus already understands the Middle Eastern oil industry better than most. He speaks the language. Assuming we can persuade David to cooperate, we will have to teach him to speak Hebrew and English with a Hebrew accent. We could change his appearance to keep him from being recognized and provide him access to our secret oil archives, which contain William D'Arcy's original Iranian oil exploration reports. Given the opportunity, David might be capable of materially changing current estimates of untapped Iranian oil potential.*'

During his voyage a week later, unaware of what was being planned for him, David had plenty of time to speculate about why he had been released. '*Why am I on a slow freighter headed to Israel? What kind of a deal was made to arrange my release?*'

Ten days later, David Marcus stepped onto the wharf-side dock of the harbor in Haifa, Israel. His curiosity was further stoked when he was met by three tough-looking, well-armed, uniformed Israeli soldiers. One of the soldiers politely stepped forward and asked, "Mr. Kahne? Mr. Alan Kahne, we have been instructed to meet you and deliver you to Mossad headquarters. There are some important people interested in meeting you."

"There must be some mistake, my name is Sir David Marcus."

Alan Kahne's first day in the Mossad training camp was devoted to having his *before pictures* taken. He was weighed, given a complete physical examination, issued boot-camp uniforms, and assigned to the bottom bunk of a long line of military metal beds in the new-recruit barracks. By three o'clock that afternoon, he was standing at attention in the parade ground, where he received his first military order - to complete a five-mile run-walk before dinner.

After dinner, exhausted, feeling pain in every joint, Alan entered the shower room. He wanted to scrub off the grime of his long day. Standing under the hot water, waiting for his pain to subside, he wondered, '*What kind of hell have I gotten myself into?*'

On the second day, he was standing at attention, in formation with his fellow recruits. It was 5 a.m. Early morning drills had to be completed before he could go to the mess tent for his second exposure to Mossad field cooking.

Following breakfast, he and his fellow recruits were assigned, and were expected to attend, classes that corresponded to their post-completion assignments. Afternoon classwork was followed by two hours of physical conditioning and another five-mile run. Any hope of a relaxed dinner, a hot shower, and a good night's sleep was eliminated when he was assigned to *advanced training* evening classes.

By the end of the first forty-five days, Alan's appearance had begun to change. His waxed bald head was now deeply tanned. His bushy red eyebrows had been shaved off and replaced with artfully applied black makeup. Previously unnoticed when he had a full head of long, red hair, his large ears stuck out from his head. Now fully evident, they had become his most prominent feature.

With the loss of weight, his facial characteristics were beginning to change. His somewhat bloated, pudgy face, a well-deserved result of way too many years of good living, had become gaunt. The bone structure of his face had become noticeable. His chiseled nose, the thin line of his lips, and his close-set big blue eyes were now framed by the strong eyebrow line of his forehead, high cheekbones, and the square set of his jaw.

But it was the transformation of his body that attracted the most attention. Gone was the 190-pound, thick body appearance. He was beginning to resemble a short, well-conditioned, slightly built, wiry combatant. He was learning to speak and write Hebrew. When he could speak in English, he spoke, as he had been trained to do, with a heavy Hebrew accent. He had become a skilled communications officer, trained to use a wide variety of equipment located in some very strange field locations. He had been instructed in the use of small arms and the martial arts.

After completing his evening orientation classes, he spent time in the Mossad archives. Fortunately, Iran's early contract oil exploration expert, William D'Arcy, had kept detailed records. How they ended up in the Israeli archives was a closely guarded secret. Alan was rapidly expanding his already extensive knowledge of the Middle Eastern oil industry.

By the end of ninety days, Major Alan Kahne walked out of the main gate a newly commissioned officer. Those who knew him best described him as a bald man with big ears, a quiet, strong-willed, analytical mind, and a sharp tongue. Those familiar with his file appreciated him for his knowledge of the Middle Eastern oil industry.

Only one test remained. Both he and his Mossad handlers needed to assure themselves that he could fulfill both the technical requirements of his new role and remain unrecognized in the presence of familiar people, even his old friends. Trial appearances were being arranged with his former Sentinel colleagues, Middle Eastern oil clients, and his earlier financial and investment clients.

Chapter Fifteen
"Birthing the Third Alternative"

NEW YORK: July, 1953

Informing each of the individual members that comprised the Independent Oil Company (IOC) of their "Third Alternative" plan would require Cecelia and Mike to travel to each company's headquarters. But the time required, and the security coordination needed to do so, would have exceeded the time and the resources that Mike, and Cecelia had available.

Instead, they invited the IOC executives to a conference on "Competitive Bidding for Iranian Oil." The meeting was scheduled to convene at ten o'clock on Wednesday, July 15, 1953, in the executive conference room atop the Stone City Bank building in New York. Mike Stone would be presiding.

Given the importance of presenting the latest estimate of the Iranian oil potential, Mike – at Smohl' s suggestion – had arranged for Major Alan Kahne to make himself available to the cooperating members before the big meeting.

The day of the IOC meeting arrived. Mike, Cecelia, and the rest of his team were sitting around one end of a big conference table. Alan Kahne and each of the independent executives were seated around the balance of the table.

Before calling the meeting to order, Mike made his way around the room to say hello and thank each executive for attending. Chair by chair, Mike Stone's efforts drew him closer to Alan Kahne.

Mike's brief stops gave Alan time to think. *'Will Mike recognize me despite the changes I have made to my appearance? How long has it been since we had our last conversation? Will he recognize my voice?'*

Stopping beside Alan's chair, Mike showed no sign of recognition. "Mr. Kahne, I have been hearing compliments regarding your research and your many contributions to different members of the Middle Eastern oil patch," Mike said. "Recently, your contributions have made it possible for me to inform each of the IOC members of the unusual opportunity they have to invest in Iranian oil. Thank you for your work."

"Thank you, Mr. Stone," Alan responded. "From everything I have learned, it appears you are on the right track." As the meeting progressed, it soon became obvious that each executive was impressed by Alan Kahne's research and by his belief that the size of the oil reserves materially exceeded historical estimates. To support his comments regarding Nation's oil potential, he pulled out a map depicting the locations of Iran's oil reserves. Without the benefit of specific seismic studies, Alan continued, "It is apparent that existing petroleum reserves, most likely, are located under the four hundred thousand acres of Nation's farmable acreage. We are talking about a significant amount of oil."

Responding to a question from Mike, Alan Kahne suggested, "For the purpose of our discussion, it is important we understand there are many moving parts involved in the ultimate passage of our proposed Oil Bill by the Iranian Majlis. Should we fail to achieve ratification of the Competitive Bidding Oil Bill, our proposed 'Third Alternative' could fail. Based on the probabilities contained in my analysis, I believe a backup plan is indicated. Why shouldn't you consider negotiating a separate agreement with Naraghi-Roth for the development of Nation's oil?"

Everyone in the room was surprised by Kahne's suggestion. Everyone but Mike. He was lost in thought. *'How could anyone who did not know about the Versailles Summit Conference be able to make such a novel suggestion?'*

Enthusiastic over the possibility that their young company might be able to create a *'back-up'* opportunity, the president of Independent Oil, Ltd., asked, "Mr. Kahne, why do you believe Naraghi-Roth might be willing to talk to us?"

"The preservation of Nation has been an important consideration of Naraghi-Roth for an extremely long time," Kahne answered. "Since the conclusion of the last war, Nation is no longer the beneficiary of Allied protection from German encroachment. They are in the need of a new deterrent.

"Becoming a recognized foreign investment interest of the United States, Nation would be classified as an 'American Foreign Investment Interest' and would thereby qualify for its protection. Assuming the appropriate protections of their above-ground farming interests can be negotiated, they might be very motivated to talk to you."

Tempering their excitement was the Independent's concern about how they could protect what could become a substantial investment. Accordingly, they were interested in learning what evidence Mike had that the president was prepared to recognize the proposed venture as a legitimate "American Foreign Investment Interest" deserving of its military protection.

Mike did not disappoint. He pulled from his suitcoat pocket a transcript of his meeting with the president and began to read aloud: "Subject to fulfilling all the requirements to qualify as a legitimate American Foreign Investment Interest, the president has indicated he is prepared to issue the required executive order."

Mike asked: "What criteria do we need to fulfill to ensure the president will endorse our agreement? His endorsement would have to be a condition of any deal we will be asked to sign."

On that note, Mike believed he had been authorized to proceed with all possible haste to implement the two suggested plans. With the last of his salutations complete, Mike Stone motioned for Alan Kahne to accompany him from his conference room to his private dining room.

A few minutes later, after they were seated and had finished giving the waiter their orders, Mike asked, "I am confused; how were you able to raise the question of an Independent-Naraghi-Roth association? How could you possibly be aware of what only a small group of us have the privilege of knowing?"

Bemused by the question, Alan was trying to decide how to answer when Mike unexpectedly asked, "How were you able to conclude the appropriate executed agreement might be regarded as an effective deterrent by Naraghi-Roth? The only time I have ever heard of that phrase being used was at the Versailles Summit meeting. I don't recall seeing you there!"

Alan answered, "Mike, have you overlooked Smohl Cantor's presence? I have had the privilege of being included in many of his discussions. Although it was not discussed in my presence, I am convinced the Anglo-Americans are planning to prevent the vote on your 'Oil Bill' from taking place and thereby eliminate the last remaining obstacle to their Ajax plan.

"My point is, while oil companies may be able to prevent the Iranian government from consummating a deal with the IOC, they cannot stop Naraghi-Roth from executing a similar arrangement."

Reminded of Smohl's presence at the Versailles Summit meeting, Mike shifted from his bit-by-bit analysis of what they had been discussing to trying to understand the connection between Alan Kahne and Smohl.

"Perhaps you would explain why Smohl would share such confidential information with you? It's common knowledge that the Stones, the Roths, and the Naraghis, together with Smohl, have worked together for many years solving Nation problems. We are talking about long-term relationships of trust, confidence, and respect! I would find it very unusual if any of the members were to talk about such serious subjects with anyone else."

Alan responded, "Smohl is not a friend of mine; he is my boss. I am a member of the Mossad. I was recruited and trained to be retained by the British and American oil companies as their oil consultant in the Middle East, and more particularly Iran. Apparently, your people needed someone on the inside to report what was being planned.

"Don't be confused by the charade playing itself out in Iran. The British government and the Anglo-American oil companies have only one objective: to seize control over Iranian oil. They have authorized Kermit Roberts of the CIA and General Fazlollah Zahedi, the former commander of the Iranian Army, to accelerate and intensify public demonstrations that were previously authorized by your former president."

"Wait just a minute!" Mike said, "I have it on reliable authority that the current president is not prepared to authorize the final phase of Operation Ajax. Quite the opposite! We have been assured, subject to implementing the 'Third Alternative,' we will have the full support of the White House.

"Kermit Roberts and General Zahedi have been promised financial support from the Anglo-American oil companies to encourage the anti-government demonstrators. According to Kermit, they no longer require financial assistance from the American government. He and General Zahedi believe it will only be a question of time before the demonstrations will develop lives of their own. Once that occurs, no further assistance or authorization from the United States will be required to affect the intended regime change."

Thoroughly incensed, Mike asked, "Is there anything that can be done?"

"Yes, we need to obtain approval from the Iranian Majlis before they can complete their planned regime change."

Believing it was time to conclude their meeting, "Alan Kahne" stood up and placed his glass on the table, then said, "Mike, are you truly aware of what we are trying to stop? I do not care to speculate about what the consequences of failure might be. It is difficult to imagine what might happen to a resource-rich, traditional agrarian economy should Iran become a despotic government under the shah's rule, '*open for business*' to foreign investment interests."

Snapping into his formal military posture, Major Kahne announced, "The time has come for the world to appreciate how valuable the Naraghi-Roth Nation of Citizen Farmers has become. Time to go to work!"

Chapter Sixteen

"The Anglo-American Conspiracy"

TEHRAN, IRAN: July, 1953

Senior executives of the British and American oil companies had become aware of the Sentinels' interest in, and possible opposition to, their carefully crafted plan, Ajax.

The meeting was chaired by British Oil's senior-most executive, who opened it by saying, "Now that the Iranians have nationalized their oil industry, absolutely nothing can be allowed to upset our plans or jeopardize the implementation of Ajax! Provided we retain the continued support of the United States government, I don't see any reason we should fail to improve our grip over Middle Eastern oil production."

Unexpectedly, one of the other British Oil directors interrupted. "I am confused," he said. "According to Mr. Kahne's research and calculations, the real quantity of Iranian oil could be considerably more than one hundred billion barrels, not your forty-billion-barrel current estimate.

"By my rough calculations, the potential value of this two hundred fifty percent increase in oil reserves exceeds what you hope to gain by attempting to preserve our eighty percent revenue participation. Why would you want to jeopardize our control over the total field by insisting on preserving terms and conditions that are no longer competitive?

"The effect of providing the Americans with a fifty percent interest in exchange for their cooperation and contribution of fresh capital doesn't make sense. Our remaining forty percent participation is ten percentage points less than the fifty percent participation the Iranians have already agreed to.

"Then, there is the problem of inviting the Americans to play an active role in Ajax. Over time, how are we going to prevent them from emerging as the dominant partner? What am I missing?"

Thoroughly annoyed, the chairman emphatically responded, "The problem we are trying to solve is how to improve Western control over Middle Eastern oil, not how to maximize British revenues."

No longer willing to remain silent, the director asked, "What has convinced you the Americans will provide the final approval of our Ajax plan? How could anyone familiar with the situation fail to conclude that our quest for control is, in reality, a blatant exercise of economic imperialism? Given a choice, why would the United States choose to be labeled as a greedy imperialist in a world of emerging, independent sovereign nations?"

Shocked by the unexpected comments, the group's attention shifted to Kermit Roberts, the American CIA case officer, recently arrived in Tehran. They were looking forward to his explanation.

Standing up, Kermit Roberts said, "European countries that rely on Iranian oil are becoming increasingly alarmed over the prospect of declining Iranian oil production. In addition, they are questioning what may occur should the reduction in domestic oil revenues adversely affect the Iranian economy.

"Should Prime Minister Mossadegh decide to turn toward Russia for assistance, that would be a risk that the United States and Great Britain are not prepared to accept. I have been informed by a reliable source that the American government is totally opposed to any plan that would allow the Russians to gain a toehold in the Middle Eastern oil patch. Given no alternative, the previous president felt compelled to provide preliminary approval of the early stage of Ajax!"

Still not satisfied, the director asked, "If the need for American influence and control is so critical, what should we do in the event the American president becomes convinced that the Sentinel Plan, which calls for competitive bidding, represents a viable alternative?"

The mood in the room suddenly changed. Confidence and bravado had been replaced by anxiety and uncertainty. Sensing the change, the chairman asked, "Surely the CIA and MI-6 must have a backup plan?"

Responding, Roberts said, "Yes, sir. We have developed two different plans. For purposes of discussion, I think we need to assume Prime Minister Mossadegh has the votes to assure a razor-thin majority vote for the Sentinel Oil Bill. One of our plans calls for us to persuade one or more of the country's sub-culture leaders, who represent fifty percent of the seats in the Majlis, to abstain or vote against the Oil Bill. Without a one hundred percent participation, the prime minister will not have the votes needed to approve the competitive bidding legislation.

"Our second plan calls for us to accelerate and enhance the initial stages of Ajax. By encouraging a more rapid escalation of the planned public demonstrations, we hope to encourage the growing public dissatisfaction to develop a life of its own. By framing a pending change in regime as the result of a popular revolution, we might succeed in removing Prime Minister Mossadegh's government before the Majlis can vote on the Oil Bill.

"Already, the distribution of American dollars to some of these demonstrators is purchasing new loyalties from some unusual and surprising parties. Of particular interest has been our recruitment of General Zahedi, the former commanding officer of the Iranian military; the shah has assured Zahedi he will be appointed to be the next prime minister. Accordingly, the general has indicated that he is prepared to withdraw his military support for the current prime minister. His fellow generals, who have clearly stated they do not wish to engage in combat with their fellow citizen soldiers, have agreed to stand aside should that occur. In such a case, the remaining loyalists would not be able to protect the prime minister.

"Once Prime Minister Mossadegh is arrested, removed from office, incarcerated, and charged with treason, the young shah is prepared to return from exile. He has agreed to declare martial law and recognize the validity of the twenty percent royalty oil agreement that Britain brokered with Iran in 1941."

"Wait just a damned minute!" the senior American oil executive declared. "Let us not assume that we are not working inside some tightly sealed vacuum chamber. Despite the fact that it has been reported, on occasion, that you people in the CIA pursue covert operations without the express knowledge and approval of the White House, how do plan to energize the second phase of Ajax without the American president's approval?"

"Are you asking how the second round of public demonstrations could occur without his approval and commitment to authorizing the funding necessary to support the final phase of Ajax?" Roberts asked.

The leading British Oil executive broke in. "If you don't mind, I would like to answer that question," he said. "Where does it say that the Anglo-American oil companies can't agree to provide the necessary funding, without the approval of the American government? How do you expect the president to react when he learns the IOC oil plan will not have been approved by the Iranian Majlis? What choice will he have?"

There being no further questions, the British senior officer declared the meeting adjourned.

Chapter Seventeen
"Making Their Case"

TEL AVIV: March, 1953

By 1953, leaders of Iran's Populace National Front could see that the nationalization of the country's oil production had led to less oil being pumped out of the ground, which had led to more economic and political problems.

Prime Minister Mosaddegh's mission was simple: find a way to preserve his government and obtain the cooperation of a foreign oil production company with the technical know-how to get production back on track.

Before the Sentinel Plan, "The Third Alternative," could be set into motion, the Iranian Majlis needed to approve the "Competitive Bidding Oil Bill." That would require the votes of each elected representative of the six sub-cultures. While the interests of the diverse populace varied, the cultures had shared goals: limit foreign intrusion; preserve Iran's representative government and its rule of law and recover the missing thirty percent of its oil revenues.

Harshim, Jacques, Smohl, and Sam had requested a meeting be convened in Tel Aviv, where each of the sub-culture leaders would gather to learn of the Sentinels' plan. They were expected to ask questions and, if appropriate, authorize the Majlis to proceed with the vote on the Oil Bill.

On the appointed day, the people sitting around the table at the meeting represented a diversified collection of the responsible leaders. They had gathered to listen to the three Sentinels -- Mike Stone, his brilliant wife, Cecelia Chang Stone, and the legendary Jacques Roth -- present their "Third Alternative" plan. They were joined by Alan Kahne, the fast-rising petroleum consultant. He had been invited to answer technical questions regarding anything to do with Middle Eastern oil in general and Iranian oil in particular. He had also been invited to test whether the attending Sentinels or any of his former clients would recognize him.

This meeting represented the last opportunity for the six Iranian leaders to discuss the Sentinels' daring plan before bringing it to the floor of the Majlis for an up-or-down vote. Each of the leaders had arrived with a list of questions.

The Iranian subculture leaders understood that the introduction of competitive bidding represented an interesting approach to separating the political control of national petroleum interests from the management of oil production. They were aware that the plan's adoption would end the viability of the Anglo-American plan to take over control of their government.

In discussions among themselves, one could be heard asking, "Before making such a far-reaching decision that includes inviting an American oil producer into our midst, don't we need to learn a lot more about the details of the Sentinel Plan? Should we start by asking if there are alternatives we need to consider?"

After an hour of unproductive debate, sensing their collective growing frustration, Alan Kahne asked, "Smohl, if this dilemma was being argued in front of the Israeli Knesset, what criterion would the members apply?"

Though he was surprised by the question, Smohl answered without hesitation. "They would apply our historic Israeli doctrine of 'Pushing Back the Desert,'" he said.

To that, Alan asked "Do you mean literally or figuratively?"

"Both. By introducing water to the desert, we push back the boundaries of an arid land. By making it bloom, we extend the boundaries of the people who perform the work!"

Dr. Mossadegh then asked, politely, "Smohl, are you suggesting that, should our government achieve a fifty percent interest in its oil revenues, we could use the extra thirty percent of the revenues to better satisfy the needs and aspirations of our working classes? Wouldn't the modernization of our economy and the enhancement of peoples' lives be another example of what you refer to as 'Pushing Back the Desert'? If that is what we are discussing, to be supportive, why shouldn't we concentrate on learning the details of the Sentinel plan and identifying the key challenges that must be solved?"

Cecelia got right to the point. "This is not the first time the problem of protecting oil reserves from foreign interests has arisen. In 1946, the newly formed Indonesian government was faced with a similar problem. The Dutch were threatening to reassert their colonial rule over the island nation by declaring that their control of the oil was necessary to protect it from the threat of spreading communism. The Dutch, in seeking the support of the United States and the recently formed United

Nations, were playing on the public's fear of spreading communism to plead their case. Wasn't that fictitious threat similar to what certain parties are now alleging in connection with Iran?

"We first became aware of the Indonesian problem when we were seeking Asian support for our Energy Development Fund. Knowing that the Sentinels and the 'Friends of the Sentinels' were committed to breaking the grip of the Oil Club, our friends invited us to develop a plan to block the Dutch agenda of reasserting their historical colonial rule over the recently emerged sovereign state. That is when we came up with the idea of introducing competitive bidding between qualified oil companies.

"That was the easy part. As with our present situation, we had to assume Royal Dutch Shell's fellow Oil Club members were not prepared to bid against each other. We knew that, when faced with this dilemma, we had to create a new, qualified oil development and production company.

"A quick survey of existing independent oil companies revealed that they lacked the necessary qualifications and the capital resources. However, when we cataloged the unique skills of the individual companies, we concluded that, if we could organize the right coalition, we could create a company able to manage the development and production of Indonesian oil.

"Following our observation, we decided to break the problem into two parts. It was Mike Stone, the man sitting at one end of this table, who introduced the idea of solving the development and production problems by combining the right independent oil companies into one master organization capable of fulfilling all the different requirements.

"It was Jacques' suggestion that we form an International Energy Development Fund. To finance our estimated need for fifteen billion dollars, we decided to appeal to motivated entities beyond the long reach of the seven-member 'Oil Club' and their loyal and supportive financial institutions.

"Before proceeding, we needed the support of the White House, the Federal Reserves, and the Treasury Department. That is where Mike Stone helped. Interestingly, he discovered the American president needed a second option if he hoped to withstand the political pressure of the Dutch and the lobbying efforts of the collective members of the 'Oil Club.' Today, six years later, you only have to look at Indonesia to see that our plan worked then and that it is working today.

"We believe the same solution can be implemented in Iran. But there are two big differences. Today, we have a qualified oil company to act as a competitive bidder, and we have access to the International Energy Development Fund capable of providing development capital."

Cecelia's presentation was interrupted when Prime Minister Mossadegh asked, "Are you asking us to believe your new plan has the support of the White House? What do you know that we don't?"

Standing up, Mike said, "Maybe *I* should answer your question since I was involved in the decision. The question you *should* be asking is, what has changed to encourage the American president to re-evaluate his position?

"Ajax has never had the final approval of the American president. In fact, his predecessor approved it in the preliminary stages only to buy the time he needed to search for an alternate solution. Were you to study the press reports, you would discover that the American president has remained silent on this matter. Without the benefit of 'The Third Alternative,' he would have to yield to the pressure of the British and the American Oil lobbyists.

"The demonstrations you have been witnessing represent only the preliminary stages of Ajax. Financially, they have been organized and funded by the American CIA and the British MI-6. If their support is withdrawn, the demonstrations will likely die down.

"After we presented our plan to the chairman of the Federal Reserve, we were assured, contingent on our presenting a done deal to the president, that he is prepared to withdraw any further support for Ajax."

For the first time, the esteemed leader of Iran's Bazaritum, the Iranian subculture that represents markets of the bazar and connects it to markets in Asia, India, North Africa, and Europe, rose to speak. "And just what are you expecting us to do?" he asked.

Before Mike could answer, five hands shot up into the air. He recognized Ayatollah Khasani, who asked, "Gentlemen, do I speak for the rest of us when I say we are all in agreement? If so, I suggest we use the balance of our time discussing what needs to be accomplished before we can place the IOC Bill on the floor of the Majlis, Iranian Senate, for formal ratification."

In the days that followed, each of the cultural leaders returned home and began to reflect on the significance of what they had tentatively decided to do during the meeting.

Sam Naraghi, remembering his training and experience in establishing the Naraghi-Roth Trading Company, tended to look at serious problems from the outside in. To him, the central question remained: Could his father and his friends hold together the diverse interests that dominated each of the parties of Iran's fragile coalition? He thought, *'In approving competitive bidding between the British and an American independent oil company, the Majlis will be asked to consider a problem quite different from the one addressed in voting for the nationalization of Iran's oil industry.*

'Each of our cultural leaders can be expected to base their decision on what they think is in their sub-culture's best interest. Who knows what private agendas they may be harboring? Despite their non-binding votes in Tel Aviv, how can we be confident that none of them will change his vote or abstain?'

Over the next few days, Sam began to question, *'If Nation is considering the development of a backup plan, might some of the other leaders be doing the same?'*

Taking advantage of his friend Jacques' habit of charting diagrams of sequential logic, Sam began to make a list of each of the coalition's supporting parties and their designated leaders. Next to each name, he noted the goals, objectives, and any possible side agendas the leader might be considering. After more than an hour of concentrated thought, Sam sat back and looked at his chart. Surprised by the presence of so many blank spaces, he quickly realized how little was known about the private agendas of their sub-culture leaders.

Sharing his doubts and concerns with his father, Sam asked, "After dinner could we talk about the problems of possible secret agendas?"

Sam was asking questions and taking detailed notes. Watching his father search his mind for a recollection that might suggest the presence of a hidden agenda, he couldn't help but marvel at the breadth and depth of Harshim's experiences and the accuracy of his memory.

Later that evening, after adding his father's recollections to his chart, Sam concluded there were still far too many blanks. The next morning, Sam suggested, "Father, why don't you look at the empty spaces on my chart? We still have a lot of blanks and not very much time to complete our task. Why don't you call on the people you know best, and I will take the rest?"

Chapter Eighteen
"Kermit and the Cia Director"

LANGLEY, VIRGINIA: July 1953

During his weekly phone call with the CIA director, Kermit mentioned that his team was no longer required to stoke the fires of the public demonstrations. "Quite the opposite, they are being organized without our assistance," he said. "The oil companies are footing the bill, and the crowds are growing larger and angrier."

Unexpectedly, the director, his longtime confidant and former field colleague, said, "Kermit, I want you to listen very carefully! We have been receiving reports, some of which have originated from your in-country agents. It appears the growing public unrest may be increasing the conflict between the leaders who support the conservative Muslim doctrine and those who support Prime Minister Mossadegh's Western constitutional philosophy. It may be that a crack between the subcultures is about to be revealed. All we need is one defection. If there is any way we can exploit this schism, we should do so.

"It may be a long shot, but I suggest you call on Ayatollah Khasani. No matter how remote the possibility, I think we need to help him consider which course of action best serves the destiny of Islam. Does he prefer to be a continuing supporter of the National Party and remain a minority leader of one segment of a coalition government, or would he prefer to remain patient and eventually assume control over the entire country?"

"Boss, what do you mean 'control over the entire country?'"

"The fact remains, after more than two thousand years, the people of Iran have finally achieved a constitutional government. In this environment there has been little reason for the working classes to seek an alternative form of government. But if they were to lose their constitutional government and become oppressed by a foreign political authority and foreign concessionaires, wouldn't it be reasonable to expect them to turn to Islam for spiritual comfort and political salvation?

"Let us not forget, the Muslim people can be very patient. In our Western world, we measure things in five- to ten-year intervals. The

Muslims are accustomed to thinking in terms of decades and centuries. Given the restoration of a shah-led military dictatorship and the intrusion of foreign investment interests, why is it so improbable to believe the growing national resentment could materially increase the role of the Muslim clergy? In such an environment, both the spiritual leadership and the clerical governing needs could be united under one tent, 'Muslim theocracy.'"

"Mr. Director, are you suggesting the ayatollah and his loyal mullahs could be influenced to think about a longer-term strategy, one calling for the Muslim religion to play an entirely different role in Iran and perhaps elsewhere in the Middle East? He and his fellow Muslim leaders would have to believe it will only be a question of time before the '*pot of growing public resentment*' will begin to boil over. If left unattended, it becomes only a question of time before the Iranian people will introduce a seventh century Muslim theocracy and take back their country from the shah and his Anglo-American supporters.

"Mr. Director, are you seriously suggesting if Khasani and his Muslim followers were to be convinced your prophecy has merit, he might be persuaded to abstain from voting on the pending oil legislation?"

"Kermit, keep me informed. After you have met with the ayatollah, let me know what you have learned."

Chapter Nineteen
"Ayatollah Khasani"

TEHRAN, IRAN: July 1953

For several days, the ayatollah had been anxiously waiting to greet his childhood friend, Harshim Naraghi, the respected, former leader of "Citizen's Nation." With all the recent developments, the ayatollah understood the importance of their meeting.

When he heard the early morning ringing of his doorbell, Khasani was confused. He distinctly remembered that his meeting with Harshim had been scheduled for that afternoon. Curious to learn who had come calling, the ayatollah motioned to his servant, "Please find out who our unexpected caller might be. Who has taken the liberty of showing up without an appointment?"

The ayatollah was not expecting the CIA case officer to appear without an appointment. Roberts' appearance in the vestibule of Khasani's humble abode reminded him of the seriousness of the challenge at hand. *'Before I have a wide-ranging conversation with Harshim, why shouldn't I try to find out what the "American Viper" has to say?'*

After greeting the unexpected visitor with an offer of ceremonial tea, he motioned for him to take a seat on one of the many voluminous, brightly colored, comfortable pillows that covered the magnificent Oriental rugs on the floor of his inner-most, private office.

It was after Khasani offered his guest a second cup of tea that Roberts asked, in a slow and deliberate way, "Ayatollah, have you and your friends given any thought to what might happen if the Majlis fail to ratify the Oil Bill?"

Instantly alert to the many possible implications of the question, Khasani sat back and did not answer immediately. Instead, he focused on enjoying his second cup of tea. It was only after a few minutes that he said, "Let's talk about the Majlis. As you will recall, I recently chaired the meeting in which we accepted the final language of the Oil Bill pending its presentation to the Majlis for approval. I don't recall there being any material disagreements or mention of anyone threatening to vote against it."

"Ayatollah Khasani, what might happen if the British and Americans attempt to take control of your government before the vote can occur? I have been reliably informed that the Americans and the British oil companies may start a revolution and call for Prime Minister Mosaddegh's removal from office. The fact that the people are upset with Iran's deteriorating economics suggests there is no shortage of public anger."

"Are you implying there is some plan being hatched to prevent the Majlis from voting?"

Not hearing an answer to his question, Khasani continued, "Mr. Roberts, in a different context, the mullahs have been discussing among themselves what they might expect should that occur."

Roberts responded, "Their inquiries have raised two questions: What portion of the working classes will look to Islam for comfort and protection? And what do we need to do to organize the more extreme sects to counter the Anglo-American threat?"

Smiling, the wise, learned religious leader said, "The mullahs are asking, should the shah's government be restored, how long it would take before the denial of the public's needs and aspirations results in a Muslim-led revolution?"

Kermit was thinking, '*Well, I'll be damned! The director was right. The ayatollah must be considering his options. I didn't have to introduce the idea, he practically led himself to his own conclusion. Maybe this would be the proper time for me to excuse myself.*'

Promptly at two o'clock that same afternoon, Harshim came calling. He was pleased by the warm reception he got from his childhood friend. They began to recount some of the many battles they had fought together to preserve and enhance Iran's constitutional government. As he listened to Harshim, Khasani found himself thinking, '*After more than forty years, how have we been able to achieve a voting majority in the Majlis? Why am I still unsure how stable our constitutional government may be?*'

Sitting among the ornate cushions, sipping their tea, the two old friends limited their conversation to personal stories of their shared past. It was only when the ayatollah said, "Well, dear friend, what have you come here to discuss?" that Harshim changed gears.

"After our last meeting, I began to think about the private agendas each of the subculture leaders might be harboring that could conflict with our ability to preserve our Majlis voting majority," Harshim said.

"Perhaps I should explain. My son, Sam, likes to draw charts displaying the evolving steps of sequential logic. When we began to consider what private agendas our colleagues might be harboring, we realized there was a whole lot more we needed to learn. We were hoping you could help us complete our analysis."

Over the next two hours, they discussed the suspected motives of their fellow leaders. When they finished, they talked about their own situations.

The ayatollah said, "Should foreign interests be permitted to operate in our country, current followers, future converts, and the abused may have no other choice but to seek comfort, hope, and ultimate salvation in the world of Islam. Today, the mullahs and I agree that the Muslim community is being presented with a bit of a dilemma. On one hand, we understand the importance of supporting the National Front Party and its quest to approve the Sentinel Oil Plan. There is no doubt in my mind that if we succeed in introducing competitive bidding and preserve Prime Minister Mosaddegh's constitutional government, we will avoid all the disruption involved in a regime change.

"Clearly, this course of action benefits the Iranian people. The question the mullahs have been raising is this: Under this scenario, will our Muslim followers be satisfied by preserving our present role, or do we need to establish our Muslim community as an independent theocracy, cable of controlling its own destiny?

"The mullahs have had no choice but to consider what will happen should the shah's dictatorship replace our constitution democratic government. If that occurs, and if we are patient, the Muslim religion as we know it today will evolve into a Muslim theocracy, combining spiritual and political leadership under one tent.

"The continued exploitation of Iran's natural resources could convert awareness into anger. Left unattended, anger might motivate the more radical sects to initiate proactive resistance. There are rumors the radical sects are already meeting in secret and arming themselves. The day could come when the shah's government will no longer have the support, or the resources needed to resist a broad-based Muslim revolution. A Muslin theocracy could unseat the shah's government and provide Islam with one hundred percent control over the entire country."

Stunned by his friend's revelation, Harshim could only think of one question to ask, "Khasani, why would the followers of Islam be willing to make these shorter-term sacrifices to pursue the longer-term goals?"

"That is what the other mullahs and I are trying to figure out!"

Realizing the implications of what Khasani was suggesting, Harshim knew any further conversation might be counterproductive. *'I need to inform my fellow leaders of this potential problem,'* he thought. He stood and expressed his appreciation to his friend for his honesty and hospitality. Then, in a sign of respect for his honored friend, Harshim bowed and backed out of the room.

Part Four

"Naraghi-Roth"

Chapter Twenty
"Mr. Tom"

TOM'S FLAT: February 1908

Kate's father, Tom York, was sitting on the balcony of the fifth floor flat he maintained in Paris' 9th arrondissement. It was located on the Boulevard du Madeleine, within walking distance of Paris's ornately designed opera house, Palais Garnier, and in the center of his favorite neighborhood filled with sidewalk bistros and boutique grocery stores, wine shops, and meat markets. It was the place he always returned to after completing his consulting assignments.

He had poured himself a glass of his favorite wine, a pinot noir from Bourgogne. As dusk approached, he was watching the lights of Paris begin to appear. A recording of La Bohème was playing on the phonograph.

Settled in his favorite chair, his thoughts turned to Kate. *'I wonder how she is getting along with Harshim and his world of Super Quants? Has the reality of living in the rural community of a nineteenth century country begun to make its ugly appearance? Will the Naraghi allow her to play a meaningful role? Not only do I miss her cheerful presence, but I am beginning to appreciate how much I have depended upon her professionally. Could it be, without her assistance, I am losing interest in responding to new inquiries?'*

Copies of several of the city's daily newspapers were spread in front of him. To distract his thoughts, he was studying the promotions announcing that Puccini's La Bohème would be presented at the forthcoming "Opening Night at the Palais." A lifelong student of Puccini operas, Tom was familiar with the composer's magnificent ability to combine melodic compositions with a touch of comedy to produce eloquent presentations of love and despair.

Opening Night was to be the first performance in Paris of the highly acclaimed opera. The city's Latin Quarter – known for its gaiety and pathos -- had been the setting. Tom and his friend, Pierre Roth, had been in attendance when, in 1896, La Bohème was first performed at Milan's Teatro Regio Ducale Opera House with Arturo Toscanini conducting. The signature event had left an indelible mark on both young men. It was one of the shared experiences that had helped them become such good friends.

Tom had been studying the critics' comments. *'Maybe I can persuade Pierre to join me for the opening?'* Lost in his thoughts, he was startled by the ringing of his party-line phone, two long rings and one short ring. Confused by who would be calling at this hour, he failed recognize the voice over the scratchy quality of the international call. Eventually, he recognized Kate's voice calling from Iran.

Even after she had identified herself, all he could hear was a lot of talk about constructing dams in Iran's Zagros Mountains. Each time he tried to re-orient the call to more personal topics, she responded by asking him excitedly to travel to Iran and lend her a hand. "I think I have succeeded in convincing the family of the merits of including modern, hydroelectric dams in their Super Quant distribution plans," she told him. "I've proceeded as far as I can without your help. Would you consider visiting Iran? I miss you terribly and your input is desperately needed."

Before responding, Tom thought, *'Working with her again, on a different set of problems, in an unfamiliar part of the world could be exciting.'*

"Tell Harshim and his family, as soon as my bags are packed, I will be on my way!"

Kate, Harshim, Father Isadore, and his wife, Ruth, were waiting on the Ahvaz railway station platform to greet "Mr. Tom." Most of the disembarking passengers had already passed by when they spotted a struggling porter slowly pulling a well-filled, metal-wheeled, baggage cargo wagon toward them. A smiling Tom York was walking behind the wagon, making certain none of his earthly treasures fell off.

Following her two whoops and a holler, Kate rushed forward to greet her father. She gave him one of her tightest hugs, kissed him on both cheeks, and continued to hold on to him while whispering in his ear. "Unless you can help us introduce a dam into their Super Quant plan, I am afraid there will not be a meaningful role for me to fulfill," she said. "Father, I love this man, and I want to be a part of his life. Without a serious role to play, I doubt I will be able to remain here in Ahvaz. Asking him to decide whether he is willing to let me go or live and work in another place is a question I really want to avoid!"

Stepping back so he could look into her eyes, Tom asked, "My Red Queen, have you invited me to come all this way to help build a dam or help you preserve your relationship with him?"

Harshim's attention was distracted. He couldn't help but notice the quantity of arriving baggage. '*Is he visiting us, or does he plan to stay and move in?*'

Finding an appropriate space for Tom and all his possessions required some rearranging. It was decided that Harshim's still single, next-oldest brother, Milton, should move out of the guest house and join his other brothers in the ranch bunkhouse.

For the next two days, nobody saw much of Kate or her father. They were occupied unpacking and arranging his worldly possessions exactly where Tom wanted them placed. It was during the second night's dinner when Tom unexpectedly asked, "When are we going to start searching for the site for your first dam?"

Early the next morning, Father Isadore was leading Harshim, Kate, and Tom along the banks of a fast-flowing stream that originated in the high-altitude snow fields and distributed water to the eastern approaches of the Khuzestan Desert. Each time they stopped for water or a snack, their not-so idle time was filled with Tom's questions and Harshim's and Isadore's answers. Kate was busy taking notes.

The Naraghi's had never before witnessed such a thorough examination of the mountainous terrain. Prior efforts to catalogue snowfall and the monthly melted snow runoff did not compare with the data Tom and Kate insisted they collect.

If Harshim had ever doubted that his father was the most aggressive mountain hiker he had ever accompanied, he would have been mistaken; Tom's and Kate's pace set a new standard. They had a lot of ground to cover. After inspecting the site chosen for construction of the first dam, Tom insisted they devote the next several days to cataloguing data of the other nineteen drainage basin sites. "After all, we want to make certain we lead with our best alternative."

Harshim made certain he kept pace with the long-legged, light, and well-conditioned Kate as they recorded the runoff from each drainage basin. By the morning of the sixth day, he was beginning to question if each new day's expedition represented some sort of personal challenge or was required to complete the checklist of their pending loan application.

If Harshim was worried about keeping up with Kate during the day, at night, he sought to prevent her from seeing him treating his bloody feet and massaging his strained ligaments.

Sitting in front of the bedroom fireplace with the relaxed and animated Kate, Harshim began to consider, '*While I admire Kate's determination and indefatigable dedication to whatever challenge she chooses to accept, am I capable of keeping up with the woman they refer to as the Red Queen? How can it be that a relatively well-conditioned championship soccer player is having trouble keeping up with a young woman and two older gentlemen?'*

One night, after they had retired and were lying next to each other, Kate spoke up. "Tonight, during dinner, when I wasn't directly involved in the conversation, I looked around the table. Has it ever occurred to you that everybody is so immersed in their daily problems that they have little time for more personal conversations? In our excitement to get started, have any of us paused to consider what kind of a life we may be committing ourselves to? Are you really prepared to commit the next twenty years of our lives to 'Pushing Back the Desert?'"

Aware her question required a serious answer, Harshim gathered up his courage, reached over to hold Kate, and announced, "Kate, my Red Queen, if our loan application is approved, there will be a big role for you and your father to play. I've decided I can't wait any longer for you to ask me to marry you. Everything I have learned to love and cherish is right here in Khuzestan Province. I now realize that, from the first time I saw you, I must have fallen in love. Long before we returned to Iran, I knew I wanted you as my life's partner; I just did not know how to express what I was feeling. Kate York, will you marry me?"

Unprepared for such a comment from a man who normally had a difficult time expressing his feelings, Kate was surprised. *'He wouldn't be kidding about such a sensitive subject,'* she thought. Pausing briefly to consider why she hadn't asked him first, she said, "Well, cowboy, for a man of few words, you are starting to show real promise. Of course I will marry you, if you satisfactorily answer my next question. Want to seal our bargain?"

Chapter Twenty-One
"Mr. Tom Returns to Paris"

PARIS, FRANCE: May 1908

Some things do not change. Three months later, when Tom disembarked from the train at the Gare de Lyon in Paris, he was once again accompanied by a large assortment of suitcases, cylindrical tubes, and briefcases filled with the material he would need to present his case to the Roth Bank Senior Loan Committee.

Pierre Roth, his respected old friend, his opera-going partner, and his Roth Bank representative, was waiting on the platform to greet him. As they approached each other, Pierre was studying his friend, the same man whom he had watched depart, less than three months before, from this very same train station. He immediately noticed, *'Tom is a changed man. He no longer appears to be depressed. His eyes sparkle and he looks like a man who is ready to laugh at the first hint of humor.'*

Tom was grinning, excited to see his old friend. Immersed in conversation, he almost missed seeing his wagonload of personal effects being pulled past them toward the cavernous depot. Sensing Pierre's interest, Tom said, "Well, as you can see, I have returned properly prepared to make my case."

Pierre replied, "It's important you understand that your presentation will be made to the members of the Senior Loan Committee. My only contribution was the scheduling of the meeting. At this stage of my career, you should not rely on my assistance. I am expected to listen, learn, and keep my mouth shut.

"Tom, you are only going to get one bite at the proverbial apple. Tomorrow you will be on your own. Good luck!

"Now, enough shop talk! I have our favorite table reserved at Roger la Grenouille. Christopher, our regular waiter, will be waiting to say hello to an old customer. He is expecting us to order off the menu. The kitchen staff is prepared to cook your personal preference. And, I should add, Christopher is expecting us to do some significant damage to their magnificent wine collection. Welcome home, Tom!"

Later that evening, as they finished their soup course, Pierre asked, "Tell me about Harshim Naraghi. How old is he? Where did he go to school? What kind of a man is he?"

Tom had only started to answer Pierre's questions when he was interrupted with more questions. "Is he a very big man? Did he attend the Birmingham School of Mines? Is he in his early twenties? Does he have a stunning redhead for a girlfriend who answers to the name of Kate?"

"All of the above, but how would you know?" Tom asked.

"I was in that tavern in Grenoble when Kate burst in. I thought Harshim was being uncharacteristically bold when he accepted Kate's suggestion that they challenge any two of the other patrons to a wagered game of darts. How was I to know that he would make arrangements to meet her later?"

"Old friend, there is something you need to know. That stunning redhead you described happens to be my daughter, Kate. And she has promised to marry Harshim. I'd be very careful what you say!"

"Duly noted. How is it possible for you to have such a lovely daughter that I have never met?"

"Ever since her mother and I were divorced, Kate has been living with her mother in Ireland. To pay for her education, she worked as a trainer at several of Southern Ireland's better horse breeding farms. Even now, when we complete one of our assignments, she still returns to Ireland to be with her mother, see her brothers, and visit with her old friends."

The next morning, Tom was ushered into the Roth Bank's executive boardroom. Pierre was waiting to greet him and introduce him to the members of the bank's Senior Loan Committee. From his previous presentations, Tom knew some of them on a personal basis and the others by reputation. Today would be different. He would not be acting in his traditional role as their employed consultant. He was there to present his analysis of the Naraghi Super-Mount, hydroelectric dam designed to service twenty thousand acres of Khuzestan arid desert, a project with which he was personally involved.

Aware that the board members had enormous responsibilities on a number of subjects, Tom was prepared to present his summary in less than three minutes. The volumes of supporting material stacked on a table beside him had not gone unnoticed.

Tom had come prepared to answer questions regarding the project's economic feasibility, but the specificity of the board members' questions surprised him. "Explain to me again, how many acres one dam and quant will service?" one of the directors asked. "How many more families will be needed to farm the land for each new irrigation district you are planning to develop?"

Another asked, "Where will the children go to school? What kind of medical services do you plan on providing?"

A third director asked, "Would I be correct in assuming you are proposing to do more than present a good lending opportunity to our bank? If we were to approve your loan, are you offering us the chance to be identified with what could become an exciting humanitarian exercise?"

The next director asked, "Explain to us how the Naraghi's were able to secure the mineral rights under their purchased lands from Sir William D'Arcy? Is it true D'Arcy was awarded the mineral rights where he was able to discover oil in exchange for his exploration services? Do we correctly understand, before D'Arcy was able to finish his exploration, he ran out of the funds he needed to complete his assignment? Was the sale of a portion of his mineral rights to the Naraghi family documented as a public record? Are the Naraghis' mineral rights the only subsurface rights that are privately owned independent of Iranian governmental control? Has the legality of their mineral rights been tested in court?

"How were the Naraghis able to secure the rights to the runoff waters for the twenty different drainage basins on the western slope of the Zagros Mountains?"

Finally, the chairman of the Roth Bank board of directors, Pierre's father, asked, "Are you proposing the bank provide the capital needed to fund the initial phase of what could become a very significant economic endeavor that would improve the lives of a lot of deserving people?"

"Yes, you are correct," Tom replied. "It's just that we hadn't thought of our work in those terms. We have been concentrating our attention on the questions of economic feasibility."

"Mr. York, on behalf of our committee, I would like to express our appreciation for your fine work. Now, if you wouldn't mind excusing yourself, we need time to discuss your proposal among ourselves. While we haven't discovered any inconsistencies in your usual fine work, because of your personal interest, bank regulations require us to conduct an independent verification of your work."

Twenty minutes later, it was concluded that Pierre would lead an investment research team to return to Iran with Tom for the purpose of carrying out a feasibility study. Tom and Pierre never made it to the opera.

Cablegram dated May 1908.

From: Tom York

To: Harshim Naraghi

'Met with Pierre Roth and the Senior Loan Committee of the Roth Bank. They appear to be very interested in your dam-quant proposal. The committee has directed Pierre Roth, son of the bank's president, to head up a team of feasibility experts to conduct the study the Senior Loan Committee will require before voting on your proposal.

'It has been my experience, if they didn't have serious interest in granting your request, they wouldn't have authorized this next step. I will be returning to Ahvaz with Pierre Roth and the rest of his team.

'Tom York

P.S. Pierre remembers meeting you last summer at a dart-throwing tavern in Grenoble. He wants to know what happened to the red-haired beauty, your girl and my daughter!'

Chapter Twenty-Two
"Pierre to Ahvaz"

KHUZESTAN PROVINCE: June 1908

As the train from Abadan approached the station in Ahvaz, Harshim, and Kate were speculating on how Pierre would react when he saw them standing together on the depot platform. Harshim couldn't help but wonder, 'Not only had we met under entirely different circumstances, but none of us knew each other's last name.'

Tom was the first to step from the train. After helping Pierre, Tom was quick to say, "I understand the three of you do not require any further introduction. Pierre, from your comments, I assumed you could have only been describing our host, Harshim Naraghi, and my daughter Kate."

Pierre's attention was only partially focused on the words of his old friend. He was distracted by the red-haired woman standing next to Harshim. '*She is more beautiful than I remember. Why didn't I suspect this mysterious man from the Middle East would do whatever was necessary to prevent Kate from disappearing from his life?*'

Shifting his gaze to Harshim, Pierre was thinking, '*Despite my envy, I still sense Harshim and I share the same sense of personal bonding. While I vaguely recall him mentioning he had spent the last four years studying mining at Birmingham University School of Mines, he never mentioned anything about his family's multi-generational effort to push back the deserts of Iran. Until Tom made his presentation, I had no way of knowing the importance and the magnitude of the program the Naraghi family had envisioned. On the other hand, I don't remember my mentioning anything about my family's trans-European banking interest. Doesn't fate provide surprises?*'

Without hesitating, the two men quickly approached and wrapped each other in a bear hug. Pierre, after disengaging himself, directed his first words to Kate: "Young lady, I have come a very long way to win back all that money you and your friend won from me in Grenoble. I just hope you have reserved enough time for a rematch?"

Having listened to the different recollections of that night in Grenoble, Tom asked, "My loving daughter, why don't you set us straight? I have always been curious about what really happened that night when the three of you first met."

Needing no further encouragement, Kate started to talk, "I noticed the big, handsome, powerfully built man the minute my friends and I entered the tavern. I still remember laughing at some comment one of my friends was making. Secretly, I was hoping my laughter might attract his attention. It seemed strange; I remember feeling a connection with him, even from across a crowded, smoke-filled room."

With the ice broken, the four friends were content to listen to the three of them tell their different renditions of the night in question. It quickly became apparent that each of them had their own imaginative interpretation of what had happened that night.

Kate was talking. "Later, when my friends and I had situated ourselves at the far end of the bar, I kept searching for the big man. From my vantage point, I was having difficulty seeing him, particularly when he seemed so preoccupied with his dart games. When he didn't venture down to my end of the bar and introduce himself, I knew if I wanted to meet him, I needed to take the initiative.

"Maybe one of the smartest things I have ever done was propose we challenge the bar's patrons to a game of darts. Just standing next to him, I could feel his quiet strength. The more games we played, the more I became aware of the growing bond of mutual attraction. Even before we had played our last game, I knew I had met a special man."

Looking directly toward Pierre, Kate said, "The time we spent together before Harshim was scheduled to leave for Iran gave us the opportunity to become better acquainted. With the passing of each weekend, I was becoming more convinced I wanted to spend the rest of my life with him. At the same time, I had to think about what kind of a life I would lead. What kind of a role would I be expected to fulfill? How could I be certain the rural domestic world of Iran would be properly suited to the energies and interests of the Red Queen?

"The idea of introducing a hydroelectric dam wasn't entirely mine. While I performed my own preliminary feasibility analysis, it was the family's desire to increase the irrigated land for each drainage basin from five thousand to twenty thousand acres that provided the real motivation.

"It was my suggestion that we invite Tom to visit Ahvaz to perform a professional analysis. It wasn't until he finished his study that we became convinced that a modern, hydroelectric dam needed to be installed as an integral part of our grand plan. Somehow, we needed to find the capital."

Impressed, Pierre kiddingly asked, "And just what new idea are you planning to introduce next?"

Not expecting an answer to his rhetorical question, he was surprised when Kate said, "Just wait until I have an opportunity to tell you about my lease-to-own idea for transferring title of the land to our tenant farming families. Successfully implemented, it will help us turn the growing multitude of tenant farmers into a nation of proud, land-owning citizens."

Just as Harshim was starting to apologize for Kate's outburst, Pierre shushed him. "No, no, I want to hear more about Kate's intriguing idea, perhaps some other time," he said.

For the better part of the next three weeks, members of Pierre's group were divided into teams to research separate segments of the Naraghi operations. Each team concentrated on verifying different parts of Tom's report. During the days, they worked at separate locales and had no opportunity to see each other's work or share what they were discovering. At night, when they gathered around the Naraghi family table for dinner, the members of each team were encouraged to relate their day's more interesting discoveries and relevant observations. It didn't seem to make much difference who was leading the discussion; invariably, they were confirming Tom's earlier report.

With the passage of each day, it was becoming increasingly apparent that the different segments of the plan were beginning to fit together. As days turned into weeks, with their level of excited anticipation rising, Pierre and his team were growing more anxious to return to Paris and submit their analysis.

Chapter Twenty-Three
"Congratulations"

AHVAZ, IRAN: July 1908

Dinners without Pierre and the Roth Bank research team were no longer as stimulating. The discussions around the table had become less animated; the excitement that had accompanied the questions and comments of the bank analysts seemed to have left with them.

Harshim was questioning what would happen next. *'Would there be a cablegram asking for additional information? Would Harshim receive a transnational phone call from Pierre? Would they be asked to travel to Paris?'* With the passage of time, frequent, unexpressed anxieties were becoming more apparent.

In Paris, the wheels of Roth Bank progress were slowly turning. Assured that the overall economics would justify granting the loan, members of the Senior Loan Committee were focusing their attention on the other problems that invariably accompany any major loan request. They were asking, "How do we secure our investment should the construction of the dam fail to complete?"

During a family dinner, Pierre's father asked, "If we were to assume the Naraghi family lacks the resources to secure the bank's loan until construction is completed, how would you propose we solve the problem?"

"Father, one of the many pleasant things we learned in Ahvaz was that excellent farming records have been maintained. At present, the Naraghi's charge each of their twenty-acre tenant farmers a percentage of their farm revenue. After studying the history of these agreements, we have tentatively concluded that 'lease-to-own' contracts, when packaged together, might constitute an appropriate source of interim collateral."

Pierre asked, "Should it be determined that the value of the existing lease contracts is not sufficient to secure the entire amount of the loan, what can we do to preserve such a fine venture? How would you feel about our family using private funds to supply the balance in exchange for a suitable participation in the operation? From everything you have said, I suspect, at some point, that we would be pleased to be partners with the Naraghi family and to be associated with all they hope to accomplish."

A senior loan officer raised the question, "Why does it make sense for the bank to be an equity investor with the same team that will be responsible for managing both the farming and the construction of the dam?

"Give us one good reason why we should become involved in a major project in a foreign country, about which we know very little."

Pierre was ready for the questions. He started by saying, "If you look beyond the economic reasons that clearly support the investment of the bank, when would we have a more attractive opportunity to gain a financial presence in the Middle East? It will be only a question of time before Middle Eastern oil will be recognized for its global strategic value.

Should we be able to confirm the presence of oil beneath the 'Nation's Land' and verify the Naraghis' ownership of its mineral rights, we would see that the economic potential of the petroleum reserves should provide the additional economic resources we will need to protect and justify our investment."

One week later, Pierre's father summoned him to a private conference. "Son, first of all, I would like to compliment you on a job well done. Without your support of the Naraghis and all they stand for; I seriously doubt the Senior Loan Committee would have recommended the Naraghi project for my approval.

"Several members told me they were impressed with your answers to their questions. Your willingness to accept personal responsibility and risk your career also impressed them, as did your vision for the future of the Middle East. But the most impressive item was your pointing out that we have been presented with an opportunity to be identified with what might become a great humanitarian effort.

"Pierre, you have just taken some very big steps; I couldn't be prouder of you. But there are three important questions I need you to answer before I could accept the loan committee's recommendation.

"How much thought have you given to the adverse consequences, should the project fail to be completed and our loan would become nonperforming? What kind of a role would you expect to play? Are you concerned about how your career within the Roth Bank could be affected?"

"Father, providing a custodial, administrative brand of leadership within the bank's bureaucratic organization has never been an appealing idea to me," Jacque responded. "I have always considered myself to be an imaginative, entrepreneurial problem solver. Given the choice, I would prefer to identify worthy projects and apply my financial expertise to assist the bank to achieve its goals. The Naraghi project is a good example of what I am talking about.

"Undoubtedly, a project of this magnitude, requiring three years to complete, will provide us with enough time to accurately assess the worthiness of our investment. If serious problems were to occur, I would expect to be actively engaged, work with the Naraghi's and assist the bank to protect its credit."

Two days later, Pierre's cablegram arrived in Ahvaz. "Harshim, congratulations, your loan has been preliminarily approved. When will it be convenient for you, your father, Kate, and your lawyer to come to Paris? We still need your assistance to resolve some of the finer points and approve the final language before we can execute the loan agreements."

Family members who had been waiting with bated breath to observe Harshim's reaction to Pierre's cablegram were confused by his silence. Kate was the first to respond. "I guess it was too much to hope for?" she asked.

"Not exactly," Harshim said, smiling. "The Roth Bank has approved the full amount of the requested loan, but they are requesting our presence in Paris to assist in resolving some of the finer points. I can't but wonder what *'finer points'* really means. Somehow, I suspect we do not have as much of a done deal as I had hoped. On the other hand, why would Pierre request we make the long journey unless he is convinced that we have a solvable problem? I suggest we accept his invitation."

Twenty-Four
"Naraghi-Roth"

PARIS: SEPTEMBER 1908

Their first three days in Paris were devoted to the Naraghis' acceptance of Pierre's invitation to visit, dine, and be entertained in the best of Parisian style. Box seats had been arranged for the opera and the ballet. Harshim understood Pierre's earlier friendship was partially responsible for their 'grand tour.' He also wondered, 'Is Pierre showing off for Kate?'

Any discussions of the alternate collateral problem had been carefully avoided, at least until Harshim and Pierre found themselves standing on the spacious balcony outside his guest room in the Ritz Paris hotel. Unable to contain himself, Harshim asked, "In your letter, you referred to resolving the 'finer points.' Are you having difficulty evaluating the collateral value of our land-purchase agreements?"

Taking his time to respond, Pierre said, "It's important you understand the Roth Bank and how things work. My father and I believe in what you are hoping to accomplish. We look forward to having an extremely rewarding and enjoyable relationship with you. Wouldn't it be nice if we can talk about the alternate collateral problem in the same relaxed manner that we have grown accustomed to discussing other matters with you?

"Quite simply, we have concluded the revenue production of your lease-to-own contracts does qualify for alternative collateral-lending purposes. Unfortunately, the total collateral value of the existing contracts makes up only approximately fifty percent of the amount that the bank will require to secure its loan until construction is completed. How would you feel if, to satisfy the bank's stipulation, my family was to contribute the remaining fifty percent as permanent equity in exchange for a fifty percent interest in any new lands we jointly develop?"

Harshim did not immediately respond. Instead, he walked to the far edge of the balcony. Looking out at the peaceful, azure Mediterranean Sea, he thought: *I may be inexperienced in this kind of situation, but if the Roth Banks and the Roth family are extending to us the courtesy of a partnership, it must indicate they believe in what we are attempting and have confidence in our family's ability.'*

Turning to face Pierre, Harshim replied, "Your offer has caught me by surprise. The idea of having your family as a partner had never occurred to me. If I interpret your offer correctly, the Roth family participation suggests you are willing to stand beside us as equal partners as we face tomorrow's challenges. Over and above the capital contributions, I do not know how to estimate the intrinsic value of your sponsorship as compared to the present-day value of our undeveloped land, water rights, and subsurface mineral rights. But maybe that is not so important. I think I can speak for the others when I say we would be flattered and pleased to have you as an equal partner.

"Perhaps I need to remind you, though, that we are talking about adding, on a one-at-a-time basis, nineteen additional irrigation districts. Although we would be able to adapt the alternate collateral of the first loan into successive loans, it could take us more than forty years to complete the development of the more than four hundred thousand acres we presently own or control. This would ultimately create livelihoods for more than twenty thousand deserving families. Are you certain you want to be involved?"

"Harshim, it's your dreams that influenced our decision to become involved. Let's shake hands before we join the others."

Chapter Twenty-Five
"Getting Underway"

KHUZESTAN, PROVINCE: January 1909

Kate York Naraghi:

With the alternate collateral-financing problem resolved, the funding for the first stages of the construction loan had been made available. Getting underway was the order of the day.

Kate, sensitive to the importance of converting tenant-farmer agreements into the higher-revenue lease-to-own contracts, arranged to sit down with some of the more progressive farming families. Using the production records of the subject parcel, she helped them understand how much crop revenue they had generated in each of the previous five years. After subtracting their annual rental payments, she calculated how much money would have remained available to pay for their farming and living expenses.

Once they understood the numbers, she introduced the idea of their purchasing the land by converting their tenant-farming agreements into lease-to-own contracts. Revising her calculations to include the added burden of amortizing the purchase cost of their land, and her estimates of the increased production derived from more prideful interest, Kate calculated how much money would be left over for farming and living expenses.

Kate had expected that each of the families would need time to consider her proposal before responding. But when, after a few days, she had failed to receive any responses or requests for more information, she became nervous. Keenly aware of the problems that would be created should she fail to obtain an assignment of executed lease-to-own contracts, she sent invitations to the same families requesting follow-up meetings.

On the first day following the delivery of her messages, strange things began to happen. Twelve executed contracts arrived at her office. On the second day, she received dozens more. By the third day, the momentum was continuing to improve.

Pleased, but confused, by the positive reactions, Kate decided to visit the families who had sent her the executed contracts. She asked them, "I need to understand. Why have you elected to proceed?"

As she moved from house to house, she became aware of and surprised by their enthusiasm. Grinning, they told her what had happened. Kate divided their responses into four basic categories:

1) From the elders, she learned that the grateful families had concluded the added revenues generated by the new contracts would make it possible for the Naraghis to extend the benefits to more needy families.
2) The new contracts assigning private ownership represented an opportunity to add any additional production revenues into the equivalent of a forced savings account.
3) The savings would be used to achieve private ownership of land that their children could farm, sell, or use as collateral to acquire additional parcels.
4) Most importantly, she was impressed that the farming families trusted the Naraghi family.

Mr. Tom:

When word began to circulate of the opportunity to construct Iran's first major hydroelectric dam -- under the supervision of Tom York and funded by the Roth Bank -- letters of inquiry from qualified international construction companies began to arrive in Ahrav. So, too, did exploratory teams and their test equipment. When they had finished their work and it was time for them to leave, each of the construction companies expressed enthusiasm for the project and their interest in submitting a bid.

On occasion, Tom was heard to say, "If we are fortunate, we might be able to create competitive bidding between qualified international construction companies."

Unaccustomed to seeing such strange activity, local citizens were asking questions. The idea of constructing big dams, digging long and large underground aqueducts, irrigating tens of thousands of acres of arid desert, and generating electricity was difficult to comprehend.

Curious local residents, government officials, and subculture leaders were asking questions. Tom, Harshim, and Kate spent part of each day carefully explaining what they hoped to accomplish.

The building of the massive dam was scheduled to occur in stages. Construction of the first stage couldn't start until the river's flow could be channeled around both sides of the designated dam site. The drilling of the diversion tunnels through solid granite required the installation of Mont Cenis-type modern mining equipment and the importation of rotary drill bits from the American Southwest.

Each time a ship carrying the equipment would dock at the relatively peaceful Persian Gulf port of Abadan, locals, watching the big crates being unloaded, were impressed not only by their size and volume, but also by the variety of origins marked on each of the containers.

Harshim and Tom looked like nervous, expectant parents. One of them could nearly always be found standing dockside. With the aid of their trusty clipboards, they would carefully write down the bill of lading numbers, prominently printed on the sides of each cargo container. After cross-checking each number against the number on their copy of the purchase contract, they would check their warehouse manifest before designating where the arriving materials were to be stored. Failure to follow these plans to the letter could have resulted in lost materials, indescribable confusion, and delays.

Taking advantage of the large warehouse space, Harshim, Tom, and their team of consultants began to pre-assemble the parts, tubes, and valves with all the different mechanisms they would be employing. Even the copper-reinforced pneumatic hoses, needed to transport the compressed air to the generator, were being connected to the valves.

The ease of assembling all the parts of the air-compression system on a flat surface, in a climate-controlled, interior space contrasted sharply with the difficulties they would encounter when they attempted to reconstruct the system in remote, high-altitude, cold, and windy locations.

One bystander was heard to comment, "The sight of Harshim and his crews; the use of liberal amounts of profanity; the striking of rubber-covered sledgehammers; and a whole lot of elbow grease reminds me of a group of men wrestling with a very large bear!"

The topping-off of the dam was a seminal day, marked by the gradual closing of the bypass tunnels. Local residents, standing on top of the dam, watched with rapt attention as the level of the water began to creep up the convex, lakeside, vertical surface.

A year later, as the rising water approached its designated maximum height, engineers threw the big toggle switches that activated the flow of water through the generator turbines. The streetlights along the side of the road on top of the dam flickered briefly, then emitted uninterrupted, bright glows that illuminated the massive concrete structure.

Back at construction headquarters, Harshim picked up the ringing telephone. He heard Kate say, "The panel is lit, you can throw the switches!" They watched in fascination as the hydroelectrically generated power caused the massive multi-bit mining machine to start to turn.

For the next eighteen years, the Naraghi family's disciplined, dedicated, maximum efforts were devoted to the installation of nine more irrigation districts. An ambitious goal was gradually becoming a reality. By 1927, the Nation of Citizen Farmers included two hundred thousand acres, provided homes and livelihoods for more than ten thousand formerly disenfranchised Middle Eastern families, and employed another twenty thousand service workers.

In 1919, Kate and Harshim's first son, Sam York Naraghi, was born. He had inherited his mother's red hair, and his father's large, muscular frame.

As his early years passed, Sam became an outstanding student, blessed with industrious work habits. He was intellectually curious and determined to complete whatever he started. Dissatisfied with the limits of his school's curriculum, he would often request additional assignments. He became a serious thinker and an exceptionally talented and driven student, while remaining a polite, soft-spoken young man who listened more than he spoke.

By the time he entered high school, the future family leader was beginning to make his mark on whomever and whatever he touched. His unusual achievements in school and on the soccer field were attracting the attention of foreign university coaches and scouts.

It was during this period that his family noticed a difference between his own and his father's interests. Sam was spending his spare time visiting with the people who sold Nation's produce, filled orders, and arranged transportation. It was becoming apparent that Sam seemed more interested in learning about the trading and distribution aspects of the business.

For some time, Nation's production had been pushing the limits of in-country, Iranian demand. To continue to grow, it needed to develop out-of-Iran markets. During his summers, on the first Monday following the last Friday day of school, Sam would join his father on his travels to new markets. Together, they studied each market's needs and methods of distribution and identified any problems. As part of the process, they formed personal relationships with the men who managed the terminal produce markets.

During each visit, Sam would listen to his father's conversations, take careful notes, and reserve his questions until he could discuss them over dinner. Over the course of three summers, Sam's notes grew to contain a wealth of information. When he summarized what he had learned, on a market-by-market basis, he felt he had identified the problems Naraghi-Roth would have to resolve and defined the products and the special services it would have to offer to gain entry into foreign markets.

On the occasions when Sam shared his notes with his father, Harshim would say, "Sam, the wealth of information you have collected reminds me of the database I helped Father Isadore collect. It was that information that formed the basis of our efforts to acquire a high percentage of the drainage rights to the western slope of the Zagros, and to purchase title to the high-desert grazing lands that fanned westward from the base of the mountains. I predict the day will come when your information makes it possible for you to convert our early primitive export efforts into a full-scale, vertically integrated agribusiness operation."

But that day would prove to be distant. Sam found that life after high school was complicated. For as long as he could remember, his father had expected him to attend Birmingham's School of Mining. Hoping to pursue an academic career in international commerce, Sam quickly learned that discussing his personal interests with his father was not a conversation he looked forward to having. His family didn't share Sam's dreams. Disagreement with his father was not encouraged.

As his departure date from Ahvaz approached, Sam found himself in a strange place. *'Should I silently obey my father, or should I express my true feelings?'*

Unsure of which path to pursue, Sam decided to seek his mother's advice. *'Mom has been successful in plotting her own course through the Naraghi labyrinth of traditional thinking. Who would question the contributions her fresh ideas have made possible? Why couldn't my interest in international trading and commerce have the same result? Maybe I should introduce the subject during one of our family dinners?'*

Not long before Sam was expected to depart for Birmingham, England, he began to discuss the possibility that his four-year college education might be better spent studying international trade and commerce instead of engineering.

Secretly pleased with their son's independent thinking, Harshim and Kate, late at night, in the privacy of their bedroom, discussed the growing seeds of conflict. Rather than risk a difficult and confrontational discussion with their strong-willed son, Harshim and Kate decided to shift the responsibility for resolving the dilemma back to Sam. They agreed, '*What is wrong with allowing Sam to manage his own life, make his own decisions? He will be leaving us for a long time. Maybe the time has come for him to take charge?*'

Sam understood he had been handed his first test for future leadership. At night, he would write down what he understood to be his parents' critical thoughts on the left side of a page in his notebook. On the right, he would list his own interests, goals, and the education and training he would need to accomplish them. The conflicting goals and expectations only made his decision more complex. '*The more I think about the problem, the more I realize that no matter what role I will ultimately fill, I will need to have a practical understanding of the family's dam-quant operations, its farming programs, and at the same time, the international trading and commerce markets.*'

Nobody was sure when the idea of expanding his education from four to six years was introduced. But it soon became apparent that attending the Birmingham School of Mines and the London School of Economics and spending his summer vacations interning at international trading companies, insurance companies, and export-import banks could be a practical solution.

When the day arrived for Sam to embark on his long journey to England, the older members of his family and their friends were reminded of the gangly, tall, and driven young man who had preceded him twenty-seven years ago. His brothers were waiting to kid him; "Sam, what kind of a woman do you plan on dragging back here? Will she have red hair? Will she be able to pass the inspection of the Red Queen?"

Chapter Twenty-Six
"The Christening"

KHUZESTAN PROVINCE: June 1912

Three years following the completion of construction of Iran's first hydro-electric dam, the stored water ready to begin flowing onto the Khuzestan desert was big news. The commencement of the operation of Iran's only hydroelectric dam and its production of surplus marketable electricity was big news. The longer and greater capacity of the new Super Quant with enough volume to irrigate twenty thousand acres was big news. The irrigated land's subdivision into one thousand twenty-acre parcels was big news. The creation of lease-purchase land contracts designed to transfer title to the families who farmed the land was big news. The construction of safe, modern homes was big news. The construction of a village commercial center to house emergent care centers, schools, and the sale of food and needed supplies was big news. The employment of one thousand service employees was big news.

Justifiably proud of what they were accomplishing, the Roth and Naraghi families were anxious to expose the results of their vision, their problem solving, and their years of hard work to as many of Iran's influential citizens as possible. Pierre, his father, and members of the Roth Bank Senior Loan Committee had been invited to the christening of the first their "Big Dam" and the "Super Quant." They were joined by the leaders of each of Iran's six subcultures, who represented eighty percent of Iran's population. The mayors and important civic leaders of Iran's cities, towns and villages had been included. The prime minister, members of his cabinet, and elected members of the Majlis were invited. The shah, his administration, and the central figures of his Loyalist Party were in attendance. The Muslim community was well represented. The ayatollah and the mullahs had agreed to attend. Key military officers, dressed in their parade uniforms, could be seen standing among the crowd. Members of the international press had been invited.

The tour began with their inspection of the dam, the Super Quant, and the twenty thousand acres of crop-ready fields. Open-air buses had been hired to move the guests around. Surprised by the size of the dam, the enormity of the lake behind the dam, and the sophisticated turbine equipment used to generate electricity, the invited crowd began to utter comments of amazement.

"This is so much grander than I was expecting," said one. "How much land are you planning to irrigate just from this dam?"

"How much surplus electricity are you planning to generate?" asked another.

"Is it true you are contemplating the installation of nineteen more dams in separate drainage basins?" asked a third.

After completing their inspection of the dam, its generation equipment, and the control room, Harshim suggested they tour the command center of the "Super Quant," its command center with the control boards used to illustrate the flow of water and oil through its system. Guests observed the illumination of little blue lights indicating the progress of the water as it began to pass through the system.

One man asked Father Isadore, "How were you able to visualize the transformation of two-thousand-year-old, hand-dug underground aqueduct technology into what we have seen today? Why have the Naraghis' and the Roths' chosen to pursue such ambitious goals requiring decades to complete?"

A smiling Father Isadore responded with a simply question: "How else would we be able to help improve the lives of displaced families who roam the Middle East?" he asked.

The largest number of people were gathered around Harshim. One of them asked, "Are you aware of any similar efforts to introduce so much water to an arid desert? Without a working example, how were you able to design, engineer, and construct what we are seeing today?"

Pleased with the question, Harshim said, "While there are no similar installations, different projects contain many of the same elements we have borrowed and incorporated into our Super Quant system."

Kate was asked, "By introducing new housing equipped with electricity and sanitary running water, what are you trying to accomplish?"

Smiling at the question, she answered, "It's part of our intent to push back the personal boundaries of deserving people. Ownership of modern, comfortable, safe housing is an essential part of our plan. We are committed to appealing to the pride and dignity of the young families on whom we will depend on to farm their land."

Another person asked, "About the village you are constructing, is it true you will introduce commercial, medical, and educational service facilities to support the everyday living needs of your citizen farmers?"

Kate answered, "Today, we will be providing only a portion of the medical and educational services that are needed. By providing emergent care and triage services, we are limited to what kind of medical assistance we can provide. Tehran's UDEH, a government-supported purveyor of medical services, is located more than three hundred fifty miles away and is virtually inaccessible to people with more extreme medical needs. Until we find a way to extend medical services to our desert communities, our people will not have access to the medical support system they deserve. Until that happens, our job is not complete.

"In addition, there is the unresolved issue of higher education. At present, our educational system will provide instruction only through the senior year of high school. Until we find a way to provide our more gifted students with the advanced education they will need to be accepted by top-flight foreign colleges and universities, our job isn't finished. Someday, we are going to find a way to solve that problem.

"It's important that you understand that constructing more Super Quants is only one part of our plan. Focusing on meeting a more complete range of human needs of our Citizen Farmers must be regarded as a critical part of what we envision."

"Ms. Naraghi, how are you planning to pay for the administrative, educational, and medical services you plan on introducing?"

"From the revenues created by selling off our surplus electrical power," Kate replied.

Then came a final question to Harshim: "What do the red lights mean? Why are we seeing some red lights begin to light your board?"

"They signify we are beginning to replace the water and install the oil we plan on using to protect what we have created from outside predators. If we assume we will be creating something of value, we need to consider our security. When water enters our system, its presence is denoted by the little blue lights. When the red lights appear, they tell us we are refilling our system with oil, which is needed to energize our security system. For centuries, the use of burning oil has been used to drive away invading locusts that can devour entire crops in a matter of days. Our system has been designed to take this centuries-old technology one step farther and protect us from a different form of predator.

"If we detect the presence of an invading military force, we drain the water from our system and replace it with oil. Once the flow of oil reaches our farming lands, we allow it flow out into the fields, to be ignited and engulf invading armies in burning fields. We hope the fear of being burned alive will act as an effective deterrent to unwelcome armies."

Following his explanation, Harshim invited the guests to accompany him out of the command bunker and to climb the fifty steps that led to the big observation deck. After waiting for everyone to catch their breath, he signaled to a man standing in front of the command bunker.

A loud *'Whoosh!'* ensued, followed by the ignition of miles of checker-boarded fields filled with burning oil. As far as the crowd could see, the sky was filled with orange flames and black smoke. It was impossible for anyone witnessing the fire to not imagine the horrorifying scene that would greet any invading army caught in the burning fields.

One of the shah's generals asked, "Will the rest of the world learn about your defense system? What a deterrent! Unless someone develops a solution to remove it, I have a difficult time imagining why an invading ground force would risk invading."

Following the anti-invasion spectacle, the guests climbed aboard open-air buses to tour the non-burning portions of the property. Twenty thousand acres represents an area of about thirty square miles, or a rectangle of approximately five miles by six miles.

Their route called for them to follow the six-mile underground path of the quant. The only visible evidence of the underground aqueduct were the ventilation stacks and concrete irrigation boxes used to direct water into concrete-lined ditches that delivered the water to the twenty-acre farming parcels. Each of the parcels was denoted by the completed construction of the building site of a future home.

Those who remained and attended the reception were impressed. People standing next to strangers could be heard asking, "Were you prepared for the sophistication and scale of a modern Super Quant?"

"Are they serious when they talk about adding nineteen more irrigation districts?" asked Ayatollah Khasani. "When have you ever heard of a family voluntarily transferring title of their property to the people who farm their land? Can you imagine what kind of worldwide attention they are going to attract? Someday, when discussing the work of Roth and Naraghi, I wouldn't be surprised to learn if people will debate what is their greatest accomplishment, their development of a mammoth, vertically integrated agri-business that affects the economies of the entire Middle East, or their creation of one of the world's finest humanitarian establishments."

Part Five

"The Next Generation"

Chapter Twenty-Seven
"Sam Naraghi Meets Jacques Roth"

PARIS, FRANCE: June 1934

Following through on his invitation, Jacques was leading Sam along his familiar night trek through the back streets of Paris's Latin Quarter. It had taken years for him to identify and make friends in the 'right' bistros, cabarets, and private clubs. Common to all of them were the availability of good wines, the presence of interesting people, and the opportunity to meet attractive young ladies.

Jacques and Sam were sitting at the crowded bar of a small bistro, their third stop of the evening, when Jacques noticed Sam hesitate when the bartender offered to pour him a second glass of wine. He watched with curiosity when Sam placed his hand over his empty wine glass and ordered instead a bottle of sparkling mineral water with a wedge of lime.

Sensing Jacques' curiosity, Sam explained, "Your nighttime world is a new and strange place for this farm boy from Iran. Drinking wine is not a regular custom in our home and is well beyond the reach of my monthly school budget."

Smiling at Sam's earnest nature, Jacques said, "I was not aware about any rules that govern the consumption of wine, but how do you feel about meeting attractive ladies?"

"Now there is a new habit I could look forward to cultivating!"

That didn't happen until their fifth stop, a late-night jazz club located half a story below street level, in a cave-like setting. Fittingly named Le Cavern, the smoke-filled club was filled to overflowing. A popular American jazz quartet was performing on the stage at the far end of the room.

They entered the club and made their way past a line of people waiting to be seated. Sam followed Jacques to the only vacant table. Sam had no way of knowing it was regularly reserved for Jacques and any guests who might accompany him. As they weaved their way among the crowded tables, Jacques would stop at one table and then another to say hello to his friends and introduce Sam as his great friend and fellow captain of the British soccer team.

While he was waiting for the conversation to include him, Sam gazed around the room. Impressed by the attractive women sitting by themselves or waiting for tables, he was trying to decide, if he could have his pick, which one would he choose. With his inspection complete, he could not refrain from tugging on Jacques' sleeve. After gaining Jacques' attention, he shifted his eyes toward the two women who were standing just inside the entrance, near the head of the line of people waiting for a table.

Needing no further encouragement, Jacques suggested, 'Sam, why don't you take charge of the table while I determine if those two young ladies would care to join us? The blonde looks vaguely familiar. I might have met her at an art exhibit not so long ago. How about those gorgeous, long legs?"

Standing among the people waiting for a table, Harriet Hollenbeck and Sally Raphael were having a difficult time hearing the music. Sally was straining her eyes in an unsuccessful attempt to see if she recognized any of the American musicians. Harriet was startled when Jacques suddenly appeared in front of her. Recognizing Jacques, she remembered, *'Isn't he the much-celebrated captain of the French national soccer team? For some time, I have been following his exploits on the soccer field and have attended some of his games. I also read about some of his nighttime adventures, frequently featured in the society section of Paris newspapers.'*

She remembered how pleased she had been when he introduced himself to her at the opening of a recent art exhibit. And how disappointed she had become when, after a short but pleasant conversation, he had excused himself to rejoin his date of the evening.

Never at a loss for words, Jacques asked, "It's Harriet, isn't it? Didn't we meet at the Metropolitan Art Exhibition not too long ago? In case you forgot, my name is Jacques Roth. I have reserved a table up front, near the stage. It is an excellent place where you can hear the music, watch the musicians, and if you like, we can order a nice bottle of wine. My friend and I were wondering if you two ladies would like to join us."

Turning toward Sally, Harriet couldn't help but notice that she was already directing her attention toward the big, red-haired man standing next to an empty table. Even from the distance, she could see he was well-conditioned, with warm, brown, smiling eyes. After receiving Sally's confirming nudge, Harriet accepted Jacques' invitation.

Jacques, no longer concerned about his new, non-drinking friend, was concentrating his attention on the tall, very friendly, physically attractive blonde sitting opposite him. After five minutes, Sally realized that her friend was not willing to take the chance that Jacques might become distracted by talking to someone else. That was the moment when she perceived, '*If I want to get to know this big, handsome, red-haired man who seems to be at a loss for words, I am going to have to initiate the conversation.*'

Unsure of what to say. Sam had been sitting quietly while studying the tall, pretty woman with coal-black, curly hair and piercing blue eyes. He was thinking, '*Tall by Iranian standards, but not too tall, she must be at least five feet eight inches. Blessed with strong, broad, square shoulders and long, well-muscled arms, she must be an athlete.*'

Sally understood what was happening. This was not the first time she had been the object of masculine inspection. To break the ice, she asked, "Have you and Jacques been friends for a long time? Is this the first time you have played against each other in a championship game? Are you planning to stay in Paris for a while? What are you planning to do after you leave?"

Fascinated by Sally's stream of questions, Sam found himself answering each one. But when he began to talk about his family's work in Iran, she interrupted.

"Did Jacques say your last name is Naraghi?" she asked. "The same family that is known for their work to push back the desert and to create better lives for so many deserving people?"

Astounded by her question, he asked, "How would a tennis player from the United States be aware of my family's work?'

"Sam, I was raised on a kibbutz in Palestine before attending college in Cambridge, Massachusetts. Anyone who has been part of a decades-long effort to transport water to the desert, make it bloom, and create a secure life for Jews seeking sanctuary is familiar with what your family has been working so hard to accomplish in Iran.

"As for being a tennis player from the United States, I was lucky. In high school, I was an internationally ranked amateur tennis player and a high-performing student. My applications to most American universities were well received. Never in my wildest imagination did I expect to be admitted to Radcliffe College, the female equivalent to the all-male Harvard College."

Now it was Sam's turn to ask questions. "Why would a Jewish woman educated in the United States want to return to such a troubled world?"

"It's all a part of a much larger process. The Jewish population of Palestine looks forward to the day when we become an independent state. To achieve statehood and become a protected sanctuary for the world's dispossessed Jewish population, our fledgling movement is going to need all the help it can attract. Female participation in military service is expected and can be an important criterion when applying for admittance to graduate school or applying for a job.

"I have been trained as an educator, specializing in teaching advanced education programs for gifted children. By helping them gain admittance to good colleges and universities, we hope to make it possible for them to push back the boundaries of their lives."

Sam felt compelled to ask, "Are we pursuing the same objective from two different directions?"

Suddenly, Jacques paused what had been a nonstop conversation with Harriet and stared at Sam. To his amazement, Sam had ordered an expensive, older-vintage bottle of premium fine wine and four glasses. Turning to his new-old friend, Jacques asked, "How does the non-drinking soccer player from Iran know how to order that particular wine?"

"Ah, you forget that I have spent five summers working in London. Why is it so unthinkable that a farm boy from Iran can't acquire some unusual habits?"

Later, not wishing for the evening to end, Jacques suggested, "Instead of ordering a second bottle of wine, why don't the two of you join Harriet and me for a visit to Les Halles, the great Parisian produce market? Located in the center of Paris where all the train lines that service Paris converge. Its twelve pavilions contain all the facilities to receive and display the finest, freshly harvested French produce, wines, fruits, nuts and fish, poultry, lamb, pork, and beef. If we arrive early enough, we can watch the arrival of the vendors as they unload their vans, open their stalls, and artfully display the finest and freshest produce in all of France. Buyers from the better restaurants, the higher-quality delicatessens, and the upscale neighborhood boutique grocery stores go there daily to make their selections.

"If you watch closely, you will learn the buyers represent an interesting collection of food and beverage experts. Not only do they know what they are buying, but they take pride in their ability to haggle for the lowest price. Bargaining over price is a long-established tradition. Observing the process can be entertaining. When you think you have seen enough, we can walk to a marvelous bistro, located in one of the front-most pavilions, that serves the world's greatest onion soup that we can wash down with a bottle of Pouilly-Fuissé. The grapes for this white wine are grown and the wine is bottled by some of the finest wine makers in Bourgogne.

Sally didn't need any further encouragement. Any signs of fatigue from her long day and longer journey had disappeared. She wasn't so sure she wanted to go to Les Halles, but she knew that she wanted to become better acquainted with this exciting, gentle giant.

Sam had long since stopped studying the physical attractiveness of this beautiful and intriguing female powerhouse sitting next to him. Never in his life had he met any young woman who was so exciting, shared so many similar interests, and was so enjoyable to talk to. He may have not realized it, but in some ways, Sally's adventurous spirit reminded him of his mother, who was still occasionally referred to as The Red Queen.

Sally was talking. "My Russian Jewish family migrated to Palestine in 1917, before the outbreak of the Bolshevik Revolution. They arrived in time to experience the early turmoil created by British, French, German, and Arab nationalist armies seemingly intent on taking advantage of the breakup of the Ottoman Empire. Each of the combatants was attempting to establish control over the countries that now represent the sovereign nations of the Middle East. It was a dangerous time for a dispossessed Jewish family. Personal security and economic survival were of primary importance.

"Becoming part of Kibbutz Dagania Bet seemed like their best alternative. It was one of the first kibbutzim to be organized in Palestine. Constructed inside a stone-walled citadel, the kibbutz provided us with a home, work, and limited protection from Arab threats. Schooling for the children was a high priority. Upon graduation from middle school, students were encouraged to apply for admittance to foreign universities."

After touring the market and speaking to several vendors and buyers, Sally and Sam entered the restaurant and joined Jacques and Harriet at a small table. After Jacques placed their order, a waiter quickly appeared and placed a basket of bread and a small dish of unsalted butter on the table, then served the onion soup and opened the well-chilled bottle of white wine from Bourgogne.

Later, thoroughly engaged in deep conversation, Sally and Sam were only vaguely aware when Jacques and Harriet stood up to leave. It was then that Jacques said, "Take your time. When you are ready to leave, have them put the bill on my house account."

Not wishing for their conversation to stop, Sally and Sam continued talking while sampling the soup and fine wine. It was 7 a.m. and the city was coming alive. Conscious of their lack of sleep, the sharing of two bottles of wine, and more than nine hours of stimulating conversation, Sam hesitantly asked, "May I walk you home? The extra time will provide us with the opportunity to finish our conversation."

"What do you mean 'finish our conversation,' Mister Iranian Citizen Farmer? We have barely scratched the surface. Don't think, by offering to walk a girl home in a town where neither one of us knows our way around, you are going to get off that easy! It's already Sunday morning. After you hail a cab and deliver me to Harriet's apartment, I suggest you get a good day's rest and plan to call for me at five this afternoon. I have been told an evening cruise and dinner on a Bateau Mouche can be a very romantic way to see the night lights of Paris."

Chapter Twenty-Eight
"Finding Sally"

PARIS, FRANCE: July 1934

Excited by the prospect of spending more time with this fascinating woman, Sam made certain he arose from his nap in time to take extra care with his shower and shaving. He selected his best outfit from his limited supply of clean clothes. Next, on his trusty map, he carefully marked the route from Jacques' flat to Harriet's apartment.

Failing to get lost, and not accounting for the brisk rate of his accelerated pace, Sam arrived at the flat fifteen minutes early. When the front door opened almost before he finished knocking, it was Harriet who appeared at the door. One look at her teary face, and Sam knew, *'Something must be terribly wrong.'*

Before he could ask, Harriet said, "Oh Sam! I'm so sorry Sally isn't here. She left in a hell of a hurry within thirty minutes of the time you dropped her off this morning. There was a telegram waiting for her. It was from her father in Palestine announcing her brother, Paul, had been killed, along with six of his friends who were standing guard at their kibbutz's forward observation bunker.

"In spite of her rush to leave, she took the time to sit down and write this note she left for you. I don't know what she said in her note, but you might observe she was very careful to write her address on the back of the envelope. That ought to tell you something!"

In another part of town, Jacques, who was not expecting to see Sam that night, had decided to visit one of his favorite neighborhood bistros, order a pastis and ask the waiter to bring him an order of steak tartare complete with his favorite variety of accoutrements. Seated at a sidewalk table, enjoying his drink, he was surprised to see Sam approaching from the direction of Harriet's flat. Sam's head was bowed as he moved slowly, taking small steps. He wasn't walking in a straight line. This was not his new friend who had planned to spend a romantic evening with the enchanting Sally Raphael!

Before Sam had reached his table, Jacques said to the waiter, "The situation has changed, please cancel my order and bring two snifters of your best Napoleon Cognac."

Sam, not expecting to see Jacques, gratefully accepted his offered snifter and sat down. Lost in his thoughts, Sam remained silent. After several minutes, he reached into his breast pocket, withdrew Sally's letter, and handed the tear-stained note to Jacques without comment.

Jacques read the note twice, then put it down and asked, "When do we leave for Palestine? If Sally didn't want you to follow her, why did she write down her address?"

"Leave for Palestine? Do you realize how far it is? I am not even sure I know how to get there."

"That's my point! I need to make certain you don't get lost. Besides, I understand July can be a perfect month for tracking down an American tennis player."

Jacques' suggestion caught Sam by surprise. *'Was Jacques seriously offering to accompany me to a remote kibbutz in Arab-dominated Palestine?'*

Jacques, guessing what Sam was thinking, announced, "Partner, how is a farm boy from Iran expected to find his way to Palestine, much less find Sally's kibbutz? I would never forgive myself for not offering you my assistance, my company, and an opportunity to become better acquainted. Somehow, I believe this is not the first challenge the two of us will face together!"

Knowing he was expected to be home in Ahvaz, Sam was trying to explain what could justify his extended absence, when he thought, *'What would our fathers say if they knew what their two oldest sons were planning? Traveling to Palestine has to be a potentially dangerous journey. All this to find a girl we have known for only one day?'*

Sam's plan to travel on an Iranian passport to Palestine without a visa created a problem. But Jacques, familiar with the complicated travel practices of Roth Bank's Jewish personnel and customers, knew how to ask the proper questions in all the right places. Within a day, Sam had been issued a French passport. The next day, they found themselves aboard a tramp steamer scheduled to weigh anchor in Marseilles bound for Larnaca, Cyprus, fewer than one hundred fifty miles across the Mediterranean Sea from Haifa, Palestine.

Jacques had been warned by his father, "Arriving in Cyprus may be your lesser challenge. Traveling from Cyprus to Haifa could be much more complicated. The British immigration officials are smart, determined, and experienced in preventing unauthorized immigrants from entering Palestine. Independent of any sympathy they may hold for these dispossessed and desperate refugees, the British military is required to enforce the Balfour Accord, which limits entry into

Palestine to properly documented immigrants in accordance with mutually agreed quotas.

"When you arrive in Larnaca, go to the Roth Bank and check for messages. Next, you will need to contact my old, valued, and trusted friend, Smohl Cantor. Originally a Polish water engineer, and an early emigrant to Jewish Palestine, he was sent to Cypress to assist disenfranchised Jews in their efforts to enter Palestine. He is someone you can trust. Smohl will help you arrange the next leg of your trip to Palestine."

Unprepared for the exhausted condition of the old ship, the putrefaction of everything below decks, and the inedible food, Sam and Jacques spent the warm days and cool nights on deck. During the days, when they weren't trying to buy extra food from other passengers, they spent their time talking to some of the dispossessed people who had been forced to flee their homes to seek sanctuary in the kibbutzim of Palestine.

Curious to learn more about what had caused people to flee their homes and seek sanctuary at such great risk, Jacques was holding court near the bow of the ship. Sam was talking to another group near the stern. Both groups were anxious to tell their stories and compare their experiences with those of their fellow travelers.

After listening to story after story, Jacques and Sam began to better understand what had caused these disenfranchised people to uproot their lives and, at considerable personal risk and expense, seek unfamiliar new lives elsewhere. Although the circumstances varied, Sam and Jacques were learning, first-hand, about the difficulties that led people to accept significant risks to reinvent themselves in better, safer places and to provide better futures for their children.

At night, hungry, cold, and waiting for sleep to come, Jacques said to Sam, jokingly, "If we hadn't decided to track some girl you have only known for a few hours, we might not have learned to appreciate what generations of your family and mine have worked so hard to achieve.

"Sam, if we are ever fortunate enough to find Sally, I strongly suggest you listen very carefully to what she has to say. Her world of kibbutzim and your family's Nation of Citizen Farmers may have more in common than you realize."

Responding, Sam said, "Once we find Sally, how would you feel about extending your journey to Iran? Come and meet my family and take the opportunity to see, first-hand, what our two families have worked so hard to accomplish."

Their impressions of the desperate plight of so many dispossessed people were further amplified by their arrival in Cyprus. After one visit to what might best be described as a tent-city refugee camp, Jacques and Sam became keenly aware of how people were arriving in Cyprus by the bucket load and were leaving by the teaspoon.

Each time they would visit what passed for the camp hospital, they were shocked when they observed a line of litters carrying sick people being transported into one end of the overcrowded field hospital and another line of litters being carried to a cemetery of unmarked graves.

When Jacques checked with the Roth local bank for messages, he was handed two notes. The first one read, '*Don't make any plans to complete the next leg of your journey to Palestine until you talk to Smohl Cantor. Wait at the bank until he makes contact.*

'Pierre Roth.'

The second note was from Smohl and gave them a time and directions to a nearby restaurant.

Not wishing to be seen with two strange visitors, a cautious Smohl Cantor had arranged to join the two sons of his dear friends in the safety of a private, upstairs dining room with a convenient rear exit. The small, intimate restaurant was owned and operated by members of the Irgun, an underground Zionist paramilitary organization. It was considered a safe place to meet.

Smohl was sitting at his private table in the rear, right corner of the restaurant with his back against the far wall when the two bewildered young men entered. Immediately noticing Sam's bright red hair, he knew the young man on the right had to be Kate Naraghi's son. '*Who else could have hair of that color? Isn't the other man an older and taller version of the young man I met at his family's home in Paris a long-time ago?'*

Motioning for the two young men to join him, Smohl shifted his gaze toward Jacques, before saying, "I am sure you don't remember the times when I have been a guest at your family's dinner table. You were quite young, and unfortunately, you must have thought we talked in riddles when we were discussing the many problems of early Zionism, and the difficulties of a young nation. What an honor it is to meet the sons of such great fathers and dear friends! Without the generosity of the Roth Bank and the energies of the Naraghi family, what is widely known as the Nation of Citizen Farmers would not have been possible!"

Shifting his attention to Sam, Smohl said, "I don't know what your father has told you about me, but we share a number of long-term objectives. In what we hope to someday call Israel, we have been engaged in bringing water to the desert, allowing it to bloom, and creating homes and livelihoods for deserving people escaping the anti-Semitic treatment of Europe, the Middle East, and Russia.

"On a grander scale, the Naraghi-Roth program has been pursuing similar goals. Fortunately, its introduction of lease-to-own parcels has helped them meet the needs of the ever-growing numbers of dispossessed families. Not only do our two cultures share a common philosophy, but we have become interdependent on several levels. Working together has provided us with the opportunity to become close, trusted, and bonded friends, totally motivated to help as many of the disenfranchised as we can."

Enjoying their tea, Sam and Jacques were listening to Smohl describe how difficult it had become to smuggle so many desperate and undocumented people into the land of Zionism. "Now, if you don't mind, might I inquire why the two of you are so intent on completing your journey to Palestine?"

After listening to their explanation, Smohl said, "Are you telling me, when I am so busy trying to help all these desperate people, I am supposed to help you find some girl who is foolish enough to return to Palestine when she could have remained in the United States?

"Jacques, I have received specific instructions from your father to help you and Sam complete your journey to Palestine. If it were anyone other than your father, I sincerely doubt this request could be honored."

Several days later, the two friends found themselves wedged into the cramped bilge of a coastal fishing boat. They were lying beneath a metal sheet supporting a bed of ice needed to cool a recent catch of fish. The boat was one of hundreds of fishing boats that worked the waters between Cyprus and Palestine.

The sound of the fishing boat's engine reducing revolutions and the slowing of the boat interrupted any further conversation. Almost immediately, they could hear heavy military-type boots hitting the boat's wooden deck. Members of the British boarding party moved around searching for undocumented Jews. When the hatch cover directly above them was suddenly pulled open, all Sam and Jacques could do was hold their breath. They didn't want to create any movement or sound that might alert the soldiers that they were hiding beneath the fish and ice. The British troops returned to their ship.

A few hours later, safely ashore in Haifa, Sam was sitting on a park bench just outside the *'able-bodied seamen's'* entrance to the Haifa seaport.

Waiting for Jacques to return, Sam was wondering if the address on the envelope would provide enough information for them to find Sally. '*Hopefully, she is still at her old kibbutz. If she has already enlisted in the Israeli secret army, she could be impossible to find. We need to get moving. How does someone travel around this god-forsaken country, where an Arab village occupies one hill, and Jews occupy the next?*'

Engrossed in his thoughts, he failed to notice when Jacques, driving an old, dilapidated, nondescript car, pulled to a stop just in front of him. Before Sam could settle in the front seat, Jacques announced, "It may not be much, but it's all that I could arrange on such short notice. One thing for sure, it's not the kind of car that will attract anybody's attention!"

Two hours later, after they had passed through the Syrian border checkpoint, they stopped at what they concluded, after careful inspection, must have been a Palestinian version of a gas station. The man who waited on them was wearing a turban.

It wasn't until they had resumed their journey that Sam finally managed a take a deep breath. "I don't get it," he said. "That had to be an Arab gas station run by an Arab. Why was he so polite and helpful? He didn't act like he cared who was driving the car. I thought you told me we were driving into a country engaged in an ideological civil war!"

Amused by Sam's question, Jacques responded, "Given that you were raised in Iran, I am surprised that you don't understand. Not unlike what is happening in Iran, Arabs and Jews in Palestine have been coexisting for an exceedingly long time. If foreign anti-Semitic treatment of Jews wasn't driving so many disenfranchised people toward Palestine, the country's Arab community might not be so concerned. They fear that the stream of Jews entering Palestine, over time, will change their country into a Jewish-run state. Mark my words, if you were to read Ayatollah Khomeini's little green book – his collection of fatwas -- you would learn,

'Islam is the religion of those who struggle for the spirit of truth and justice, of those who claim for freedom and self-determination. It is the abode of those who learn how to fight against the oppression of imperialism.'

It was dark when Sam and Jacques arrived at Kibbutz Bet Dagania's elevated parking lot. They could see lights shining through the windows of what appeared to be a well-filled eating hall. They parked and walked along the dimly lit path leading to what appeared to be the main entrance.

As they approached, they were vaguely aware of two-armed guards standing in the shadows on both sides of the heavy, wood-planked door fitted with wrought-iron hardware. Approaching cautiously with both hands in clear sight, Sam and Jacques couldn't have been more than fifteen feet away when two helmeted sentries, carrying automatic weapons, emerged from the darkness. They focused the beams from two powerful flashlights on the faces of the visitors. Temporarily blinded, Jacques and Sam were not sure of what might be happening. They stopped in mid-motion when they heard the words, "Sam, Jacques, what the hell are you two doing here?"

Having never imagined that he would be met by the romantic object of his dreams – who was wearing a military helmet, a flak jacket, and carrying an automatic weapon -- Sam was not quite sure how to react. Hesitating for only the briefest of moments, he walked up to Sally, took off her helmet, set her rifle against a nearby wall and embraced her in one of his big hugs, before kissing her the way he had dreamed of doing.

Watching the lovely woman melt into the arms of his big bear of a friend, Jacques could not help but say to the other guard, "For someone who is supposed to be standing guard, your friend sure has a strange way of greeting people!"

Chapter Twenty-Nine
"Attack at Bet-Degania"

BET DAGANIA KIBBUTZ: July 1934

Unaware of what had just happened, all the people gathered in the commissary turned to watch the new girl, absent her helmet and weapon, escort the two large, handsome strangers to a vacant table in the far corner of the commissary. One of the girls sitting near the entrance turned to her friends and said, "Look! Isn't that one on the left Jacques Roth, captain of the French National soccer team? I recognize him from his picture in the sports section of Paris Match. Why, in the middle of the night, would he and his big friend be visiting our kibbutz? How do they know Sally?"

Any opportunity to discover the reason for the two men's presence would have to wait. The sound of a not-so-distant, deafening explosion filled the big room. Moving quickly, Sally said, "Follow me, we are being attacked."

Before Sam and Jacques could fathom what was happening, Sally had led them down a long flight of metal-meshed stairs to a large underground arsenal. It was well-stocked with military weapons, ammunition, hand grenades, and flares, the kind that burned eerily white against the night sky.

In a voice that sounded like someone trying to hail a New York taxicab, Sally yelled, "I have the flares! Grab two of those buckets filled with hand grenades and whatever weapon you know how to use in close quarters, and follow me into that tunnel over there, the one to our right! It leads to one of our forward observation bunkers!"

Following closely behind Sally, carrying buckets of grenades in both hands while running along the dimly lit tunnel, Sam could hear the "whoosh" of the flares as they ignited, punctuated by intermittent bursts of an automatic weapon. The kibbutz sentries were defending their position.

Many layers of sandbags stacked on top a high mound formed the bunker. Vegetation had been cleared for a hundred yards in all directions, giving the defenders a clear field of fire. Flares would expose any would-be attackers hiding in the underbrush beyond the perimeter, leaving them vulnerable to automatic weapons fire and hand grenades rolled down the slope of the embankment.

The two guards assigned to the bunker were putting up a hell of a battle. One of them was hurling flares into the night sky, illuminating the area above the bunker. The second guard, in charge of a Browning Automatic Rifle, was concentrating his fire, in short bursts, on the closest approaching enemy.

Sally, the first to arrive at the bunker, saw an attacker standing on the opposite side of the bunker, aiming his rifle toward the back of one of the sentries. Instinctively, she yelled and hurled a lit flare toward the attacker. Sam shot the man while he was attempting to brush the flare's burning phosphorus from his clothes.

Sally, from her position in the center of the bunker, was too busy to take notice of the dead man lying in a pool of blood. She was busy lighting flares and throwing them as far up into the air as her strong right tennis arm would permit. Occasionally, the flare of her second throw would ignite the sky before her first throw fell to the ground.

Sam and Jacques took up positions on opposite sides of the bunker to cover the two men operating the air-cooled Browning automatic weapon. From their positions, they were able to cover the remaining three-quarters of the perimeter. With the advantage of the well-lit battlefield, they pulled pins from hand grenades and rolled them down the outer slope of their bunker toward the advancing enemy. When the remaining combatants charged the bunker, Sam and Jacques shouldered their rifles and tried to pick them off before they could get too close.

Suddenly, out of the corner of his eye, Sam saw an attacker rise up behind Sally, gun in hand, aiming directly toward her. Knowing he didn't have time to shoulder his own gun, Sam roared and lunged toward his enemy before pulling him down onto the floor of the bunker. With two quick movements, he broke the man's neck.

Jacques, only feet away, watched the violence Sam was dispensing. Feeling the hairs on the back of his neck start to rise, Jacques instinctively turned, just in time to see a second man rise above the bunker, holding an automatic weapon. From his waist, he fired his Colt 45, hitting the enemy with all three shots. The attacker fell forward into the bunker and lay – apparently dead -- next to two of his dead comrades.

Too busy to worry about the three bodies and the growing pool of blood, the five defenders continued to concentrate on the enemy directly in front of them. High school students were kept busy running back to the armory, retrieving more flares, hand grenades, and ammunition.

Hour after hour, the Arab attackers, willing to risk death, continued their effort to overrun the bunker and gain entrance to the tunnel leading to the core of the kibbutz. The five defenders, aware that they were the only resistance, were determined to hold their ground.

Four hours later, when the sky to the east began to lighten and the sun began to appear over the Golan Heights, the attackers broke off their engagement and retreated under the cover of what little darkness remained.

Thirsty, hungry, and too tired to think or talk, the five exhausted defenders turned over their empty buckets, sat down, and leaned against the inner wall of the bunker. The younger children were delivering cups of hot coffee and freshly made sandwiches. Without saying a word, the five warriors sipped the coffee and eagerly accepted the food. Fully absorbed by their fatigue and their memories of the night, they seemed surprised to note that the sun was signaling the start of a new day, and that they were still living.

Like what happens when the sun shines on a flower, Sally, feeling some renewal of energy, raised her head, looked around, and surveyed the carnage. Looking over the top of the bunker, Sally concluded, from the number of dead or wounded enemies who lay there, that the Arabs had been willing to pay an enormous cost. *'If so many men are prepared to risk death, do their actions provide us with an indication of their strength and commitment to drive the Jews from their shores?'*

After no more than twenty minutes, the irrepressible Sally quietly asked, "It's 1934. If militant Arab terrorists are so intent on driving the Jews out of Palestine, what kind of lesson should we be learning?"

Too tired to answer such a weighty question, Sam asked, "Don't we all need to get out of these clothes, take long, hot showers and get some sleep? Maybe later, we can continue this conversation."

Chapter Thirty
"What Did We Learn?"

BET DAGANIA KIBBUTZ, PALESTINE: July 1934

Jacques and Sam awoke wondering if their experiences during the previous night a bad dream had been. A glance around the small room gave them their answer: it revealed blood-splattered clothes, weapons, spare ammunition, and piles of bloody, soiled towels. The clock on a small table read 2:15 p.m. The sun, already high in the sky, was shining through the one small window. Sam quickly surmised, "We must have slept for more than seven hours."

A loud knocking on their door followed by its sudden opening revealed a fully scrubbed, dark-haired woman, dressed in well-washed and -pressed military garb. The two bewildered men, standing in their underwear, were trying to fathom what was happening. Before either of them could speak, Sally announced, "A hot dinner awaits. Once you have finished, let's go for a long walk. I have something I wish to discuss, and we don't want to be overheard."

An hour later, Sally was leading the walkers when she suddenly stopped, turned, and asked, "Jacques, what the hell are you doing here? I was hoping Sam would follow me, but why you?"

Surprised by her question, Jacques paused before answering. "The best explanation I have been able to come up with has something to do with the joint mission our families have devoted their lives to achieving. Someday, the responsibility for perpetuating what they have started will pass to the two of us.

"I can only speak for myself, but I would like to think, when that day comes, Sam and I will share the same kind of relationship our fathers have enjoyed. What better opportunity could I have had to develop that relationship than helping Sam find his way to Bet Dagania? How could I have known that the three of us would end up in that bunker fighting for our lives?

"Even now, I am still trying to figure out what was really happening last night. I understand we were all fighting to protect an entrance to Bet Dagania and remain alive. But I suspect something else must have been occurring. Standing there, fighting a vicious enemy trying to kill us, was nothing like anything I have ever encountered. Strangely, I was never conscious of my personal danger. Somehow, I knew that, by supporting each other, we were generating the kind of inner strength we needed to prevail."

Responding, Sally said, "That is what I would like to discuss."

Sam and Jacques, without protest, sat on the ground, leaned against the trunk of a fallen tree and waited for her to speak.

"When I finally woke up this morning, I decided I needed to take a second shower. During the first shower, no matter how hard I scrubbed and washed, and no matter how many times I rinsed, I was convinced that I had not cleansed myself of the last of the blood and the grime of gunpowder. Standing under the hot water the second time, I started to replay the events of last night. All I remember was the three of us standing next to each other, totally dependent on each other for our survival. That's when I realized that a special personal bonding was taking place."

Sam said, "I remember watching you reaching for another flare, stripping off the igniter strip and calmly lighting flare after flare. Do you realize, for four hours, you kept the battlefield well-illuminated? Never in my life have I ever seen someone, exposed to real and immediate danger, work so calmly."

Jacques added, "Sam, it must have been when you yelled, dragged the gunman down into the bunker and killed him with your hands that the sensation of kill or be killed finally sank in for me. From that point on, our attackers no longer seemed like real people. They were an enemy trying to kill us. Realizing the three of us depended on each other, I remember thinking, *'As long as we keep fighting, we will survive.'* That is a feeling I never want to forget."

Sam, normally a quiet man who had difficulty expressing his feelings, spoke up without hesitation. "Hopefully, the recollections of all that killing will fade with time," he said. "But I never want to forget the memory of the three of us standing shoulder to shoulder, doing what needed to be done. It makes me believe, no matter where our respective lives may lead, we will always be there for each other when we are faced with real problems."

No one spoke during the walk back to the kibbutz. Each of them was lost in their own thoughts. Sam, knowing he and Jacques were scheduled to leave shortly for Iran, was thinking, *'Either I need to remain at the "Bet" to help Sally or I need to find some way of persuading her to accompany us to Iran. Maybe I should follow Sally to her room so we can have a little chat?'*

Chapter Thirty-One
"Sam and Sally"

BET DAGANIA: July 1934

The door to Sally's room had just closed behind them when Sam reached forward to engulf her in one of his gentle, warm bear-hugs. Whispering into her ear, he said, "Sally, believe me, if I didn't think of you as someone I don't ever want to lose, I wouldn't have followed you to the 'Bet.' During last night's attack, when I saw that man rise behind you and aim his weapon at you, I knew I wanted to save you, even if it might have cost me my life! That was the moment when I realized how important it was to me for us to share our lives together."

"Not so fast!" Sally said, "Since when did you decide you are the spokesman for us? We are equals, both our opinions count. I want you to sit here in this chair and listen to what your other half is about to say.

"I agree with most of what you have said, and I would like to think all we have is an unresolved problem of occupational geography. Knowing this problem might come up, I've been thinking. How was I to know I would fall in love with a great man who has chased me halfway around the world, a man whose own life is committed to providing an opportunity for other people to enjoy a better life?

"What would you say if I was to tell you, this not-so-little Jewish girl would give up her dreams to work for a future Israel if it meant that she could spend the rest of her life assisting her man to pursue his dreams?"

Before Sam could respond, Sally put up her hand to stop him. "There is, however, one thing that we need to get straight. If I accompany you to Iran, that doesn't mean I will agree to marry you. That will have to come later. Once I have become convinced there is a formidable role for me to play, then *I* will ask *you* to marry *me*."

"Sally, without your asking, I want to assure you geography will always be a secondary consideration. After I establish the new trading company, I should be able to manage it from a different location. Where we live should be determined by where you feel you can make your best contribution. Once we get settled in, after an appropriate time, if, by some chance, you haven't asked me to marry you, I will find a way to accompany you to Palestine."

Standing up, extending his arms, he waited for her to rise before he wrapped his arms around her. Secure in their embrace, he said, "There is another problem we need to discuss. You need to meet my mother. They don't call her the Red Queen without a reason. Without her approval, she could make life exceedingly difficult for us."

Pulling her gentle, giant man toward the bed, she answered, "Let's worry about that when the time comes."

Smohl was sitting at his big desk in his private office in Tel Aviv when the morning newspapers were delivered. Consistent with his normal practice of seeking to stay fully informed about current events, he carefully scanned the first paper. He sat up straight when he noticed the mention of a valiant defense of Kibbutz Bet Dagania and the role that his friend's children had played. Realizing Sam, Jacques, and Sally had become celebrated heroes overnight, Smohl was concerned that they could become the victims of further attacks. *'I have to get them out of there!'* Quickly making the necessary arrangements, Smohl called for his car and started driving towards Bet Dagania.

Early the next morning, Jacques and Smohl were the first to arrive for breakfast. Deeply immersed in conversation, they were startled when Sally and Sam suddenly appeared. One look at their showered and freshly scrubbed friends told them they were ready to discuss *'the situation.'*

It was over their first cup of coffee that Sally said, "Jacques, your friend has asked me to join him on your journey to Iran and his world of dams, quants, and irrigated farms. In the process, he has managed to convince me there is a great opportunity to organize a school of advanced preparation for the more advanced students in each of the villages. This is a role I could become extremely excited about!"

Smohl quickly reacted. "Wait just a minute! When I talked about *'moving on'* I was thinking in terms of Tel Aviv, not Iran. Maybe you might care to explain why you are prepared to sacrifice such a promising opportunity to help mold the educational future of an independent Israel?"

"Smohl, with all due respect, it seems to me the question that needs to be asked is: If we were to focus on the needs of the gifted students, what difference would a change in geography make? Once the program has been proven, why couldn't we operate campuses in both countries? When would there be another opportunity to tap into two pools of exceptionally gifted children? It seems to me that we should take advantage of the Naraghis' proposed generosity and open a School for Advanced Preparation as soon as possible."

After listening to Sally, Smohl said, "There are those of us who believe our job is only half-finished when we relocate families into our kibbutzim. Performing what is basically agricultural labor is a fair price for the parents to pay, but not for their children. It's important the children be exposed to and have an opportunity to pursue life beyond the boundaries of kibbutzim. We were hoping you would be the person to help us build an advanced college preparation educational system."

Sally was prepared to answer. "Why couldn't we think in terms of all the students in each Nation village and all Israeli kibbutzim as candidates for our advanced-learning programs? Knowing of the close working relationship that presently exists between our kibbutzim and the Naraghi Nation, I am not aware of any differences in culture, religion, language, or geography that might prevent Nation and Tel Aviv from working together."

Rarely before had Smohl witnessed three more strong-willed people able to reach an agreement. Finally, Smohl suggested, "Maybe the time has come for us to meet with Sam's father, Harshim, in Ahvaz. Before making a geographic decision, it might be prudent to determine if Nation is willing to provide the resources Sally will require. If they are, their generosity would facilitate the *'getting started'* problem. Why don't I arrange suitable accommodations for the four of us to embark on a Naraghi-Roth chartered, seagoing freighter bound from Haifa, Palestine, to Abadan, Iran?"

Chapter Thirty-Two
"Sam Returns"

AHVAZ, IRAN TRAIN STATION: August 1934

History has a strange way of repeating itself. Twenty-seven years after Harshim and Kate stepped off the train from Abadan onto the railroad station platform in Ahvaz, Sam, Sally, Smohl and Jacques would be stepping onto the same platform.

The waiting women were speculating '*Had six years of foreign study, five summers of work experience, and his relationship with some Jewish girl from Israel changed Sam? Why would he be bringing home a girl he had only recently met? Is she visiting or will she be staying? Is she a woman of substance or some opportunistic woman he has met along the way?*'

The men were worried. Why had Smohl, Pierre's close friend, Jacques, and some strange woman accompanied Sam on his return home? '*What new ideas would Sam be bringing home? Is something important about to happen for the community?*'

Ever since they had boarded the train in Abadan, Sally -- in anticipation of making her grand entrance -- had been asking questions. Sam would hear her ask, "Am I properly dressed? What's going to happen when I am thrust into the midst of so many people, many of whom I don't share a common language with? Will they be wondering what kind of woman Sam has brought home? How will people in Iran feel about my Jewish heritage? Is this rural community ready for another female *spitfire*, committed to making changes? What can I expect from your mother?"

"Sally, whatever is waiting for you can't be any more difficult than when the three of us were forced to defend our position that first night at the Bet. No matter what, I can assure you, nobody will be carrying guns or hand grenades. All we have to do is stick together, relax, and we will be fine."

For Sam, the idea of returning home was turning out to be less than exciting. '*What kind of a problem have I created for Sally? What kind of reaction will the waiting people have when they meet Sally? Will they appreciate that she is a highly educated educator and a world-class amateur tennis player who is committed to pushing back the educational barriers faced by disadvantaged children? Will she be given a fair chance?'*

Harshim, Pierre, and Kate were standing near the exit of the rear car when Sam emerged. They couldn't help but think, *'Who is this giant of a man with red hair and such broad shoulders?'*

After stepping from the train, Sam immediately moved toward his mother. He picked her up in a big bear hug and whispered in her ear, "Mom, I have been missing you for six years. You have no idea how grateful I have been for your encouragement and support; I would never have had the opportunity to attend both schools without your help. I hope you will be pleased by what I have learned."

Harshim waited until Sam had set his mother gently down on the platform before he moved forward to embrace his son. After stepping back to examine the formerly gangly young man who was returning from a strange and bigger world, he said, "Welcome home, son! Let's see what six years has produced." The first thing he noticed about his son was that he was at least two inches taller, possessed very broad, strong shoulders and, except for his red hair, closely resembled a younger version of himself.

Any thought of engaging in more welcome-home pleasantries was quickly forgotten. Harshim's attention was focused on the entrance to the last car. His first image of Sally was that of a very pretty girl, tastefully dressed, in a loose-fitting afternoon cocktail dress. Her makeup gave her the look of Semitic mystery and intrigue. Wearing high-heeled shoes, she appeared much taller than her 5'8" height. It was a tall, slim, and well-muscled former professional tennis player who energetically stepped from the train. Harshim's first reaction was, *'She certainly doesn't resemble a woman who has been recently engaged in close military combat!'*

On her best behavior, Kate waited until the greetings and small talk were finished before she reached forward to touch Sally's arm and invited her to move off to one side. Kate then said, "Sally, I am looking forward to having some quiet time we can use to become better acquainted. Sam has mentioned in his letters that you are bringing some fascinating ideas for improving our educational system. I am anxious to learn more about what you hope to accomplish. Perhaps that will create an opportunity for me to learn why you have chosen to follow my son home? You must have concerns about fitting into our rural world of quants, and our traditional family environment?"

"May I call you Kate?" Sally asked politely. "Do you believe in love at first sight? From the very first time we met, after eight hours of talk, I knew I had fallen in love with the man of my dreams. How was I to know he would follow me all the way to my kibbutz in Palestine? Following the night attack, as tested 'Bunker Buddies,' we all felt a strong bond. In my mind, it was never a question of whether Sam and I would devote our lives to loving each other. Unresolved is the question of occupational geography.

"You have no idea how threatened I feel by the idea of being set down in a world of strange women, committed to performing domestic chores, raising children, and keeping their men happy. If I am to survive, I need to have a mission of my own, one that will allow me to make a material contribution to what you have started."

Totally surprised by Sally's directness and candor, Kate, the strong-willed women, took a step backwards to get a better view. Kate understood the implications of her response. '*She doesn't waste any time, coming right to the point. Is she trying to test me to determine if I expect her to become an enemy or a supporter?*'

Despite her earlier promise to remain quiet, Kate asked, "What will happen if you aren't offered the financial support needed to start the new school?"

Ready for the question, Sally said. "Sam and I have already discussed that possibility. I think it is only fair I explain. The fledgling state of Israel has already agreed to support my program. Sam and I are committed to spending our lives together. We have both agreed our home will always be located where we can pursue our individual interests. It is yet to be determined if we will be living in Ahvaz or Tel Aviv!"

Kate didn't need a roadmap to understand that this kind, gentle-appearing woman was, in effect, a highly intelligent, strong-minded woman, determined to help gifted children and to love her son.

Sam, unaware of the serious nature of the two women's conversation, interrupted when he approached them and reached for Sally's hand. "There are a lot of people who are waiting to meet you. Mother, would you mind if I steal Sally away for a few minutes?"

Not expecting Pierre Roth to be in Ahvaz, Smohl and Jacques wasted no time in making their way over to where Harshim and Pierre were standing. With all the commotion over Sally's introductions, Smohl, Harshim, Pierre, and Jacques were left standing alone, well out of earshot of any interested listeners.

Pierre was talking, "We have a lot to discuss. Sam and Sally aside, I know we are planning on talking about proceeding with another ten irrigation districts. But there are several sticky situations we need to resolve before we are asked to make a final decision.

"Not the least of which are the recent developments in Germany! An enormous amount of power is being consolidated under the tent of a new reform leader who is suspected of having his own secret agenda of Aryan supremacy. Let's make certain we reserve whatever time is needed to understand what the Germany implications may mean to Nation."

As Sam and Sally approached the nearest group of waiting people, Sam was thinking, *'Am I going to enjoy introducing this brunette version of the younger Kate who stepped from the same train twenty-seven years ago!'*

After each introduction, Sam would step back from Sally just far enough to make sure he would not be engaged in the conversation, but close enough to be of assistance should his services as translator be required. He was anxious for Sally to exude her charm and her mastery of several languages.

As she waited for Sam to complete his introductions, Sally would smile, look into the eyes of the person she was meeting, and hold their attention as she listened to Sam describe each person's history and interests. In each instance, Sam provided Sally with enough information to enable her to ask informed questions.

Unaccustomed to meeting an attractive, well-educated, multilingual woman from another culture, his concern about his friends' possible apprehension was quickly relieved.

Sam could not have been prouder. For someone who had difficulty communicating with people he had just met, he was impressed by how seamlessly Sally moved from one group to another. As the topics of conversation varied, she never seemed to be at a loss for words. *'Drop Sally into the midst of strangers, and it doesn't take much time before she is creating her own fan club!'*

Chapter Thirty-Three
"The German Problem"

HARSHIM'S STUDY IN AHVAZ: August 1934

The Roths and their guests were gathered in Harshim's library, with its big fireplace, comfortable chairs, and a deep, leather-cushioned davenport. Taking advantage of the time before the women were scheduled to appear, Pierre was using the cocktail hour to continue his discussion about Germany. "Internally, Hitler and his industrial support are adjusting their power base away from the workers' socialist movement in favor of the military industrials, and the army's powerful generals.

"Rearmament programs are advancing at an alarming rate. Already 'Arsenals for Peace' are being converted into 'Arsenals for War.' There doesn't appear any doubt Hitler and his military establishment are committed to expanding Germany's geographic borders. It appears they are intent on creating a military force capable of standing against the French, the British, and the Russians, in their quest for a trans-European Aryan supremacy.

"Their current threats notwithstanding, I have it on reliable authority that the German High Command does not want to become involved in a military conflict before they are ready to engage in an all-out war.

"Then there is their oil problem. Fortunately, for the rest of the world, Germany does not possess an adequate supply of domestically produced oil to engage in a long war. The lack of oil compromised their World War I ambitions, and they don't want to make the same mistake again. Any plan Germany may be harboring will depend on its ability to occupy an oil-rich country or negotiate a treaty with a privately owned source of oil."

Pierre continued, "I believe we need to recognize the possibility of Nation's potential oil reserves being one of the only sources of new oil that isn't under the control of a sovereign government. All Germany would have to do is consummate a private agreement with Naraghi-Roth."

Hesitantly, Harshim said, "The process you describe may have already started. For the last three months, a coalition of German industrialists has been offering us a very lucrative arrangement in exchange for the development rights to our oil. Over the course of the prolonged discussions, we assumed they were negotiating as a private party, independent of the German government. They led us to believe it was their intention, once they had obtained control, to offer to sell their oil production to the German government, much the same way they do with so many other items they manufacture and supply.

"After we turned down their final offer, I perceived their subsequent threat to bomb our dams and our Abadan commercial facilities to be serious. Since their interests are focused on our oil and not on the agribusiness activities of Nation, they would have no reservations about demolishing Nation's agribusiness complex."

Pierre leapt out of his chair as if he had been shot out of a cannon. "Harshim, you and I have been working closely together on this recent interest by the Germans. But this is the first time I have heard of their threat. I believe, if Allied governments were to learn of Germany's attempt to solve its oil problems with Nation, they would become genuinely concerned.

"It's no secret there is an informal understanding that Middle Eastern Oil requires all the major powers to observe a *'hands-off'* policy. I believe if the French, the British, the Russians and perhaps the Americans were to learn about the German threat, they might decide to pay serious attention."

Jacques, always the conceptual thinker, said, "If the Allies are prepared to respond militarily to any German attack, have we identified our next effective deterrent?"

Uncertain of what Jacques was suggesting, Sam asked, "'Effective deterrent?' What are you talking about?"

Jacques answered, "Could it be the Germans are not prepared to become involved in a major military conflict before they are ready? Is it reasonable for us to assume, if they are aware of the Allies' willingness to militarily protect our oil, we may have achieved the effective deterrent we need?"

"What an interesting concept!" said Pierre, who was fascinated by Jacques' argument. "I wonder how long we can rely on American protection. I predict, sometime in the future, under different circumstances, we will need to create a different version of an effective deterrent if we are to protect ourselves from future world power temptations."

Moving to a different subject, Harshim interjected, "I have been informed that, with the introduction of new mining technological improvements, we should be able to reduce the construction time required to install all the components of a new irrigation district to less than two years. At that rate, we could complete the next nine quants in less than twenty years. Should we decide to proceed, we could increase our annual need for refugee farming families to one thousand from our current demand of seven-hundred fifty. Changing the lives of two-hundred fifty additional families annually makes a big difference if you are one of those families."

Smohl responded, "As attractive as this goal may be, I question why we should commit to the extra burden and risk of developing another drainage system until we are certain we have solved our effective deterrent problem?"

Unexpectedly, Sam said, "Wait a minute, I can understand why we might not wish to commit to nine more irrigation districts, but why not just one? Won't the commencement of work on one more dam-quant prevent us from creating a lot of confusion and not materially increase our exposure?"

Any further discussion was interrupted when Kate entered the library and announced dinner was ready to be served.

Dinners around the big family table could best be described as passionate, interesting, and complicated. For decades, the highly polished mahogany table had been the place where big decisions were discussed and settled. Tonight, though, was different. At one end of the table, Harshim was huddled with his oldest son, Sam. More than six years had passed since his introverted, tall, skinny, eighteen-year-old son had left for England. Wanting to learn more about the gentle giant who had stepped from the train, Harshim needed to have an uninterrupted talk with him.

At the same time, Sam needed his father to understand that his six years of study and five summers of work had included more than an education in modern mining technology. "Father, it's important to me that you appreciate my two extra years at the London School of Economics, and my five summer jobs of international trading work experience," he said. "I've never forgotten our international trading conversation we had before I left. I can only hope that my returning home will enable us to pursue that dream."

Unexpectedly, Harshim said, "Until we have adopted a new plan for establishing additional foreign demand for any new production of electrical power and farm products, we are precluded from developing any additional acreage.

"Someone needs to re-visit prospective markets, learn about their unfilled needs we can resolve, and develop trusting and durable relationships. Sam, as soon as you and Sally are settled in and you have had time to become familiar with the new changes in our operations, why don't we continue this conversation?"

Late the next morning, before lunch, Kate asked Sally to join her. Almost immediately, it became obvious to the others present that Kate and Sally were huddled in a serious, do-not-disturb conversation.

Kate would make a statement or ask a question and Sally would take her time to provide what she hoped would be regarded as a thoughtful response.

Finally, Sally summoned the courage to ask the question she had been waiting to ask ever since she had arrived. "Kate, I would like to know your version of what took place twenty-seven years ago, when you first arrived in Ahvaz," Sally said. "What transpired when you began to ask questions normally reserved for *'male-only'* conversations? How did they react when you started to express your own ideas, make your own suggestions? How did the other women react to your non-traditional behavior?"

Appreciating the question, Kate responded, "It was hard to tell. I could not be sure if they resented my presence. It was only after I began to introduce a discussion about the advantages of including hydroelectric dams into their 'Super Quant' concept that the men realized I knew what I was talking about. If you hope to be asked to join the Boys' Team, it's not the women you will have to convince; it's the men."

Kate continued, "After so many years, I understand why a talented woman attracted to a Naraghi man wants to be allowed to play a big part in supporting her man and contributing her share to the family mission. I would like to believe my efforts have opened the door and have made it possible for subsequent generations of Naraghi women to play productive roles."

Sensing Kate had provided her with an invitation to express her views, Sally plunged onward. "If I choose to remain in Ahvaz, I would like to dedicate the professional side of my life to improving the educational opportunities for Nation's more gifted students," she said.

"The idea of using established tools of education to provide children with advanced educational preparation is not new. Properly implemented, Advanced Prep would allow the more gifted and motivated students to extend their boundaries by pursuing their education from some of the world's better schools of higher learning. It could also be perceived as another way we will have of differentiating our humanitarian program from others."

Growing more confident that this exciting young woman might be capable of introducing her own brand of constructive change, Kate asked, "Now, what is all this nonsense of you and Sam living someplace else? If you are worried about developing an opportunity to pursue your own interests, you can depend on my support."

Engrossed in conversation, the two women were surprised when they finally looked up and noticed they were the only people left at the table. Lunch had concluded, the dishes had been cleared away, and the tall clock read 4:30.

Three days later, buoyed by the encouragement she was receiving from Kate and Sam, Sally was prepared to introduce her "Advanced Preparation Educational" concept to the family. After standing up at the family dinner table and asking for recognition, she announced, "If my math is correct, at the present time more than five thousand children are attending your one through twelve village schools, one thousand of whom will graduate from our high schools each year. Historical studies have concluded that, at a minimum, fifteen percent, or one hundred fifty of these students, would qualify as gifted scholars, and become candidates for Advanced Prep.

"I know it's difficult, but if were to include Advanced Prep as part of our curriculum, imagine how these graduates could push back the barriers of their lives by attending foreign colleges and universities, and later by gaining employment by some of the world's leading companies. You might prefer to think of Advanced Prep students as future Nation Ambassadors."

After pausing to allow what she had just said to be absorbed, Sally continued, "It is important that my proposed program includes provisions for the teaching expenses, tuition and living costs of our graduates. We could be talking about a great deal of money. Unless that kind of money can be made available, what is the point of creating an opportunity for these children of lower-income parents?"

Finished with her presentation, Sally returned to her chair and sat. For almost a minute, no one said anything.

Finally, Kate rose to speak. "What the hell is wrong with us? We've just heard a very gifted and motivated woman present her ideas defining new advantages we need to introduce into our galaxy of improved living advantages. Did we hesitate when we had the opportunity to convert our tenant farmers into land-owning, citizen farmers? Did we flinch when we decided to use a portion of our surplus electrical power revenues to support our medical clinics and schools?

"I have no idea how much money ten more irrigation districts will generate, but I'd bet we could be talking about very large numbers."

Quick to respond, Smohl said, "Maybe Nation won't have to absorb the total cost of educational expenses for our successful graduates. Our Zionist movement has demonstrated that a large number of people support our work in Israel and are prepared to vote with their wallets. I don't see any reason why these same people wouldn't be willing to assist in the endowment of the educational expenses of Advanced Prep graduates."

Later that evening, in the privacy of their bedroom, Sam asked Sally how she felt about the evening's conversation.

Sally slowly turned toward Sam, put an arm around his shoulder and whispered in his ear, "I think I am going to like it here. According to your mother, there are two mistakes I need to avoid making. One, I could stop loving and supporting her son, and two, I cannot just sit around and fail to develop a project of my own. Since I don't plan to do either, how would you like to marry me?"

Chapter Thirty-Four
"State of Nation 1934"

AHVAZ, IRAN: August 1934

The next morning, Sally, Sam, and Jacques were last to arrive at the table for breakfast. Noticing Harshim, Smohl, Kate, and Pierre were involved in what was obviously a *not-to-be-disturbed* conversation, they stopped long enough only to help themselves to breakfast rolls and coffee.

Sam had insisted he be allowed to lead Sally and Jacques on a driving tour of some of the more important features of the Nation. "No tour can be complete without your understanding all the critical parts that need to be meshed together before the overall operation of Nation can effectively function," he said.

Sally's incessant stream of incisive and penetrating questions was interrupted when they noticed they were approaching what appeared to be the roof of a large, underground building. It was made even more conspicuous by the fact that it was located amid thousands of acres of lush, green, irrigated, and well-cultivated crops and surrounded by a donut-shaped lake.

Sam was leading them toward the strange-looking building when he said, "Survival in this part of the world is not something we can take for granted. I can assure you, if trouble comes, we could find ourselves all alone and forced to rely on our own devices.

"After the attack at Dagania Bet, I suspect you understood why it was necessary to construct this underground armory, dig all these trenches, and construct these outer perimeter observation bunkers."

Jacques could see the guards, the automatic weapons, the anti-tank guns, the artillery, and the mortars located behind the inner perimeter of the lake. Descending to a tunnel that ran underneath the lake, they were greeted by a cast-iron door that opened into a large, cold warehouse. It was filled with freshly harvested, perishable fruits and vegetables and large blocks of ice, formed from water that had frozen during the winter.

Sally asked. "How are you able to produce so much freezing cold air clear out here in the middle of the desert?" "How do you make the room so cold?"

Smiling at her questions, Sam said, "This big room is, in reality, an evaporative cooling chamber we use to store perishable produce in the summer and make ice. You are looking at a modern version of an ancient evaporative cooling system engineers designed more than two thousand years ago. It captures the cold air, created by the evaporative cooling of the water moving long distances through the systems of underground quants. The cold air is collected at the terminal base of each of the Super Quants. We have simply improved on the technology."

Nodding to indicate her understanding, Sally asked, "Where do you store the military supplies?'"

After descending halfway down what looked like a three-story set of heavy, perforated metal stairs, Sally paused to look around. The enormity what she was seeing was impressive: the thirty-foot-high ceiling and the below-ground armory. The two-story high ceiling was supported by rows of evenly spaced, steel-reinforced concrete columns.

Against the far wall, Jacques was looking at a series of big metal tanks when he asked. "What do those contain? Is this where you store the oil you use for your 'Light the Candle' system of defense? What happens, during a prolonged attack, if you deplete your stored oil? Why wouldn't an invading army make the kind of feints that would cause you to ignite your ditched fields, and then wait until you have used up your oil supply before attacking?"

"Good questions," Sam said. "Buried under the reservoir are the pipes we use to pump oil from our artesian-fed oil ponds. They provide a continuous supply. All we have to do is to open the valves and turn on the pumps."

Not sure of what he had just heard, Jacques asked, "How much oil do you think exists under Nation's farmed land?"

"We don't know," Sam answered. "Pierre and Harshim have prevented any exploration from happening. A long time ago, they decided the humanitarian benefits derived from the farming of the surface lands should not be interrupted by the surface activity required by introduction of oil drilling, pumping stations, storage tanks, and the road systems needed to transport oil to the Port of Abadan."

"Sam, I seem to recall Pierre telling me that part of the Roth Bank's decision to become involved with your family's venture depended on proving ownership of the Naraghi family's sub-surface mineral rights. Was the presence of these ponds the compelling cause for validation?"

One of Sam's sly smiles was the only response Jacques would receive.

After looking around, Sally and Jacques saw that the rest of the storage area was filled with loaded pallets stacked three high. Even from her vantage point she recognized some of the markings on the crates. Hand grenades were stored in one long row. Rounds for mortars and artillery were stored in the next row. Ammunition for automatic weapons was stored in the third row. Automatic weapons, rifles, and handguns were stored in the fourth row. Neatly arranged along the right wall, near the underground entrance, were tanks, tank ammunition, spare parts, and a machine shop.

Sally asked, "Sam, should we conclude the terminal cooling chamber is both a cold storage facility and a military arsenal?"

Sam had anticipated the question. "In Israel you have to defend yourself from bands of local terrorists," he said. "Here, we need to be prepared to defend ourselves from well-equipped, mechanized, modern armies."

Horrified by the vision of an army engulfed in flames, Jacques asked, "Have you ever been required to light the candle?"

"Only twice. Prior to World War I, in 1914, a German military brigade invaded the western reaches of what was then our first irrigation district. More recently, in 1927, an armored detachment of unknown origin tested our perimeter defenses. In both instances, we concluded the vision of curtains of burning oil not only discouraged any further advancement, but it also succeeded in creating public awareness of our deterrent. Today, we would like to believe that the knowledge of the effect is a more valuable defense than its actual use.

The drive back to the family compound was subdued. There was no talking. Their minds were filled with the images of immolated armies. Before departing, Sam said, "Tomorrow be prepared for an early start. We are going to Abadan. It's important that you see the port, and our industrial park where we store, process, and prepare our produce for shipment. In the afternoon, after we inspect one of our dam sites, I am planning to escort you to one of the Nation villages, Hopefully, once you talk to the citizens, you will better understand our humanitarian efforts."

Chapter Thirty-Five
"More Pins, More String"

AHVAZ, IRAN: August 1934

The next morning, Harshim, Pierre, Kate, and Smohl resumed their discussions. Pausing only long enough to help themselves to cups of coffee and rolls, Sam and his disciples climbed into the jeep and were off on their day's adventure. As they approached what looked like a sizeable industrial park, Sam said, "The Iranian seaport of Abadan in the Persian Gulf is the principal port through which Iran is connected commercially with the rest of the world. Located next to the port, Naraghi-Roth's commercial center for receiving, processing, and shipping Nation produce resembles what might best be regarded as an agribusiness industrial complex within a bigger industrial park. The storage buildings, administrative offices, crop-processing facilities, and ship, rail, and truck loading operations make for an impressive sight. The long line of ships waiting in the harbor to be moored dockside serves as a visible barometer of the commercial activity needed to support both Iran and Nation."

Impressed by the magnitude and complexity of the industrial compound, Jacques asked, "How long did it take for us to construct and how much did it cost? How much time and money would be involved if it were destroyed?

"Those are questions we hope we don't have to answer. Unfortunately, they fall in the same category of what we would have to consider should the dams be bombed."

"Should we presume, if any of these events were to occur, they could destroy the economic viability of Nation?"

"The answer to that would depend on the extent of the damage. Nation reserves a sinking fund adequate to fund a one-year interruption in operations. But, without outside financial assistance, it is doubtful if we could survive a second year."

In the afternoon, Sam drove them to where they could see a recently constructed hydroelectric dam, the electrical generation equipment, and the flow of water entering the mouth of the quant.

Neither Jacques nor Sally was prepared for the scale of the dam and the size of the lake behind it. It was Sally who first spoke. "I would never have believed the scale and complexity of what is required to service just one irrigation district. Do I understand that you have installed similar facilities in nine other drainage basins? Nothing you mentioned gave me a hint of what your family has accomplished and is planning for the next fifteen to twenty years."

Jacques, similarly impressed, said, "For as many years as I have been listening to my father, Harshim, and Smohl discuss what they intended to accomplish, I never envisioned he was talking about this kind of scale. When you add another ten thousand-family-strong Citizen Farmers, I must believe we are envisioning much more than some modern regional agribusiness operation! Nation's productivity supports an enormous humanitarian accomplishment. This is a story that needs to be told and retold on a global basis."

Their final stop was at the Naraghi-Roth underground command center. A map, punctuated with multi-colored pins and strings, was attached to a long wall in the main conference room. The map included Iran, the other Middle Eastern countries, Western European Mediterranean nations, and the major population centers of North Africa.

Confused, Jacques asked, "What do all these pins and strings represent?"

Sam answered, "The colored marks on the map demonstrate where each crop is to be delivered and identify the means of transportation that is used. Over the years, we have learned to use this model to help us determine how much of each crop we need to produce. Once we have those numbers, we can work backward to determine processing capacities and transport arrangements. The color of the pin denotes a particular crop. You may notice there are more yellow pins. A yellow pin represents our biggest crop, wheat.

"The different colors of string represent our methods of transport. The blue string represents sea-going; the red string represents rail; and the white represents long-haul truck. By studying this map, you can quickly deduce how many crops we produce, who purchases them, and how we deliver each particular crop.

"The contours of the map are the same, but in the five years I have been away, a lot more pins and strings have been added."

Jacques jokingly suggested, "If we are seriously considering adding another two hundred thousand acres, aren't we going to need to expand our markets, streamline methods of transport, and introduce trip insurance and in-transit financing? It would appear we are going to need a bigger map and a lot more strings and pins."

In response, Sam said, "We are going to need a lot more than pins and strings. We should be talking in terms of establishing an international trading company. We need to think of Nation as a vertically integrated international agribusiness and trading company."

"Sam, now I understand why you have been so driven to expand your education to include the international worlds of commerce and trade. What a terrific new opportunity for Nation and the Roth Bank to work together.

Part Six

“Creating the Foundation”

Chapter Thirty-Six
"The Almost War"

ROTH VERSAILLES CHÂTEAU: November 1934

Pierre's cablegram was explicit: "Important we convene in the security of the chateau at your earliest convenience. I've talked to my friends, and it appears we have a serious German problem requiring our immediate attention!"

Harshim, Sam, Smohl, and Jacques were gathered in Pierre's study. Pierre was reporting. "When the German industrialists mentioned 'military intervention,' my friends interpreted that to mean they are operating in concert with the German government and its military. From other sources, we have been able to learn that Hitler has an interest in testing the Allied appeasement policies. Hitler has been heard to say that, if the Allies fail to respond, 'Much of Western Europe is ours for the taking. The problem is, until Germany possesses an adequate supply of foreign oil, we are prevented from using our military to expand our borders.'

"Further conversations have revealed the German military establishment regards a surgical strike, at this time, to be premature. They are resisting any kind of confrontation and possible reprisals until Germany's rearmament program has reached military parity with those of the French and British.

"Left unresolved, one of Germany's only remaining options is to contract with a non-sovereign source of oil. Nation has to be on their short list! Policies of appeasement aside, the three Allied governments agree that allowing Germany to make a private treaty with Nation would not be acceptable.

"Should Germany choose to attack Nation, its actions would be regarded as unacceptable. Any violation of the Treaty of Versailles requires an Allied military response."

Harshim asked, "From Hitler's viewpoint, doesn't he have to weigh the possibility that a surgical strike would be met with a similar Allied response somewhere in Germany? How could he be certain that aerial attacks would not escalate into a broader war? Is this a risk Hitler is prepared to accept? If Hitler were to invade Iran, how confident could he be that the Allies would not retaliate?"

Two weeks later, Pierre Roth, Smohl Cantor, France's prime minister, Britain's prime minister, and the American president, together with their secretaries of the military, state, and treasury were huddled together in a private conference room in the Carlton Cannes Hotel.

Secure in their well-guarded sanctuary and not afraid of being overheard, the governmental leaders had been quizzing Pierre and Smohl for the previous half hour to better understand the situation. Essentially, they were all asking the same three questions: "Are you prepared to allow the German government, by private treaty, to obtain the extra oil it requires to wage war? Is the threat of Allied retaliation enough to offset Hitler's appetite for more oil? Is he bluffing or is he really prepared to bomb their dams and their commercial facilities should Naraghi-Roth refuse to negotiate with the German industrialists?"

Smohl said, "Maybe we need to look at this problem from a different point of view. How do you think Hitler might react if he were convinced the Allies are encouraging him to attack to provide the public with the justification they need to abandon their longstanding policies of appeasement? If they were to attack Germany militarily, before Hitler's rearmament program has reached or exceeded parity with the British and French forces', it could be argued they would be avoiding a larger and more costly war."

Impressed by Smohl's logic, the French prime minister turned to his British counterpart and asked, "What do we need to do to convince Hitler of our retaliatory intent?"

"Why couldn't we relocate our heavier bombers on your French airfields closest to Germany? And, at the same time, reposition our longer-range artillery, our tanks, and our infantries at strategic locations opposite Germany's western border? The problem is, repositioning our forces is one thing, but having the authority to commit them to battle is another issue."

Responding, the French prime minister said, "I don't believe a deliberate violation of the Versailles Treaty requires government approval to attack Germany. If, on the other hand, Hitler were to learn that legislation authorizing a retaliatory attack on Germany was being fast-tracked through the American Congress, the French and the British Parliaments, wouldn't he have to pay serious attention?"

It was decided that all three governments would introduce the requested legislation. Transatlantic and English Channel underwater transmission cables were being used to communicate coded messages among the three diplomatic corps. In anticipation of receiving confirmation that the legislation had passed, each of the three Allied governments requested a meeting with their respective German ambassadors. They wanted to make sure the German High Command was accurately apprised of their intentions.

Hitler and his supporters were debating, 'Short of a military invasion of neighboring oil-rich nations, what alternatives did Germany possess to secure its needed oil supplies? If the conquest of a neighboring country is inevitable, why shouldn't we test the Allied response to a lower-level, private-treaty arrangement, at this time?'

The German military vehemently opposed Hitler's suggestions about attacking Nation. The generals continued to argue among themselves, "A premature attack could result in a defining defeat for Germany's fledgling military and destroy our longer-term agenda for trans-European conquest. Is this a risk we should be taking at this time? By being patient, can't we achieve the same objective and delay the risk until we are ready?"

Absent a timely response by the German government, the Allied governments interpreted the continued delay to mean that Germany had decided to not test Allied resolve at this time.

Observing the efforts of the opposing powers to protect their best interests, Pierre, Harshim, Smohl, Jacques, and Sam watched the implementation of the Allies' larger agenda with interest from their perch. It was these policies that provided Nation with the "effective deterrent" they had been seeking.

With the removal of their last remaining obstacle, the Nation leaders were excited to proceed with their new plans for the development of the next two hundred thousand acres. Excavation and construction of their "Super Quant and Dam" projects for the next ten irrigation districts would incorporate the technological tools that had been steadily modernized over the previous twenty years.

The additional energy revenues would provide the financial means to support their introduction of the changes that they hoped would improve the quality of life for their citizen farmers and their corps of service employees. The introduction of state-of-the-art medical services and Advanced Prep educational programs would complete their quality-of-life improvements.

Chapter Thirty-Seven
"Advanced Prep"

KATE & SALLY NARAGHI; Ahvaz: January 1935

Kate's attention was focused on the establishment of each of the rural villages. Coordinating the completion of the construction with the hiring of employees and helping families move into their new homes required her to work closely with the future residents of Nation from sun-up to sun-down. In the evenings, around the family dinner table, Kate was frequently asked to share any new information about life in Citizens' Nation.

One night, after a particularly difficult day, she decided to explain. "While each of the families I talk to are quick to express their gratefulness for all that we have done, they keep asking two questions."

Interrupting, Harshim curtly asked, "Kate, aren't they satisfied? What more are they expecting us to do?"

After pausing to collect her thoughts, the Red Queen decided to take the risk of speaking her mind. "Without exception, they are deeply appreciative of the opportunities we are providing. Looking ahead, they are expressing their concerns about their children's access to foreign schools of higher learning. Without the means and the competitive academic skills, what chance will their more gifted children have to pursue educational and vocational opportunities offered beyond Nation's and Iran's perceived boundaries?

"Fortunately for us, Sally is beginning to produce ideas about introducing an advanced academic curriculum. Still unresolved is how we hope to generate the funds needed to create and operate the Advanced Prep schools."

Silence was not one of the reactions Kate was expecting, but that's what she got. It was Harshim who broke it. "Maybe the question Sally should be asking is, '*Shouldn't we be prepared to implement Smohl's original suggestion of creating an international educational endowment fund?*' If we can make it work, we would effectively remove the uncertainty and be able to proceed on a more positive basis."

Smohl had been heard to say, "In Palestine, our Zionist movement never has enough funds to support existing programs, much less any new programs. To keep moving forward, we are forced to appeal to our friends located beyond our borders. Fortunately, they are learning to vote with their wallets. Why, with our assistance, couldn't Nation develop a similar program of international support?"

Tom York, who had been carefully listening to the discussion, said, "In my opinion, solving Sally's problem is so important; we should consider all the possibilities. What is wrong with the idea of asking our electrical power customers to accept rates that include the cost of our advanced student program? We could use those revenues, particularly in the early years, to fund any shortfall we may experience in appealing to our global friends.

"Why shouldn't we commit to establishing the rate of future electrical power contracts and remove any uncertainty, and encourage Sally to proceed with all possible haste?"

Following the removal of the financial uncertainty, organizing her start-up faculty became Sally's top priority. With curriculum in hand, Sally still faced the challenge of persuading top-rated instructors to leave their positions of tenure and personal comfort and move to Ahvaz, Iran. On a person-to-person basis, she needed to convince her targeted teachers employed by other universities of the importance of creating a new kind of program to be built around their strongest teaching skills.

Sally's efforts were beginning to attract international attention. As highly regarded teachers joined Sally, word began to spread. Copies of proposed curricula, circulated to targeted foreign colleges, were alerting their admissions committees that highly qualified, self-supported candidates would be applying for admission from a new source.

Conscious of the universities' growing interest, Sally committed to shortening the time before qualified graduates of Advanced Prep would begin submitting their applications. Unwilling to wait for construction of the new school to be completed, she reconfigured existing warehouse space into classrooms so that teaching could begin. Two years later, applications for enrollment were being received by administrators at foreign colleges and universities.

Sally arranged for each of the applicants to tour the campuses of the schools of their choice and participate in in-person interviews. Frequently, when any of her graduates were asked back for a second interview, Sally would accompany them, explaining, "Fit is a two-way street. I want to make certain each of our students' principal attributes and interests properly fit with the curriculum and goals of your school. It's important both parties get off to a good start."

By the summer of 1939, momentum was building. Advanced Prep graduates were being admitted to top-rated colleges and universities and annual contributions to Friends of Nation were rising.

Chapter Thirty-Eight
"N-R Trading Co. Ltd."

SAM NARAGHI; ABADAN, IRAN: January 1935

Identifying the most-opportunistic markets and the most-qualified distributors had to wait. Almost immediately, Sam discovered two critical problems that needed solving before he could hope to convert their terminal, customer-by-customer distribution system into a modern international trading company.

International trading law required that the cost of each shipment be paid to the supplier of origin prior to transport. The receiving customers were required to pay for their purchases only upon delivery. The problem of funding the gap in ownership represented a new problem. Totally frustrated, Sam called Jacques.

He was surprised by Jacques' response. "What took you so long to call? The Roth Bank regularly provides credit facilities for legitimate shippers and receivers in other markets. There is, however, the question of trip insurance. With all the craziness going on in our world, you can understand why in-transit cargo insurance is required. Properly organized, with the right kind of assistance from Lloyd's [of London], we might be able to combine both services into one to better meet your needs or those of any other related supplier.

"By the way, have you estimated the total value of cargos you will have in transit in any given time period?"

Prepared for the question, Sam responded with the high and low ranges of Nation's transport cargoes, by commodity and on a season-by-season basis.

His estimates surprised Jacques. "Sam, we are talking about some very large numbers," he said. "Do you know how unusual it is for a new trading company to come to market with such a large volume of business, financed by someone as credible as the Roth Bank?

"Once you are able to organize the records documenting your prior shipping experience, why don't we plan to meet in London? Insurance companies are known to move slowly. I believe we are going to have some idle time. In London, there is the theater, the musical stage, and the ballet at Covent Garden. In addition, there are private clubs, incredible restaurants, small bars, and bistros. Then there is the Soho district, London's equivalent of the Latin Quarter in Paris. After all we have been through, don't you think another *Captains' week-out* might be appropriate?"

Any excitement Sam may have felt evaporated when he mentioned Jacques' invitation to Sally. Immediately, she asked, "Are you suggesting that you meet Jacques in London without me? Don't forget, I was there in Paris, and I watched how you two operate. If you think, for one minute, I am going to allow you to meet Jacques in London without taking me along, you are out of your mind. Besides which, don't you think it's time for the three bunker buddies to celebrate our baptism by fire?

"While you and Jacques are spending time, during the day, in all those boring insurance meetings, I plan to call on English colleges and universities. My question is, at night, what will you be planning that will include me and be fun?"

Chapter Thirty-Nine
"Visiting London"

LONDON, ENGLAND: February 1935

As predicted, the combination of Sam's projected shipping volume, the creditworthiness of the Roth Bank, and the offered stewardship of the two exceptional young leaders caught the attention of Lloyd's and its market of experienced and reliable insurers.

In their first meeting, one of the insurers asked, "Do your plans call for you to collect and deliver other foreign-produced cargos? With your ability to efficiently solve the transport insurance and in-transit funding problems, you should be able to generate additional revenues and substantially reduce or possibly entirely offset your own shipping expenses.

"In addition, have you ever stopped to consider the added value you would be creating if you were to use a portion of your voluminous supplies to help smaller shippers fill out their loads so that you would thereby qualify for more attractive rates?"

The significance of the comments was not lost on Jacques or Sam. When the opportunity presented itself, Jacques asked, "Sam, have you stopped to consider what effect the Naraghi-Roth Trading Company might have on the Roth Bank? Over the years, the expansion of the bank's financial services could represent an attractive opportunity for it to increase its exposure to new markets."

As anxious as they were to receive answers from the insurers, Sam and Sally were learning that Jacques' early prediction that the wheels of the insurance industry would turn slowly was becoming a reality. Excited about researching international trading opportunities, Sam and Jacques made full use of any available holes in their schedule to call on the managers of terminal markets, which receive produce from shippers of agricultural produce generated from a broad geographic origin. The markets display the vegetables, fruits, fish, beef, and poultry in booths for sale to local jobbers, who then sell them to local restaurants, grocery stores, hotels, and delicatessens.

The more they learned, the more convinced they became of the need for a modern, well-financed, full-service trading company capable of reliably providing, high quality product at affordable prices.

By extending the reach of their management to include each element of the distribution chain, Sam and Jacques saw an opportunity to improve a system that hadn't changed for a very long time.

Excited by the prospect of introducing a new kind of trading company, they devoted their free time to developing a business plan for what they called the N&R Trading Company.

Each day, Sally called on new admission administrators. Word of her mission preceded her. In anticipation of hearing her proposals, the school representatives were preparing questions of their own. Almost without exception, the discussions led to the forging of strong personal bonds and an ongoing interest to learn more about the qualifications of "Advanced Prep" graduates.

Nights were different. During their free time, they began to explore how they could take advantage of London's impressive array of things to do and places to visit.

One evening, following a particularly difficult day and before anyone could suggest an alternative, Jacques asked, "How would you like to accompany me to the French Club near St. James Palace. It's a small bar-bistro that serves great onion soup. On any given night, you never know who you will meet. Historically, it has been the local watering hole for the Royal Air Force and the French and Polish aviators. If you think meeting the patrons would be an interesting experience, wait until you meet the irrepressible proprietor, Miss Maggie. Put all the pieces together and you will have a difficult time finding a more fun and entertaining experience!"

Naturally suspicious of anything Jacques might suggest, Sally asked, "Maybe you should tell us more about your Miss Maggie?"

"It's not difficult to describe her," Jacques said. 'She is a big woman, maybe six feet tall, with broad shoulders, enormous breasts, peroxided blond hair, and she possesses great physical strength. She generously applies a very red shade of lipstick to her lips. I can't remember a time when she hasn't picked me up off the floor while planting one of her patented bright red, wet kisses on me, before making some sarcastic remark, and setting me back on the floor."

A half hour later, Sally discovered that Jacques' description had been on target. The minute Maggie spied Jacques entering her pub, she let out two loud whoops, wrapped him in a bear hug, and lifted him well off the floor. Looking directly into his eyes, she exclaimed, "Jacques, where have you been? I was beginning to think you had forgotten your dear ol' Maggie." Before Jacques could answer, she planted a bright red, wet kiss on and around his lips. Then, lowering him to the floor, she said, "Take a look in the mirror, I've left my mark all over your face!"

Uncharacteristically, Sam stepped forward. "Maggie, we've met before. I regret that you don't remember me. On the several occasions after our Birmingham side played soccer matches in London, win or lose, we would retire to the French Club."

Amused by his comment, Maggie said, "Sam Naraghi, do you really believe Miss Maggie would forget a really big, handsome man with all that red hair? Step up and let ol' Maggie pays you a proper hello!"

When his feet touched the ground, his face well-smeared with Maggie's red brand, Sam was at a loss for words. Not sure of how he was expected to react, he reached behind her, grabbed a well-frosted mug of beer off the bar, and said, "Isn't time for me to have a pint with an ol' friend?"

"Not so fast!" Maggie said. "Who is this beautiful young lady you have so rudely failed to introduce? What is a beautiful, refined woman doing with you two hooligans? Has she lost her mind?"

To avoid being intimidated, Sally spoke up. "I have always wondered if you only remembered the big handsome men who frequent your establishment," she said. "I have also been here on previous occasions. After I completed my tennis matches with some of England's top-ranked amateur women tennis players, this was the first place I and my teammates would stop."

Intrigued by her boldness, Maggie stepped back to study her. "Are you the woman who played the piano and sang your marvelous renditions of Cole Porter and George Gershwin songs?" She stopped for a second in thought, then brightened. "Now I remember!" she said. "Isn't your name Sally Raphael? How is it that such a talented saloon singer reappears after such a long time in the company of such notorious rascals?"

Jacques, who had left to wipe the lipstick from his face, reappeared in time to hear Maggie mention "saloon singer." "Wait a minute!" he said. "Has the dedicated educator, the hero of Bet-Dagania, a ranked amateur tennis player, just been exposed? Are we to assume there is another person lurking beneath the surface?"

This was the first time either Sam or Jacques had seen Sally blush. Before Sally could answer, Maggie announced, "We still have that old piano and one of our patrons might be able to accompany you. Would you be so kind as to sing a few songs?"

Almost immediately, it became obvious that Sally was no rookie. She had a lyrical voice, a wide range, and the poise to sing well and confidently. Standing next to the upright piano, she sang song after song. If no one requested a next song, she would introduce one of her favorites.

Sally was having a good time, drinking her share of beer and trading comments with her enthusiastic audience.

Sam was amazed by the emergence of this new person, whose performance made it clear that she had devoted much of her life to a professional singing career. He couldn't help but notice, '*When she is singing, she appears to be in a different world. Who is this mysterious woman who happens to be my wife?*'

It was 1:30 the next morning before Sally managed to separate from all her new fans and friends and excuse herself. Buoyed by adrenaline and unsteadied by way too much beer, Sally, Sam, and Jacques, with their arms wrapped around each other, began to trek slowly back to their hotel.

At 11:00 a.m., Sam and Jacques were sitting by themselves at a table in front of a big window facing Hyde Park. The table was gaily decorated with fresh flowers and copies of the London Times. Not waiting for Sally, the two men ordered two large glasses of freshly squeezed orange juice, a large pot of coffee, croissants, shirred eggs, and kippers.

Too tired to read the newspapers, both men concentrated instead on downing their orange juice and black coffee while nibbling on the rest of their breakfast. When Sam wasn't thinking about the sharp pain in his head, he was struggling with Sally's recent revelation. He was having difficulty thinking of Sally as a saloon singer. '*The Sally I know is a loving wife and a highly talented and dedicated educator. If she spent much of her younger life singing professionally, why did she choose to pursue her educational goals, get married, and commit herself to a life in the desert?*'

By the time Sally appeared, messages had been delivered to the table. The "right" insurers had called back, asking Sam and Jacques to return for further discussions. Distracted by the promising news, neither Sam nor Jacques took advantage of the opportunity to ask Sally the questions they wanted her to answer.

The atmosphere in the insurers' offices had changed. Skepticism had been replaced by professional cordiality. Both men were surprised when the different insurers repeated some of their previous questions. "Do you anticipate needing insurance just for your own cargoes or are you interested in using your vast supplies of produce to fill out and consolidate partial shipments of other producers? Are you going to charter or own the ships you will be using?"

Both Sam and Jacques interpreted the insurers' questions to signify their enthusiasm to be of assistance. The Naraghi-Roth International Trading Company was about to be born.

Later that evening, when they were eating at their hotel, Jacques made the unfortunate mistake of referring to Sally as "Saloon Sally." It was an agitated Sally who looked directly into Jacques' eyes and said, "Jacques, I think you need to listen very carefully to what I am about to say. Earning your way through college may never have been a problem for you. There are, however, many of us who have not been so fortunate. If my singing enabled me to pursue a life as an advanced educator, why would you find that so unusual?

"Singing professionally has never been my long-term goal. It was only a means to help pay for my college education. What may sound like a glamorous career pales in comparison with the satisfaction I hope to achieve by being married to Sam and helping children to expand their boundaries."

Sally continued, "Jacques, Sam, if I choose to sing on occasion, why is it so different from your playing in celebrity soccer tournaments? Now, this is the last time I expect either of you to bring up the subject."

Properly admonished, Sam and Jacques understood that the tranquility of their quiet dinner had just ended. Sam politely asked, "Sally, Jacques and I have been so absorbed with our own work, we haven't provided you with an opportunity to tell us what you have accomplished during our stay in London."

"Thank you for asking," she responded. "While the two of you may have exceeded your expectations, I have succeeded in developing the cooperation of some of the more outstanding entrance administrators of important English colleges and universities. Their willingness to consider our more qualified students should make it possible for us to create the track record we will need if we are to encourage other outstanding colleges and universities to participate."

Jacques asked, "Sally, over time, you will be doing a lot more than pushing back the boundaries of your students' lives. Have you ever stopped to think about what a successful Advanced Prep will contribute to the perceived value of Nation's humanitarian efforts? Except for what the Zionists are accomplishing with their kibbutzim program, I am not aware of any other program in an underdeveloped country that is committed to improving the learning skills of its high-potential students. When your students graduate and find employment in good foreign companies, can you imagine what kind of influence these early Nation's ambassadors will exert on whomever or whatever they come into contact with?"

Pierre had been receiving calls of congratulations from many of his old English friends and colleagues. They were expressing their excitement over what these future family leaders were accomplishing.

Wanting to be the first to congratulate Jacques, Sam, and Sally when they disembarked in Pas-de-Calais, Pierre Roth and a full detachment of Roth Bank security personnel were standing on the dock, waiting for the ferry from Southampton.

Jacques, seeing his father among them, was both surprised and curious. *'Something very unusual must have happened. Why else would Father come all this way? Why are there so many bank security guards standing around him?'*

Jacques' thoughts were confirmed when his father, dispensing with his usual greeting, immediately ushered the three of them into one of the bank's black limousines. Without waiting for the car to start moving, he said, "Over the last 24 hours, friends of mine have been expressing their amazement over what the three of you have been able to accomplish. Jacques, Sam, almost to a person, they have been reporting their excitement over your progress toward making changes that should materially improve foreign trading practices, not just of Nation but of all the different markets you plan on serving.

"What I find so interesting is the idea that, in your quest to expand demand for Nation's ever-increasing agricultural production, you are on the verge of creating a new company that has the potential to improve foreign trading practices, revolutionize in-transit financial services, and create new sources of profits for Naraghi-Roth. Congratulations on a job well done! You make us very proud.

"Unfortunately, I have some troubling news to report. There are some unusual developments with our German friends, problems we need to discuss right now.

"First, I have been informed that no further government authorizations are required to enforce the terms of our Treaty of

Versailles. A German attack on a sovereign country would be regarded as a serious violation and met with a proportionate Allied response.

"Here are copies of the three letters, which have been signed by the president or the prime minister of each of the three principal Allied nations. In essence, the letters say that any attack by Germany on Nation would be construed as a violation of the Treaty of Versailles and would subject Germany to an Allied attack.

"To remove any doubts about the Allies' resolve, the British and the French have already started to move long-range bombers to French air bases close to the German border. Long-range artillery and armored vehicles will be moving to forward positions opposite the main transportation corridors leading into the heart of Germany. They will be supported by combat-ready infantry divisions.

"Unstated is our collective recognition of the possible consequences of allowing Germany to acquire the oil reserves it would need to initiate a major war. As strange as it may seem, I am not certain if all these arrangements are being made to discourage a German attack on Nation or to provoke Hitler into attacking while his military is still in its fledgling stage.

"It's important you acknowledge that an undeclared cold state of war exists, and we need to take precautions. Once considerations of military action are placed aside, we must assume the German government will pursue its other options, namely coercing Nation to comply with its desire to achieve contractual control over the development of its oil reserves in some other way.

"To improve their negotiating leverage, they could start using kidnapping as a real threat. Any one of us could be an unsuspecting target. It is this concern that has led me to assign a security detachment to protect all of us."

The limousine was approaching the outskirts of Paris when Jacques asked, "Father, should we conclude that Nation will benefit from the same protection the Allied governments are extending to the Middle Eastern oil-rich nations? Aren't the Allies effectively pledging their support for Nation? By aligning ourselves with political policies, haven't we found the deterrent we have been seeking?"

The deafening, thoughtful silence that followed was broken only when the limousine pulled to a stop inside the secure confines of the Roth Bank executive parking area.

Chapter Forty
"Change in Direction"

JACQUES ROTH; PARIS, FRANCE, FAMILY HOME: March 1935

Joining his father in the library, comforted by a couple of glasses of his favorite 1927 Bourgogne pinot noir, Jacques unexpectedly announced, "Once all the arrangements needed to support Sam's Naraghi-Roth Trading Company have been completed, I am planning to take a leave of absence from my position at the bank. Recent events have convinced me that I need to develop a much better understanding of what is taking place in the world around us.

"In a strange kind of way, I can understand why the German industrialists are attempting to gain control over the Naraghi-Roth potential oil reserves. Maybe the bigger question is, once they have completed their military preparedness, how are they going to obtain the needed oil reserves? The developed oil fields in Ploiesti, Romania; the Caucasus-Caspian Sea region of the Russian Ukraine; and the Middle East will remain obvious targets. Given enough time to complete his preparations, Hitler and the German industrialists' ambitions could lead the world to war.

"Earlier this year, Claudine Demaureux explained what our old friend, Dr. Tom Burdick, has been accomplishing with the International Political Science Doctoral Studies Program he is teaching at the University of California, Berkeley. What better opportunity could there be than to spend the next three years studying the changing world of international politics and commerce under the tutelage of our long-time family friend, Dr. Tom?"

Having made his announcement, Jacques was prepared to defend his decision against an irate father and employer. When he watched his father smile, he was relieved. Curious to understand Pierre's unexpected response, Jacques asked. "You must have questions?"

"Not questions, but I do need to share with you some of my private concerns," his father said. "From my banker's perch, I feel confident I am privy to the current attitudes of major governments and industrial establishments. The causes of fascism's rising popularity need to be better understood. Fascist leaders have developed an interesting way of creating major concentrations of power. You don't have to look any further than Germany, Italy, and Japan to observe the beginnings of some very powerful cartels of concentrated capitalism.

"Although the specifics may vary in each instance, major industrial resources have been combined with unfulfilled political agendas, and the support of their respective financial communities. Although each of these emergent processes may be in their early stages, I think it is critical we pay attention to the accumulation of so much power.

"Since I don't have the time to research the problem myself, my next best option is to release you from your current responsibilities. It's important that we develop a better understanding of the consequences of spreading fascism.

"That having been said, I do have one question. How much of your decision is based on what we have been discussing and how much is based on pursuing a relationship with the incredible Claudine Demaureux? After all these years, I find it interesting you have finally grown to appreciate what a remarkable woman she has become. If you are serious, there is one question you better learn to answer.

"Your interest in so many different, glamorous ladies has been regularly reported in the French newspapers. Have you stopped to consider what you must do to change your ways before you can expect Claudine to trust you?"

"Father, regardless of my true motives, which I concede I don't completely understand, I am concerned my departure could adversely affect the progress of Naraghi-Roth and its future trading company," Jacques said. "Before I leave, let's make certain we establish a proper channel of communications. If problems arise that can't be resolved over long-distance communication, I will be on the first ship home."

Chapter Forty-One
"Developing a Modern Trading Company"

SAM NARAGHI; NARAGHI-ROTH TRADING, LTD.: Ahvaz, May 1935

Sam was busy traveling to different terminal produce markets. He was determined to establish working relationships with the executives in each of his target markets. Of equal importance, he wanted to obtain a clearer picture of any problems Naraghi-Roth Trading might encounter or be able to solve.

Shortly after arriving, Sam would meet with the responsible market managers. After discussing what N-R Trading hoped to accomplish, he asked for the names of the principal broker-jobbers who could best describe how N-R could be of service. Making time to meet with each of them, Sam would ask the appropriate open-ended questions.

Not used to having access to the leader of an important international trading company, they willingly answered Sam's questions before taking advantage of the opportunity to ask questions of their own.

Not trusting his ability to digest and remember everything he was learning, Sam quickly developed the habit of taking careful notes. Each night, in his hotel room, he would transcribe his shorthand notes into separate notebooks, one for each terminal market. Brick by brick, he was building the foundations he would need before Naraghi-Roth Trading could formally approach the different markets he hoped to supply.

Each day, the terminal managers had been receiving reports from their broker-jobbers describing how much they respected Sam and his apparent interest in their problems. When he was ready to resume his talks, they would be interested. Sam discovered they were curious to hear what he had learned and raised questions of their own.

Invariably, the terminal managers asked, "What can be done to streamline the individual in-transit insurance and financing requirements of each of the cargoes?"

Sam answered, "Why couldn't N-R Trading purchase the unowned cargoes and consolidate them into a single shipment that can be serviced under our master arrangement with the Roth Bank?"

Impressed with Sam's response, they proceeded to ask their second question. "What can you do to convert transport-costly, partial shipments into complete cargoes?"

Once again, Sam explained how N-R Trading proposed to divert a portion of Nation's voluminous supplies to fill out the smaller shipments.

Pleased with Sam's answers and the goodwill he had created, one of the terminal market managers asked, "What do we need to do to encourage you to include us as one of your early markets?"

Word of N-R Trading was spreading throughout the international terminal market community. Sam was receiving invitations to expand his travels to include new markets. To make sure he made time to complete his study of each market, he was constantly adjusting his travel schedule. His trips were taking longer and were becoming more frequent. Market by market, Sam was building a firm foundation upon which the trading company could be organized.

Accompanying Sam on many of his trips, Sally met with local college administrators. She knew that one of the ways schools of higher learning measure their performance is by looking at the jobs their graduates get. In discussing the attributes of her students, Sally expressed her hope that Nation graduates would serve as ambassadors for both the subject university of choice and Nation's Advanced Preparation programs.

Graduates of Advanced Prep were being accepted into the better schools of higher learning. Individual performances were being recognized. The contributions from the "Friends of Advanced Prep" were gratefully received.

Once they returned home, Sally and Sam devoted the daylight hours to synthesizing and distilling all that they had learned on their journeys. Like Sam's desire to understand the individual needs of each terminal market, Sally was learning that each institution of higher learning had its own idiosyncrasies. Appreciating that the fit between a given school's strengths and each student's skills and aptitudes had to be carefully coordinated, she transcribed her observations and catalogued them by school.

Chapter Forty-Two
"Udeh –Nation Medical"

NARAGHI FAMILY DINNER TABLE: June 1938

During the prior three years, Kate had been carefully observing the progress of Sally's Advanced Prep program and the results it was producing. Sam's international trading achievements were becoming apparent. She knew that something of importance, beyond improving Nation's agribusiness success, was taking place. Concerned people from all over the world were becoming increasingly aware of the full range of Nation's humanitarian efforts.

One night, over dinner, Kate announced, "Now that we have solved our Effective Deterrent problem and Sally's Advanced Prep programs are progressing, I believe the time has come for us to discuss the level of medical services we should be providing.

"Perhaps I should explain. The establishment of each new village provides the space needed to perform entry-level triage medical evaluations and to provide minimum levels of medical treatment. The more extreme cases require the assistance of the UDEH Medical hospitals in Tehran, more than three hundred miles away over poorly maintained roads. The combination of the difficult travel conditions and the limited availability of suitable motor vehicles virtually prohibits access to Tehran's more advanced medical treatment. Somehow, we need to find a way of bringing UDEH Medical to Nation!"

After a thoughtful silence, Harshim asked, "Is there any one of you who would object to our encouraging Kate to solve one more problem?" He continued, "While no one will question your objectives, it will be interesting to learn if you can find a way to extend the services of a centuries-old medical complex by more than three hundred miles."

Over the next few weeks, knowing she would need the assistance of more knowledgeable people, Kate took advantage of Harshim's long-time and close relationship with Dr. Mohammed Mossadegh, the leader of Iran's National Front Party. It didn't take long before the first lady of the family had arranged to meet with the top administrators of Tehran's UDEH Medical Complex.

Kate quickly learned that the administrators were keenly aware of the need to extend the geographic range of their UDEH Medical services. One of them told her that, given the limited funding they had received from the shah government, "We have been forced to abandon any recent thoughts of expansion."

Concluding that both parties were anxious to solve the same problem, Kate realized that, first and foremost, she needed to develop an adequate source of funding. It didn't take long for Kate to visualize how some combination of Naraghi-Roth family wealth and surplus income from Nation's sale of electrical power might be sufficient to amortize the capital expenditures required to construct a world-class teaching hospital in Ahvaz and a satellite hospital for emergency care in each irrigation district village.

Consumed by her desire to put her plan into practice, Kate sequestered herself in the construction offices with her father, Tom York. Her absence from her field work was immediately noticed. Invariably, members of the family would ask, "What can she be doing that requires so much private, undisturbed time?"

Over dinners, discussions pertaining to solving the physical problems of installing new quant systems were becoming repetitive and somewhat boring. Sally's continuing success in contributing to the improved lifestyle of Citizen Farmers had become a regular subject of discussion. The more the family focused on Sally's life-improvement program, the more they would ask Kate to update them on the progress she was making with their medical treatment problem.

Not wishing to expose her plan until she and her UDEH colleagues had a finished product, Kate would sit back at the family dinner table and encourage the others present to discuss what her plan should include. On occasion, she would say, "Until we can agree on a final plan, we can't begin to develop all the different economic feasibility analyses we will need to calculate the cost of construction and the operating expenses."

It was Sam who pointed out that they were in pretty good financial shape. "Let's not forget, by the time the new medical center is ready for construction, we should have two additional revenue streams to draw upon," he said. "In addition to the improving stream of N&P profits, we should have at least one additional stream of electric sales revenue to draw upon. If we are lucky and time it right, we may be able to repay the construction loan of the medical center from future electrical power sales revenues."

But Kate was aware that it could take time to work out the details; she realized that final approval of the UDEH-Nation medical plan would be delayed, and she was concerned. *'A substantial postponement of the project could adversely interrupt the progress I have been working so hard to achieve with UDEH Medical administrative staff. Somehow, I need to find a more immediate solution.'*

Following a good night's sleep, a rejuvenated Kate concluded, *'Wait just a minute! I haven't come this far to be stopped by a timing problem over money. How do we know there isn't some other solution that won't expose our planning to so much uncertainty? Just because we are not aware of an alternate source of funding, that doesn't mean it doesn't exist!'*

Kate decided to call Smohl and explain her concerns. In typical Red Queen fashion, she came right to the point. When Smohl started to laugh, she asked, "What's so funny? I call you with a serious problem and all you can do is laugh?"

"My dear Kate, the last thing I want to do is upset you," Smohl said. "I laughed only because your problem may be quite solvable. Allow me to explain. Here in Palestine, there have been times when we were faced with similar situations. We learned there are world health organizations that regularly concern themselves with the problem of providing improved medical services to new populations of uncovered people.

"I am reminded of the International Committee of the Red Cross, religious-sponsored missionary programs, various governments, and the League of Nations, all of which regularly fund worthy medical treatment service programs. Once you are prepared to present your case, with our assistance, why don't we schedule a series of meetings with the most promising charitable institutions? We might be pleased at how people familiar with Nation's brilliant humanitarian track record will respond."

Convinced of the value of Smohl's suggestion, Kate decided to proceed with the refinement of the final plan for the UDEH-Nation Ahvaz Medical Institute.

Several months later, following the emergence of a consensus plan, Kate realized the time had come for her to introduce its conceptual portion to the Naraghis, the Roths, the Roth Bank, and to the Israeli-assisted group of international medical foundations.

Three-dimensional models depicting her team's vision for the new medical institute had been fabricated. They were accompanied by an in-depth, comprehensive study listing the services to be provided. Estimates forecasting the number of patients to be treated were calculated. Charts were made available describing the jobs and the number of employees that would be needed. Budgets detailing construction costs and operating expenses were compiled.

Armed with all the supportive information, Kate had consolidated her proposal into three parts. The first estimated the amount of long-term credit needed to fund the construction of each of the facilities. Second, she calculated what the total annual cost of amortizing the credit facility needed to be. And finally, with the assistance of UDEH Medical administrators, she estimated what the operating expenses might be.

Armed with this information, she decided to pre-test the quality of her report by presenting it to the Elders of the Nation of Citizen Farmers, the Roth and Naraghi families, and to the Senior Loan Committee of the Roth Bank and ask for questions and comments.

On the eve of her initial presentation, over the family dinner table, Kate was talking about her favorite subject when Sam interrupted. "One thing we have only briefly discussed is what the impact of the presence of world-class educational and medical support services might be on the market value of a twenty-acre parcel," he said.

"Historically, the price of each farm has been calculated as a function of the profits it produces, and the debt it can service. I can't recall a time when we have stopped to consider how much additional value is created by these two new programs. Won't it be interesting to observe the sales prices of a parcel before and after the introduction of these new services has been completed?"

"What an interesting question," Harshim said. "Now, I have one of my own. How will these two programs affect the world's opinion of what we are trying to accomplish? I suspect Kate will find out when she calls on all these charitable foundations?

"Assuming you and your program are well received, you might think about the possible problem created by our wealth. You might discover that, rather than being the only contributors, they would be more attracted if we were to match whatever their contributions."

"Harshim, my dear husband, we could be talking about a lot of money," Kate said. "Are you certain that is a commitment you should offer?"

"Kate, the answer is yes, and I make it thanks to your original suggestion that we should modify our tenant farmer leasing program to provide our Citizen Farmers with the opportunity to purchase the land. For some time, the amortization of those land-sale contracts has increase to a level where the entire amount is no longer required to amortize the cost of the next dam. Those uncommitted revenues have been adding up to a sizable financial reserve. Haven't we just identified a more valuable use for those funds?"

That night, Kate, the Red Queen, wrapped her arms around Harshim and quietly whispered in his ear, "Thank you for bringing me here. Thank you for believing in me, thank you for marrying me, and thank you for our wonderful sons. Never in my wildest imagination did I comprehend the everyday thrill of being married to you and how contributing to your family's mission would enrich my life and bring me so much joy!"

Chapter Forty-Three
"Finishing the Job"
(Thirteen Years Later)

AHVAZ, IRAN: May 1951

Left undisturbed by World War II, Nation was becoming increasingly recognized for both its agribusiness and humanitarian accomplishments. The geographic expansion of Naraghi-Roth Trading, Ltd., the ever-increasing contributions of Advanced Prep graduate ambassadors, and the expansion of UDEH Medical-Nation services added to the prestige of the Nation of Citizen Farmers. Sally had been correct when she predicted that Advanced Prep students would become effective ambassadors for Nation and its humanitarian accomplishments.

The difficult work of constructing ten dams and major quants; preparing land; and installing irrigation systems seemed to be accepted as a never-ending task. Each year, small but steady advancements were translating into major accomplishments of pride and purpose. If there was ever any doubt, the reactions of the thousand appreciative families who arrived each year dispelled it.

The years of uninterrupted personal commitment, discipline, and hard, never-ending work were never viewed as difficult or as a time of self-sacrifice. The cumulative efforts of more than ten years of the graduate ambassadors' efforts succeeded in creating an ever-growing world-wide "Friends of Nation" audience. The performance of the Advanced Prep graduates -- both academically and in the global workforce -- were making it possible for the continuing waves of Advanced Prep students to push back the boundaries of their lives.

The growing membership of Friends of Nation was doing more than encouraging people to vote with their wallets; they were becoming well-informed advocates and proactive, supportive voices in the forum of international public opinion.

Part Seven

"Birthing the Effective Deterrent"

Chapter Forty-Four
"We Don't Have the Votes"

TEHRAN, IRAN: August 1953

Prime Minister Mossadegh's nationalization of Iran's oil industry had been accomplished without any material confrontation from the British. Their only act of reprisal was to recall their managers and technical staff. Consistent with predictions, the Iranian workforce was not capable of sustaining acceptable levels of oil production. Active exploration and drilling programs were abandoned. Without regular re-supply, oil inventories were shrinking.

Leaders of foreign countries, dependent on the reliable delivery of Iranian oil, were becoming concerned. The reduction in oil revenues was affecting the Iranian economy. The drums of foreign and public concern were beginning to beat more rapidly and with greater volume.

Discontent over Prime Minister Mossadegh's inability to maintain the country's oil production, coupled with the increasing hardships of daily living, was growing. Public anti-government demonstrations were occurring more frequently.

It was not clear how many of the marchers were legitimate protesters and how many were recruited and paid by the CIA and MI-6. Public chants, placards, billboards, newspaper editorials were calling for the prime minister to resign.

The public protests were starting to take on a life of their own. With the passage of each week, the demonstrations were growing larger and angrier. The hurling of rocks, cobblestones, and the occasional Molotov cocktail was becoming more frequent. No longer confining themselves to public squares, demonstrators could be seen marching in the streets and spilling into private neighborhoods.

The need to implement the "Third Alternative" was becoming increasingly apparent. Time was of the essence. Harshim's disturbing report of his meeting with Ayatollah Khasani, coupled with the growing ferocity of the public demonstrations, indicated clearly that the Naraghi family could wait no longer to act. Sam, the family leader, was asking, "Are we prepared to proceed with the Sentinels' suggestion that we consummate Nation's' proposed separate agreement with the Independent Oil Companies, Ltd.?"

After a short family meeting, Sam placed a call to Jacques. Assured that the Naraghis were committed, Jacques then called Mike Stone. Jacques was surprised by Mike's reaction to the news. '*He didn't seem upset or surprised.*'

What Jacques had no way of knowing was that Mike was holding a copy of Alan Kahne's most recent report. It read, '*The Anglo-American complex is unwilling to wait for the Majlis' oil vote before proceeding with the final stages of Ajax. Suggest you commence Plan B at the earliest possible time!*'

In New York, all the documents had been prepared and signed by representatives of the Independent Oil Companies, Ltd., and the International Energy Development Fund. To finalize the agreement, signatures were needed from only Sam Naraghi, the U.S. president, and Iran's Majlis. To expedite its final execution, a presidential courier was dispatched to take the documents to Iran for final authorization by the Majlis before they would be presented to the president for his signature.

On the eve of the Oil Bill vote, the six subcultural leaders had scheduled a meeting to take care of any last-minute details and to determine if there would be sufficient votes to assure passage. Prime Minister Mossadegh, his cabinet, and the six subcultural leaders were assembled around the great table in the prime minister's main conference room. All those present had taken their customary seats. As he prepared to start the meeting, the prime minister, looking around the big table, noticed that there was one vacant chair -- the seat customarily occupied by the Ayatollah Khasani.

Quick glances around the room failed to reveal the presence of the Muslim spiritual leader. Khasani was notorious for arriving late. No one present that day evidenced any concern until fifteen minutes later, when he still had failed to appear. They didn't need to be reminded of the consequences of his absence. Finally, Mossadegh's chief of staff rose from his seat and asked if he could be excused to check on the whereabouts of the leader.

Thirty minutes later, the chief re-entered the room, which was filled with nervous and agitated people. Blood had drained from his face; his hands were shaking; and he was walking in short, measured steps. Proceeding to the side of the prime minister, he handed him a handwritten note. The note read, '*Khasani and his family were reported to have left Tehran early yesterday morning, whereabouts unknown.*'

By the time the ayatollah had been discovered missing, he and his family, under the protection of several mullahs, their mosques, and their most dedicated followers, were making their way north to the Caspian Sea. Upon arriving, they boarded a commercial fishing craft and headed to the Azerbaijan port city of Baku. From there, they would join the long line of petroleum and passenger railroad cars as they crossed Azerbaijan into Georgia to the Black Sea port city of Batumi. Arrangements had been made for them to then board an oil tanker that would make its ponderous way through the Bosporus Straits, past Istanbul, and into the Mediterranean. From there, the tanker would turn westward toward its ultimate destination, Marseilles, France.

With no hope of quickly finding the ayatollah, Prime Minister Mossadegh was the first to react. "Could there be some explanation?" he asked. Not hearing any response, the tall, longtime leader of Iran's constitutional movement, dressed in one of his more elegant robes, calmly turned toward one of Iran's most trusted and respected judges and asked, "Is there any compelling reason why we can't delay bringing this legislation to a vote? It seems to me that there could be any number of plausible excuses we could invoke to justify a postponement."

The news that the vote on the oil legislation had been postponed cascaded through Tehran, the British and American capitals, the boardrooms of the American and British oil companies, the Sentinels, and Smohl Cantor's office. They understood that they didn't have much time to locate the ayatollah, persuade him to return, and vote for the adoption of the Oil Bill. To a person, they were beginning to believe, '*If we fail to adopt the Oil Bill, the political order of the Middle Eastern oil world will be severely shaken.*'

Chapter Fort-Five
"The Coup"

TEHRAN, IRAN: August 1953

Kermit Roberts, the in-country CIA case officer, had arranged for General Zahedi to personally deliver a special document to the deposed shah at his Mian Poshteh Palace in the city of Bandar-e Anzali on the Caspian Sea.

After the Ajax coup was completed, the military was to have been authorized to arrest the prime minister, shut down the Majlis, declare martial law, and assume control of the Iranian government and the oil.

The evolution of fifty years of constitutional *governance* and the country's participation in fifty percent of its oil revenues were about to be crushed under the boot of Shah Reza Pahlavi's dictatorial regime. Should this occur, the shah's government would operate as a beholden '*client government*' of the British and the American governments. Control of the oil would pass to the British and American oil companies, whose executives were standing by to restore Iran's recently deteriorating oil production operations. Iran would continue to receive its historic royalty rate of twenty percent.

Alan Kahne's message regarding the possibility that a regime change could be affected before the Oil Bill could be approved had been passed along to Sam and Harshim Naraghi, Smohl Cantor, and Jacques and Pierre Roth by Mike Stone. Each of the recipients understood the gravity and the urgency of the situation.

The Iranian military had been segmented into separate camps marked by divided loyalties. Sam is concerned, "With all that has happened, how can we remain confident that what's left of the military, supposedly loyal to Mossadegh, will be adequate to defend him?"

Harshim was cautioning Sam, "Tehran is three hundred miles from Ahraz, and our people can't be absent from their regular chores for more than a few days. Let us not forget it is imperative we remain prepared to 'Light the Candle' on short notice. Given these limitations, why shouldn't we consider utilizing our highly trained force of private volunteers to augment whatever remains of the Iranian Army that is still loyal to Prime Minister Mossadegh and his government?"

The prime minister immediately understood the problem. "There is only one general whom I think we can trust. He is General Kiani, who commands the Ishrat-Abad Barracks outside Tehran. I will talk to my old friend and tell him what you have told me. Harshim, once all the arrangements have been completed for you to meet with General Kiani, I will alert you before you return to Ahvaz."

General Kiani was delighted to see Harshim, his long-trusted and much-respected friend. Born in the port city of Abadan, the two had played soccer against each other as children and were familiar with their different career achievements.

Fascinated by what Harshim was telling him, General Kiani asked, "Are you suggesting, if we can prevent Prime Minister Mossadegh's removal by these hired mobs, we might be able to stop this charade of a domestic-sponsored regime change? With enough notice, the combination of your Nation's forces and my brigade should be able to prevent an out-of-control mob from storming the palace."

The buildings where the off-duty Palace Guard and their commanding officers were normally billeted were located just outside the guarded, high-walled, fortified entrance to the prime minister's palace. The situation had changed. General Zahedi had switched his allegiance to the shah and was no longer in command of the Palace Guard. In his new role, he called on his former military officer staff. Over the course of several hours, General Zahedi discussed his plan with those of his officers who remained loyal to the prime minister. He was explaining why it had become necessary to remove the prime minister and his constitutional government in anticipation of the shah's return.

Unpersuaded by his former commanding general's best argument, the responsible officer replied, "General, while I appreciate what you are planning, I can't ask my troops to attack their fellow Iranian brothers."

Not surprised by the answer, General Zahedi responded, "Major, how would you feel about standing down your troops? Should you agree, you will be relieved of the need to attack your brother soldiers or defend the palace from our attack."

"My general," said the major, "Based upon what you have told me, I am prepared to agree. If you keep me informed of the date and time of your attack, I will arrange for my militia to be elsewhere."

Two nights later, the anti-government protesters were proceeding along a street leading to the prime minister's palace. General Zahedi, standing in the turret of his command tank, was in the lead. They approached the dimly lit medieval stone structure, then entered it through a large gate. As expected, General Zahedi quickly learned that the Palace Guard, absent the support of their militia, had assumed protected positions inside the palace.

Unexpected was the presence of members of General Kiani's military brigade. They had taken protected positions along the inside of the high circular walls surrounding the entrance to the palace. From their fortified positions, they could use their automatic weapons, small arms, and hand grenades to attack anyone or anything entering the well-lit courtyard.

The Nation's invisible army soldiers had positioned themselves behind the garden walls of the grand residences that surrounded the circular drive leading to the palace's gated entry.

The first wave of revolutionary troops and demonstrators entering the courtyard found themselves caught in a withering field of crossfire with no place to hide. Those who were fortunate enough to be able to withdraw from the courtyard were forced to contend with gunfire from the well-armed Nation forces.

Soon, what remained of General Zahedi's troops and the surviving demonstrators were forced to withdraw out of range of their unexpected opponents.

With the rise of the next morning's sun, the dead and wounded could be seen strewn throughout the courtyard and along the circular drive next to the palace entrance. General Zahedi's attack had been repelled, but at a staggering loss to his troops and the demonstrators.

Word of the costly attempt at a coup spread rapidly. The demonstrators dedicated to seeking Prime Minister Mossadegh's removal were packing their tents in anticipation of returning home. The paid organizers had departed. General Zahedi, concerned about possible personal retribution, had gone underground.

Following the defeat, Roberts was not looking forward to his next call to Langley, Virginia, home of the CIA. '*What can I tell the director? How do I explain the failure of our planned coup*?'

Chapter Forty-Six
"The White House"

WASHINGTON, D.C.: August 1953

Behind closed doors, unaware of the events in Tehran, the president and his kitchen cabinet had been discussing how quickly the pieces of the Sentinel plan seemed to be falling into place. They had learned the prime minister was planning to present the Oil Bill to the Majlis for ratification within the week. Their mood was improving. The president was growing cautiously optimistic. He had been heard to say, "How can it be that I am in charge of the most powerful country in the world and yet I find myself having to rely on the narrow majority in the Iranian Majlis to approve the Sentinel Plan? What can I do but sit and wait?

"If I am going to challenge the British government, the Washington oil lobby, and the British and American oil companies, I will need a damn good reason! Tell me again, how much progress are our Sentinel friends making? How long will I have to wait?"

A gentle knock on the outer door of the president's office was followed by his secretary entering the sacred, not-to-be-disturbed territory. She quickly handed him a note. It read, *'Excuse my interruption. Mike Stone says it is urgent that he see you. He is waiting in the hallway.'*

The president responded without hesitation, "If Mike Stone says it's urgent, what he really means is he has some important and timely news. I think we should invite him to join us."

Seconds later, Mike entered the office. Forgoing the normal greetings, he announced, "Mr. President, there are three recent developments in Iran that require your immediate attention. I have just received word from Sam Naraghi. Ayatollah Khasani failed to appear at the pre-meeting caucus concerning the final vote on the Oil Bill. Without his support, Prime Minister Mossadegh had no choice but to delay the vote.

"Sam reports the daily public demonstrations have become larger and angrier and are spreading into adjacent neighborhoods. It would appear that, through the efforts of the CIA and MI-6 and the financial support of the Anglo-American oil companies, the momentum of the demonstrations has increased without the White House's approval or continuing financial support. The demonstrations may have taken on a life of their own. Left unattended, the final implementation of Ajax could occur spontaneously, without any further authorization from the White House.

"From a reliable source, we have learned a plan is being prepared by General Zahedi and Kermit Roberts to take advantage of the growing confusion. They are going to mobilize a small, military militia, loyal to the shah, to arrest the prime minister and take him into custody.

"Upon receiving verification of his arrest, the young shah plans to return from exile, declare martial law, charge the deposed prime minister with treason, and reassume titular responsibility for governing Iran. Should all that be allowed to occur, any hope of resurrecting our 'Oil Bill' will be lost."

Had Mike exploded a bomb in the president's office, he couldn't have created a bigger uproar. The president was the first to recover. Focusing his full attention on Mike, he asked, "And just how were you able to come up with that information? Normally, the director of the CIA keeps me very well informed. If I haven't heard it from him, how do we know what you are reporting is accurate?"

"Mr. President, since we don't have a lot of time, I would suggest we need to quickly develop a backup plan."

Almost before Mike had finished talking, the enraged president ordered his secretary to get the CIA director on his line. Unaccustomed to talking in a loud voice, the president began his one-sided conversation. "Mr. Director, I have recently been provided with information suggesting the CIA and MI-6 have been staging Iranian demonstrations in anticipation of completing the planned coup before the Majlis has voted on our oil bill. Is it true Kermit Roberts and General Zahedi are planning to take advantage of their demonstrations to provide the public support necessary to justify their arrest of Prime Minister Mossadegh? Do I understand correctly that all of this was planned to take place before I authorized the implementation of the final stage of Ajax?"

Ignoring the silence at the other end of the line, the president continued, "May I suggest you make your presence in my office as quickly as possible? There are some people here who have some very interesting questions to ask you."

Taking advantage of the delay, Mike asked, "While we are waiting for the director, could we use the time to discuss another recent development? The active phase of the planned coup was initiated. From

Harshim, we received word when General Zahedi's military detachment arrived at the prime minister's palace, a combined force of loyal Iranian troops and the Nation's invisible army were waiting in position to repel their attack. This resulted in a great loss to General Zahedi's military force. During the attack, the prime minister and his party, hoping to take advantage of the chaos, managed to escape through a hole they blew in the backyard wall. At last report, they have taken sanctuary in the Bararite portion of Tehran's labyrinth old city."

"Mike, are you suggesting the coup may have failed?"

"Maybe it would be best described as 'it hasn't succeeded yet.'"

The president seemed confused. "Mike, if General Zahedi has gone underground, why are you suggesting an effort to arrest Prime Minister Mossadegh may still exist?"

Mike responded, "Following Prime Minister Mossadegh's escape, General Zahedi, concerned about possible retribution, went into hiding. If he has decided to change his mind, it's entirely possible, should he come out of hiding, with his leadership, the Anglo-American oil companies might be capable of successfully completing a second coup.

"Mr. President, there is more. There is a rumor floating around that Kermit Roberts has paid a surprise call on the safehouse where General Zahedi is hiding. Although our sources have no knowledge of what was discussed, they have advised me to anticipate a second attempted coup.

"In the meantime, Naraghi's civilian army has returned to Ahvaz and General Kiani's loyal brigade has returned to its base. Should General Zahedi come out of hiding and attempt to resurrect what remains of his military force, Prime Minister Mossadegh could be vulnerable to a second attack."

The president, by now agitated, asked, "Mike, if your information is accurate, what can we do to help the prime minister?"

"Mr. President, the first thing that needs to be done is for you to order the CIA and MI-6 to stand down. Second, there are two things that need to be accomplished immediately. We need to publicly announce that the coup attempt has failed and that Prime Minister Mossadegh, with the support of his still loyal military, remains in his rightful role as leader of the National Party. And he should reschedule the 'Oil Bill' for a vote at the earliest possible date."

"Mike, I am confused. Why does it make sense to schedule a vote before we can locate the ayatollah and obtain his support? Without him, how can we expect the Majlis to have the votes needed for ratification?"

"Mr. President, here is the tricky part. Now that the Ajax agenda has been revealed, our source reports that Harshim Naraghi and his fellow sub-cultural leaders can appeal to the more moderate members of the Royalist Party and achieve sufficient support to construct a voting majority."

"Mike, for the sake of argument, if I choose to accept your plan of action, how can I communicate with the prime minister?"

"Through Harshim Naraghi. He still maintains his position of trust with the prime minister, and he has the contacts needed to deliver and receive your notes."

"And why should I believe Mr. Naraghi is willing to communicate with me?"

"Because, Mr. President, he needs your assistance with a second problem."

"A second problem?"

"Perhaps I need to explain.

"The Naraghi-Roth Nation of Citizens Farmers could be placed in jeopardy should Iran's constitutional government be replaced. Consequently, the Naraghis and the Roths have negotiated a separate agreement with the Independent Oil Company. Only your signature remains to be added to activate their agreement."

"My signature? Why do you need my consent to a two-party business agreement?"

"Your signature is required to validate that the newly formed petroleum production company will qualify for protection as a bona-fide American Foreign Investment Interest."

"Mike, let me get this straight. In my capacity as president of the United States, you wish me to agree in writing, should this new alliance become a reality, that it will be deserving of American military support? Will someone please tell me why it's in our best interests to accept the implied responsibility of protecting the oil-producing efforts of Nation and the American-owned Independent Oil Co. Ltd.?"

Mike, knowing he was going to get just one bite of the proverbial apple, quickly responded, "Two reasons. With all that has happened, the alliance will provide the United States with the assurance that Nation's oil will no longer be susceptible to foreign interests. Perhaps of greater importance, your support will demonstrate America's interest in protecting and preserving one of the world's most deserving humanitarian efforts!"

Looking directly into the eyes of each of the men seated around the table, the president could see their confirming looks.

Five minutes later, the president's secretary escorted the director into the inner sanctum of the president's office, where his kitchen cabinet plus Mike Stone were seated.

Used to talking to his president on a confidential basis, the director questioned why it was necessary to include the others.

Ignoring the question, the president said, "Mr. Director, we have received information that Ajax has been allowed to proceed well beyond what I had approved. Perhaps you wouldn't mind bringing us up to date?"

"Mr. President, my information is two days old. For the last forty-eight hours, I have not been able to communicate with our in-country case officer, Kermit Roberts. Could you be more specific?"

The normally mild-mannered former Supreme Allied Commander and current president of the United States then asked, in his most deliberate tone, "Would you care to clarify why I am being told that an unsuccessful coup in Tehran has already taken place? Prime Minister Mossadegh is in hiding and the opposing demonstrators no longer exist. And while you are at it, perhaps you would explain, why did you let this situation proceed to the next level without my consent?"

Understanding the possible consequences of his answers, the director proceeded to answer the president's questions with the seriousness they deserved. "If it is true that the forces loyal to the shah failed to prevail in their first attempt to remove Prime Minister Mossadegh and his government, I have not been informed. If I wasn't informed about the failed coup, I certainly have no information regarding what may be planned next."

Those present appeared shocked by the director's response. They were disgusted by what they had just been told.

The director, reacting to the prolonged silence, continued. "Mr. President, I understand how you might regard all of these actions as having exceeded what your predecessor previously authorized for Ajax. Maybe we should focus on this fact: had Roberts' and General Zahedi's plan succeeded, we would have secured control over Iranian oil, removed an out-of-control, rogue government, and prevented the Russians from becoming involved. Haven't we achieved a great victory? History will report this incident as a public revolution expressing the will of the Iranian people!"

"Horse manure! You and I both know those are not decisions in-country case officers are authorized to make. You can bet that if *we* know the real story, so will others. The Iranian people have been deprived of important revenues they need to rebuild their country. Do you have any idea how much wealth will be created if Iran's natural resources are opened up to foreign investment interests? Once they become coupled with a corrupt, puppet, shah government, they will be capable of removing great wealth from Iran for their own, self-serving purposes.

"Somehow, we have allowed the British to involve the United States in a plot to destroy the Middle East's first constitutional government, plunder its oil, and violate the very foundations of American foreign policy."

"Mr. President, you have me confused. Why, when we are on the brink of restoring Western control over eighty percent of Iran's oil revenues and restoring a government loyal to the British and Americans, are you not pleased?"

"Mr. Director, it might be best if you listen very carefully to what I am about to say. Under normal circumstances, I would be asking for your resignation, effective immediately. Unfortunately, the publicity surrounding your dismissal could expose what we have been trying to hide from public scrutiny. Fortunately for you, that is a risk I am not willing to take.

"You are formally ordered to contact your on-site case officer and order him and his MI-6 colleagues to stand down. Am I making myself clear?"

Chapter Forty-Seven
"Time for a Do-Over"

TEHRAN, IRAN: September 1953

On the Tuesday following the failure of the coup attempt, Kermit Roberts was knocking on the front door of the safehouse where General Zahedi had taken sanctuary.

He was immediately ushered inside. "General, it took a great deal of effort to find you," Roberts said. "I have come here to ask you one question. Would you and your people be willing to make a second attempt to complete the coup? I have received reports saying that General Kiani and his brigade have returned to their barracks. I have also been led to believe Nation's not-so-invisible army is returning to Ahvaz. It would appear we may have a small window of opportunity to finish what we have started. All that remains protecting the prime minister is his small regiment of Palace Guards. With your help and the assistance of what remains of your army, why couldn't we wage a second attack?"

Surprisingly, General Zahedi asked, "On whose authority are you asking? Is the American president on board?"

"They must not be, I have received orders to stand down. For reasons I don't understand, no one at Langley is accepting my calls or responding to my cablegrams. It would appear we are on our own.

"I have, however, discussed the matter with the representatives of the Anglo-American oil companies. They have assured me they are prepared to provide us with whatever financial assistance we may need."

Seemingly satisfied with Roberts' answer, the wily general asked, "Is the shah still willing to support me as Iran's next prime minister? And how much time do I have to round up my team, create a new plan, and prepare to act?"

Following the failed coup, Harshim Naraghi remained in Tehran. He knew he had to talk to his old and trusted friend, the prime minister. Fully disguised and carefully guarded by their private security forces, the two long-time colleagues met at a nondescript tea house, located deep in the heart of Tehran's ancient Barite district. They were well-guarded by the ruthless Bararite security team, the same guards who once protected its Silk Road trading routes and markets.

Had anybody been watching, they would have concluded that two old friends were taking the opportunity to exchange pleasantries. After a short time, the two men decided to enter the café and continue their conversation over a cup of tea.

Seated comfortably at one of the café's secluded corner tables, waiting for the tea and biscuits to be served, Harshim, leaning forward, came right to the point. "Mohammed, my dear friend, with the exception of Ayatollah Khasani, the other sub-culture leaders have asked me to convey their interest in supporting your return to office and doing what you can do to assure passage of the Oil Bill."

The confused Prime Minister Mossadegh asked, "Without the support of the Muslim community, how can we expect to generate a sufficient number of votes to pass the Oil Bill without the support of the ayatollah?"

"What an excellent question. How do we know, when certain members of the Royalist party learn of British Oil's attempt to pirate the country's oil industry, to prevent Iran from participating in prevailing market-rate royalty fees, and to replace its democratic form of government with the shah and his despotic form of government, that they will be appalled and vote for the oil bill? Obviously, we will need to confirm we have those votes in hand before you come out of hiding and reclaim your office of prime minister."

"Mohammed, you understand the American president is prepared to support our Oil Bill. Already, he has signed a document committing the United States to defend the interests of the recently formed alliance between the Independent Oil Company and Naraghi-Roth against any threat or attack of foreign governments."

Impressed with Harshim's answer, the prime minister asked, "How do we know his consent doesn't represent a political promise that can conveniently be withdrawn?"

Having anticipated that question would be raised, Harshim reached into his inside jacket pocket and extracted what appeared to be an official U.S. government document. After handing it to his old friend, he said, "Why don't you and your people study this agreement? You can be your own judge of what it represents."

Over the next few days, Harshim, with the assistance of Kate, as well as Sam and Sally, began to call discreetly on his fellow leaders, old friends of importance, business acquaintances, and elected Royalist members of the Majlis.

Within three days, Harshim informed Prime Minister Mossadegh that he had received the personal assurances from enough of his Royalist friends to ensure passage of the Oil Bill.

Two days following his receipt of the agreement, Dr. Mohammed Mossadegh returned to his palace and resumed his duties as prime minister. Almost immediately, he began to speak publicly about his vision for the future of Iran. The supportive crowds in the streets and public squares were growing larger. Slogans that spoke of preserving their constitutional government and increasing the royalty rates to a fair level were providing his supporters with new information.

Prime Minister Mossadegh, speaking publicly as many as three times a day, was building his case. The pendulum of civil expression was beginning to swing in a new direction.

Roberts and Zahedi were watching the increasing presence of people desirous of voting with their feet. It was becoming evident that Prime Minister Mossadegh was reaching his audience. Each day it was becoming more obvious there were two highly motivated groups of demonstrators who opposed each other.

When word of the failed coup reached the White House, the president was quick to speak of his tremendous relief that a major mistake in U.S. foreign policy had been avoided. He mistakenly believed his order to stand down had been received and acted upon.

The growing number of international communications from people concerned over the safety of the *Great Humanitarian Work* were flooding into the offices of congressional representatives, senators, and the president. They were urging the president and the Congress to recognize and protect Nation.

Secret reports from Alan Kahne were being received by Smohl Cantor. In turn, he was keeping the prime minister, the American president, Jacques Roth, and Mike Stone fully informed. He was unaware of the plans that General Zahedi, Kermit Roberts and the Anglo-American oil companies had authorized.

Kermit Roberts and General Zahedi had been watching Prime Minister Mossadegh's progress. They were counting the growing list of the converted Royal Party advocates prepared to support the pending Oil Bill. Each day, they were becoming increasingly convinced, "We need to stage a second coup, before the Oil Bill is presented to the Majlis for approval."

Believing they were running out of time, Roberts and General Zahedi were operating from an underground command post, well outside any direct means of communication with Washington or the CIA director.

The not-so-spontaneous, anti-government, pro-shah demonstrators were returning to the streets. Marchers were frequently observed using freshly printed American dollar bills when they paid for their purchases. The mood of the opposing demonstrations was turning ugly. Shootings, the hurling of Molotov cocktails into adjacent buildings, looting, and the overturning of cars selected for incineration, were becoming commonplace. With each passing day, opposing mobs were penetrating ever deeper into residential neighborhoods.

On the night of the second attempt at a coup, General Zahedi was seen entering the quarters where the Palace Guard was billeted. Within thirty minutes, he was observed leaving. It would later be determined that the Palace Guard had agreed to stand down.

General Zahedi, standing tall in his personal tank, was observed, once again, slowly traveling through the assembled demonstrators in the direction of the prime minister's palace. His tank and the other weaponized vehicles had been placed in front of the main entrance, their gun turrets were pointed directly toward the palace.

Absent any resistance from the Palace Guard, Kiani's troops or the Nation's invisible army, the general climbed down from his tank and, along with a limited detachment of his troops, made his way to the main entrance of the palace.

Without the protection of his personal guard or General Kiani's Brigade, Prime Minister Mossadegh, hoping to avoid further Iranian bloodshed, appeared at the open door, unarmed and unprotected. Wasting no time, General Zahedi approached the prime minister, his former leader, and handed him a several-page, official-looking document, embossed with the letterhead of the deposed shah.

Standing back, the general waited to give the prime minister time to read and study the document. When the prime minister appeared to have finished reading the document, General Zahedi motioned for his guard to move forward to handcuff the prime minister and escort him into a waiting van.

Roberts and General Zahedi were proceeding to execute the second phase of their plan. Provisions had already been made for the shah's return. His private police, the SAVAK, had already returned to their customary quarters inside the shah's palace compound. Externally, commanders loyal to General Zahedi and the shah had been ordered to assemble their troops and remain prepared to provide whatever protection might be needed. The world was informed, the people of Iran had spoken.

Unprepared for the shocking news, White House staffers watched with concern as the young shah immediately issued four proclamations. First, he declared martial law. Second, he charged Dr. Mossadegh with high treason. Third, he appointed General Zahedi to be prime minister, and fourth, he revalidated Iran's eighty percent royalty agreement between Iran and the Anglo-American oil companies.

Ajax had been accomplished!

In Washington, the news was carefully managed. It was important that the public not learn the real story behind the story. How could it be explained that a coalition of Anglo-American oil companies, coupled with British and American information agencies acting without the consent of the American president had seized control of the world's fourth-largest oil reserves? Almost immediately, the big refinery at Abadan was returned to its online status. Pumping stations were restarted. Pipelines were returned to service. A line of oceangoing oil tankers, waiting to transport Iranian oil, were moored in the Abadan Port. Formerly vacant administrative office buildings were reoccupied. The consequences of the regime change were becoming apparent.

Chapter Forty-Eight
"The Diagnostic Test"

AHVAZ, IRAN: October 1953

In Tel Aviv, Alan and Smohl were still trying to obtain a clearer understanding of all the changes taking place in Iran. Alan was asking his mentor, "Smohl, have you ever considered the possibility that CIA and MI-6 field agents initiated the final stages of Ajax without the knowledge or approval of the American president? It makes you wonder who is really in control, the Big Oil companies and the intelligence agencies or our elected political leaders.

"If the former is the case, how do we know the Anglo-American thirst for oil will not stop with their confiscation of the Iranian oil? I predict it will only become a question of time before Nation's undeveloped oil potential will attract the attention of the shah and his Anglo-American oil company support group."

Nodding his assent, Smohl suggested, "It is going to be interesting to determine if the American government will respect the Naraghi-Roth-Independent oil agreement, given the influence of the American oil lobby. Somehow, we need to test the American resolve to protect its foreign investment interests."

Fascinated by Smohl's suggestion, Alan, thinking out loud, said, "Somehow, on a more limited basis, I think we need to find a way to create a diagnostic test that will determine how reliable the American protection will be. I wonder what can be done to provoke the Anglo oil companies into challenging this new arrangement?"

Smiling, Smohl asked, "Alan, I have a second question I plan to raise in Versailles. Now that the Naraghis, the Roths, the American Independent Oil Company, and the American president have executed the agreement, might it be prudent for us to initiate discussions regarding its activation? Don't we need to create a diagnostic test to determine America's willingness to step up?"

Whenever Alan saw Smohl's whimsical grin appear, he knew something unpredictable was about to happen. Immediately, he asked, "Has the time arrived for Alan Kahne to go back to work?"

Nobody except the shah was certain when he became aware of how valuable the concession for producing Naraghi oil might become. No one, including the shah, knew for sure how much oil lay under the four-hundred thousand-acre Nation of Citizen Farmers property. The services of Alan Kahne were needed.

The shah's ambition became apparent the day the SAVAK ranking commander, General Apgar, together with the shah's private military detachment, appeared at Nation's main entrance. The on-duty guard was told that the general was there to deliver a letter from the shah to Sam Naraghi.

The senior guard, who had not been informed of the pending arrival of a large military detachment or of the shah's letter, became suspicious and called Sam Naraghi for instructions.

Sam responded, "Why don't you escort the commanding officer and his military detachment to Field Fifty-One, whose wheat as recently harvested? You might tell them that their heavy vehicles will do no damage, since only the stubble remains. Advise the general I will be right out to take receipt of the shah's letter and to talk about anything he may wish to discuss."

Twenty minutes after the military detachment had reached Field Fifty-One, the commanding general was arraying the armored vehicles and the artillery in a widely spaced formation that would provide maximum military defense in the case of a surprise attack.

General Apgar was pleased. He had gained entrance to the property on an uncontested basis and completed the deployment of his considerable military assets without encountering any resistance. His attention was now focused on how long he would have to wait for Sam Naraghi to arrive.

After forty minutes of standing under the hot sun, General Apgar was thoroughly upset by the continued absence of Sam Naraghi. Taking advantage of the time, the general noticed the strange-looking building that housed Nation's evaporative cooling chamber and wondered why someone would build such an unusual building in the middle of farmed land. He failed to notice that the water in the doughnut-shaped lake was being replaced with oil.

Shifting his gaze in the direction of the Naraghi command bunker, he noticed a fast-moving jeep, followed by a plume of dust, headed in his direction. '*Sam Naraghi is finally on his way.*'

Turning to his second-in-command, he said, "Tell the men, as soon as I give Mr. Naraghi the shah's letter and conclude whatever we need to discuss, they should be prepared to proceed to their previously designated control positions throughout the entire Nation property." With his attention focused on the approaching jeep, the general failed to observe the thin blanket of oil that was seeping through the wheat stubble.

Sam was walking briskly toward the waiting general. After exchanging the usual pleasantries, General Apgar handed Sam the shah's letter and suggested that he immediately read it.

Sam had finished reading the document for the third time when he asked, "Why have you found it necessary to bring an entire military detachment to deliver one letter?"

With the general's next remark, the cordiality of the meeting ended abruptly. "I have instructions to occupy your Nation of Citizen Farmers until this matter of mineral rights ownership has been resolved," the general said.

Sam, without hesitating, presented the general with a document of his own, saying, "It might interest you to know that my family no longer owns the mineral rights to the land in question. Some time ago, Roth-Naraghi executed an agreement with the American Independent Oil Company. This agreement, among other things, provides them with the authority to prospect and develop any oil reserves that may exist under the property. It's all described in this document.

"You may also wish to note that the document's signatories include the American president. His signature evidences the American government's recognition of this new entity as a legitimate American Foreign Interest, subject to protection by the American military."

Following a long, strained silence, the general said, "I don't know about your letter. I have been ordered to spread my detachment over your entire property pending the successful adjudication of the mineral rights. Surely, you don't believe this document is going to stop us from accomplishing what we have come here to achieve?"

Nodding to indicate his understanding, and without further comment, Sam and his driver retreated to his jeep, climbed in, and drove away in the direction from which they had come. Sam was not smiling when he descended the stairs leading to the underground command bunker, where Harshim, Kate, and Sally were waiting for him.

After explaining the situation, Sam said, "I think the shah just presented us with the limited threat we need to test the enforcement of our agreement with the Americans. "If we light the candle, wouldn't we be sending a strong message to the Americans that we are being threatened by the shah government and the Anglo-American oil cartel? Does anybody object to my ordering the 'Lighting of the Candle'?"

When Sam had failed to return within thirty minutes with his response to the shah's letter, the frustrated SAVAK commander turned to walk back to his detachment. That was when he first noticed the black oil seeping from the ground where his vehicles were parked. Flares intended to ignite the oil were beginning to land nearby. It was apparent that, if the entire detachment didn't move quickly, the men and their equipment would be engulfed by a curtain of fire. Wasting no time, the commander motioned for his military detachment to proceed with all possible haste to the entrance and exit the property.

Standing atop the command bunker, the four Naraghis watched as this once-menacing military detachment, with flames nipping at the rear-most vehicles, raced pell-mell toward the main gate. General Apgar was standing in the turret of the lead tank, talking on his two-way radio.

Any pleasure the four Naraghis may have felt was tempered by their appreciation that Naraghi-Roth-Independent Oil had just thrown down the gauntlet. By challenging the authority of the Anglo-American Oil companies and the puppet shah government, they hoped to test the willingness of the U.S. government to protect its Foreign Investment Interest, in the event that the shah government chose to retaliate.

Chapter Forty-Nine
"The General's Report"

TEHRAN, IRAN: October 1953

Apgar's initial report, delivered from his fast-moving tank, was difficult to understand. Exiting Nation's main gate, General Apgar noticed the shah's helicopter setting down in a vacant parking lot for visitors. 'It must be waiting to take me back to Tehran. Based on my scrambled report, I can only imagine what must be going through their minds.' The one-hour helicopter ride to Tehran provided the general with the time he needed to organize his thoughts into a concise, written outline.

Judging from the haste with which he was escorted from the landed helicopter into the crowded boardroom, he was not surprised to see the concerned and agitated looks of the senior leaders of the Anglo-American executive oil team. Appreciating that his next comments could alter the future of Iran's petroleum landscape, General Apgar raised his hand. "Before we start, I think it might be better for us to pause long enough for my notes to be copied and distributed to you," he said.

"While we are waiting, I have a question for you. Why would Sam Naraghi openly challenge our military presence? He must understand, in unleashing his 'Lit Candle' defense system, that he is challenging more than the authority of the shah. He is a smart man. What was he thinking? What possible combination of circumstances could have caused him to challenge the entire Anglo-American government and oil community, and believe he could escape unscathed?"

Alan Kahne stood up, with the general's report in his hand, and suggested, "Before we begin, you may wish to study the Naraghi-Independent Oil Company agreement that Sam Naraghi delivered to you. In essence, it not only describes the agreement Nation has executed with Independent Oil, but it defines the government's commitment to protect its new foreign investment interest.

"You have to assume any retaliatory attack on your part could trigger a response by the American military. Not only would you be faced with a superior force, but you would be giving U.S. officials an excuse to reconsider their support for Ajax. Is that a risk you are willing to take?"

Intrigued by the question, the senior American oil executive asked, "Mr. Kahne, would you be so kind as to explain how the Naraghi-Roths were able to make a separate arrangement with the IOC?"

Standing erect in his best military posture, the short, muscular, bald, big-eared consultant said, "Because I suggested it!"

"You did what? Didn't you stop to consider the possible consequences on our position?"

To Kahne's credit, those gathered in the room were curious to learn how the brilliant petroleum consultant would defend his actions and stand up to the now thoroughly agitated senior American oil executive. They watched as Kahne paused. Presumably, he was carefully weighing his response.

Then, speaking slowly and in a firm voice, he said, "Perhaps we need to clear up some misunderstandings. First, my services have been retained by you, and I have signed your agreement, and I understand its terms and conditions requiring me to comply with well-defined confidentiality stipulations.

"But it's important for you to understand that I have never consented to work exclusively for you. My engagement agreement specifically states I am entitled to work for anyone I might choose. The record will reflect that my services were employed by the IOC for estimating the capacity of the oil reserves underlying Nation's four hundred thousand acres. During our discussions, I simply raised the possibility of Nation entertaining the idea of consummating a separate agreement with the IOC.

"I believe the minutes of that meeting will reveal that the adoption of an agreement provides the IOC with an alternate incentive. As the record clearly demonstrates, there was a lot of discussion regarding the possibility that the Oil Bill might fail to win approval by the Majlis. The idea of consummating a separate arrangement with Naraghi-Roth was interpreted to suggest, in the event the Oil Bill failed to materialize, that the IOC would not go away empty-handed."

The British oil executive asked, "Mr. Kahne, while you are correct on your right to work for whomever you choose, did you stop to consider what loyalty expectations you might be violating? I am afraid that any future consideration regarding your professional services must depend upon our ability to resolve this loyalty issue to our satisfaction."

Needing time to think, Kahne asked, "Before I respond to your question, may I be excused for a few minutes?"

Standing in a locked toilet cabinet in the men's room, Alan sat down to consider how he was going to answer his own question, *'What kind of life would I like to pursue? Do I prefer to return to my former life of wealth and privilege and continue to pursue my career as an international petroleum adviser? How would I feel about giving up the life of a pursuer of beautiful women and a connoisseur of fine wine and cuisine? Or would I be happier remaining inside the Mossad and committing myself to assisting Israel to achieve its goal of providing safe sanctuary for the disenfranchised and threatened people of Jewish faith?*

'Then there is the second problem. The solution to the current Iranian problem may not be the end of major-power appetites for Middle Eastern oil. Aren't we just beginning to understand the problems that the growing importance of Middle Eastern oil may be creating?

'Could our current problem be the conclusion of a major power act of imperialism in Iran? Or, could it just be the star?. If I remain in my present covert position as a petroleum consultant for the Anglo-Americans, I should be able to gain access to valuable and important information.'

With his mind made up, Alan reappeared in the conference room, prepared to announce his wish to remain a consultant in the employ of the Anglo-American oil cartel.

Not convinced of Kahne's sincerity or trustworthiness, the British Oil executive asked, "Would you mind sharing with us how you were able to reach your decision? Perhaps you might explain what you regard as the most important problems we might create, should we choose to interfere with an American Foreign Investment Interest?"

Aware that his answer would affect his prospects of being able to continue in his present role, Alan was thinking about how he might disseminate the kind of information these men would find timely and valuable. He walked to one end of the big conference table and stood in front of the executive lectern. Now that he had everyone's attention, he began, "There are three overriding factors that will have a tremendous influence on the future of the Middle Eastern oil industry.

"First, we don't completely understand what the magnitude of the Western World's demand for petroleum and related products will be. In 1950, the United States became a net importer of oil, and the experts are predicting the world's demand for oil will double every ten years. It's only a question of time before the world's growing appetite for oil will shift the center for petroleum production from the Gulf of Mexico to the Middle East. Accordingly, we must assume both the demand for, and the value of Middle Eastern oil will rapidly escalate.

"Second, the future revenues generated from the sale of oil will bring unprecedented profits to the Anglo-American operating oil companies, and royalty revenue to the shah government. We are about to witness a redistribution of wealth and a concentration of power within the shah's Iran. There are bound to be consequences.

"Third, there is the problem of Nation's oil production. Fully developed, Nation oil could represent both a significant source of competition and a target of opportunity for conquest.

"Should you wish to prevent a military engagement with the United States, it's important that you accept that the interdiction of Naraghi-Roth shipping is no longer an option. You would be challenging the Americans' policy of protecting their Foreign Investment Interests, and they would have no alternative but to respond.

"Fourth, are you prepared to create an open conflict between the British and the American navies? Do you really want to create a significant rupture in your relationship with the American government? Is that an outcome you really want to test?"

After another thirty minutes of discussion, it had become clear there was no consensus. It was only when the American and British executives asked for a motion of adjournment that the animated discussion concluded. No further mention of Alan Kahne's future employment had been mentioned.

That night, alone in his hotel room, Alan began to replay in his mind the events of his incredible day. *'Sitting on top of a toilet in the men's room of the Anglo-American Oil headquarters seemed like a strange place for me to be making such a life-defining decision. One thing for sure, had I not been invited into their meeting, I would not have been given the opportunity to participate in such an important discussion. I need to talk to Smohl.'*

Chapter Fifty
"Alan Kahne or David Marcus?"

TEL AVIV, ISRAEL: October 1953

Following Alan's return to Tel Aviv, he and Smohl soon found themselves sitting in their regular booth of their favorite bar. Alan was explaining his dilemma. Seeking to encourage Alan to help him think through his situation, Smohl said, "Even if Naraghi-Roth has consummated its agreement with the IOC, they still have to qualify operationally as a legitimate American Foreign Investment Interest. Until the necessary criteria have been satisfied, how can we expect to be the beneficiary of America's protection?

"Don't we have to concern ourselves with the possibility that the British will attack before Nation-Independent has fulfilled all the requirements?"

Continuing his line of thinking, the wily veteran said, "Similar to the British efforts to prevent the Majlis' passage of the Oil Bill, I think we can assume they will do whatever they can to prevent Nation-Independent from achieving certification. Somehow, we need to discover what they are planning. The need for your services is clear. The question is, are you still interested in playing your role as Major Alan Kahne of the Israeli Mossad?"

"Smohl, I agree. For some time, I have been thinking about my life, both past and present. The question you are really raising is, do I prefer to pursue a life of helping troubled people or do I prefer to return to my previous world of self-indulgence? Having been exposed to your world, if I were to return to my former life, I would always wonder what I might have been able to contribute.

"Now that I have made my decision, I think it's best that I don't attend Jacques' Versailles retreat. Following my last meeting, where my loyalty was questioned, I must assume someone is following me. Being seen in Versailles in the company of the Sentinels could destroy my already tenuous relationship with my Anglo-American employers. That is a risk I should not take. Then there is the problem of maintaining my identity as Alan Kahne. Once so many of my friends know of my dual role, how can I remain confident I won't be exposed?"

The next morning, following his regular three-mile run, Alan agreed to have breakfast with Smohl before he was to be picked up by the Roth Bank company plane. After breakfast, Smohl was standing near the gate of the private-plane terminal, rehearsing how he would explain Alan Kahne's last-minute decision to decline Jacques' invitation.

Chapter Fifty-One
"Alan Kahne's Dilemma"

BEACHFRONT HOTEL; TEL AVIV, ISRAEL: October 1953

Alan's life was becoming more complicated. For some time, during his early-morning runs, he had been noticing a shorter, mature, soft-appearing, yet athletic and attractive woman jogging along the same path in the opposite direction. As they approached each other, he would nod, smile, and show some sign of recognition. But she would continue without responding. By the end of the first week, watching her approach, he slowed his pace before pulling to a stop in the hope that she too would stop so that he could introduce himself and start a conversation.

Ten minutes later, they were sitting on the sunlit veranda of a nearby beachfront hotel. Over several glasses of water, no ice, they were engaging in small talk when she said, "My name is Suzanne Strauss, and I am employed by the Weizmann Institute as a nuclear scientist."

Anxious to reciprocate, Alan said, "My name is Alan Kahne, and I am a major in the Israeli military."

Skillful at asking questions, Alan quickly learned that Dr. Suzanne Strauss was a third-generation Palestinian Jew, educated in the United States, who taught nuclear engineering at the Weizmann Institute. Married to an early Israeli military hero, she became a widow when he was killed in Israel's 1947 war of independence. The woman spoke of raising her two daughters, continuing her nuclear research, and pursuing her doctoral teaching career.

Intrigued, Alan asked, "How does an Israeli-born student qualify for admittance to one of the few American universities devoted to nuclear research?"

"Alan, have you ever heard of Iran's Advanced Prep educational program? Are you familiar with the name Sally Raphael? An old family friend, Smohl Cantor, took me to Iran and introduced me to Sally. Three years later, I was one of the first students to complete her program. I was admitted to the University of Chicago's Physics Department. Following graduation, I applied for admittance to the University of California's Lawrence Livermore National Laboratory.

Upon graduation, I was invited to join some of my previous instructors on a special project, code-named the "Manhattan Project."

"The Manhattan Project?" asked Alan, "Wasn't that the secret American operation organized to develop the atomic bombs that were dropped on Japan? What an opportunity it must have been to work with Enrico Fermi and Robert Oppenheimer, unquestionably two of the world's brightest nuclear engineers."

Continuing, Suzanne said, "After the war, I was invited to return to Israel and teach nuclear engineering at the Weizmann Institute."

Alan was faced with a dilemma. *'How can I reveal my association with Smohl, the Naraghis, and the Roths without compromising my identity?'*

To break the tension, Dr. Strauss said, "Ever since my husband was killed in Israel's war for independence in 1947, I began to accept invitations to provide guest lectures at leading nuclear engineering universities all around the world. If I choose wisely, I am afforded the opportunity to visit fascinating places and meet interesting people. Over the years, I have prided myself on my ability to balance a serious, demanding life in academia with one that includes room for the adventure of travel and the rewarding friendships I encounter along the way."

Alan understood the moment he dreaded had finally arrived. "Rather than talk about how we make our livings, why don't we devote our time to becoming better acquainted?"

"Alan, you have no idea how long I've been waiting for some man to ask me that question! One of the things I find interesting about meeting someone dressed in jogging clothes is that they portray nothing about the person. If we are planning to become better acquainted, perhaps it would be nice if you would tell me about your life?"

Impressed with Dr. Strauss's candor and directness, he thought, *'I've heard how disarming and intelligent Jewish women can be. The question she is raising requires me to make a decision about how much sensitive information I am prepared to divulge.'*

"Suzanne, to answer your question with honesty and completeness, I would need to divulge some sensitive and secret information. Regardless of how our adventure turns out, can I trust you to treat what I am about to say confidentially?"

"Ah, Mr. Kahne, so there is a dark side to your life?"

"Not so dark, but other peoples' lives could be harmed by its public disclosure. Do I have your word?"

"Your secrets will always be safe with me. For your information, my former husband was engaged with the Mossad. Maybe you have heard of him. He was referred to as 'Wild Willy Strauss.' He earned the name by leading covert operations behind enemy lines that helped upset some of our Arab enemies' more aggressive attacks.

"As his wife, I was frequently exposed to sensitive information. In addition, in my position as a nuclear engineer, I must adhere to strict security requirements. I think you can rely on me to keep a secret."

Satisfied by her answers, Alan proceeded. "Suzanne, my real name is Sir David Marcus. I am the fourth generation of the Marcus family that worked for English Oil, Ltd. Desirous of pursuing my interests in the oil industry from a different direction, five years ago I resigned my executive position.

"I had become convinced that, in a post-world-war industrial revolution environment, it would only become a question of time before the center of gravity of oil production would shift from the Gulf of Mexico countries to the Persian Gulf countries. It was obvious to me, as the shift began to occur, that the value of Middle Eastern oil would dramatically increase. This would be accompanied by a transfer of political influence and a great redistribution of wealth.

"Rather than remain employed by English Oil, Ltd., and be considered an adversary by the Middle Eastern oil establishment, I decided to become a part of the emerging process. There is a saying by the host oil countries, 'To become involved with the Big Oil companies requires them to dance with the devil.'

"That is when I started my own independent petroleum, economic research, and investment advisory firm. Committed to winning the trust and cooperation of oil-rich Middle East governments, I quickly discovered that my understanding of the British and American oil company business practices was quite valuable.

"Along the way, my services were requested by my old friend, Jacques Roth, and his Sentinel colleagues, who had decided to break the grip of Big Oil. My participation with the Sentinels continued until MI-6 kidnapped me to prevent me from disclosing the pending implementation of an Anglo-American covert plan to seize control over Iran and its oil fields. It was codenamed Ajax."

Alan, suspecting even Suzanne, a veteran of work in nuclear proliferation, would be overwhelmed, was surprised when she said, "Alan, David, whatever your name is, how would you feel if I were to suggest we spend the next three weeks learning to become better acquainted?"

Part Eight

“Let’s Not Repeat Our Mistake”

Chapter Fifty-Two
"Retreat"

THE ROTH CHATEAU, VERSAILLES, FRANCE:
November 1953

A gathering at the Roth Chateau had been called hastily. Sequestered inside Pierre's study, Smohl got right to the point. "Alan reports the British and American oil executives are considering lobbying the British Parliament to provide the Royal Navy with the authority to block Nation-Independent's oil shipments.

"According to Alan's reports, the American and British oil companies have been advised that the legitimacy of the Naraghi-Roth mineral rights is in question. The British believe, until the ownership issue has been resolved, they are entitled to protect what might be their historical interests. Absent the certification of minimum deliveries of oil to commercial customers, Nation-Independent Oil will not be able to fulfill all the American Foreign Investment criteria. Should that occur, we would no longer be immune from attack."

Not liking what he was hearing, Jacques asked, "Are you suggesting we are engaged in another horse race? What is so different between this issue and the resourcefulness that the Anglo-American oil cartel exhibited in delaying approval of the Majlis for our competitive bidding bill?"

Harshim, who had been carefully following the logic of the conversation, asked, "What if we remove that option? Why don't we exercise our option with Nation-Independent Oil and do whatever is necessary to comply with all specifications of an American Foreign Investment before the Royal Navy receives authorization to interdict?"

"Jacques, since you and Mike have had the most experience dealing with the president and Roger Malone, why don't you excuse yourselves and deliver copies of our notice to exercise to the IOC and the White House? At the same time, it would be helpful if you could draw up a list of what we need to accomplish to qualify as a legitimate American Foreign Interest."

Early the next morning, standing on the tarmac of Paris' Orly Airport, Sam and Jacques were watching the plane carrying Mike and Cecelia from New York land before taxiing slowly to its designated gate near where they were standing. It was the same plane that was scheduled to take them to New York. Watching the passengers disembark, they were pleased when they saw Mike and Cecelia emerge from the cabin door.

A Paris Tribune reporter, waiting near the gate, was observing the four well-dressed friends hugging and kissing before breaking into animated conversation. Turning to his colleague, he asked, "Isn't the tall one Jacques Roth? I wonder what could be so important as to bring him all the way to Orly and greet the two arriving passengers in such a familiar manner?"

Separating themselves from the other people, the four old friends found a vacant area inside the terminal where they could talk and not be overheard. After explaining the situation, Jacques said, "Mike, I am suggesting that you and I pay another visit to the president and his staff. Normally I would have invited Sam to join us. But his presence is needed in Ahvaz to help coordinate the oil production installation."

Understanding the seriousness of the situation, Jacques asked Cecelia if she would prefer to return to New York with them or accompany Sam back to Versailles. Before either Sam or Mike could react, the Mighty Warrior from Hong Kong said, "If Mike doesn't object, I would prefer to continue to Versailles. I am looking forward to meeting Sally and Kate. For a long time, I have heard stories about how these remarkable women have succeeded in improving the quality of life for the citizen farming families and the service employees. Someday, we may wish to introduce what they have achieved into the Sentinel Institute's teaching curriculum."

Before anyone could react, Cecelia reached over to give Mike a goodbye kiss, before saying, in a kidding manner, "Who knows, driving to Versailles with Sam could prove very interesting!"

As was the custom, the Roths and their guests assembled at 6:30 p.m. in the family library. Orders for drinks had been taken. Freshly prepared pommes soufflées were being served. Madame Roth was explaining, "Pommes soufflées resemble a thin slice of potato, puffed up to look like a lightly salted French-fried ping-pong ball. Preparing them and cooking them in separate vats of hot oil, heated to different temperatures, is considered a rare culinary skill. Only a limited number of chefs have mastered the art. We are fortunate to have one on our staff."

After the Roths and their guests had retired to the grand dining room, Pierre rose to make his traditional first night toast. As was his custom, he intended to include everyone at the table in his remarks. But in midstream he was interrupted when he was handed a transatlantic cablegram from Mr. Morgan Stone. It read, *'It is imperative we immediately talk about a recent development that has occurred in Washington, D.C.!'*

Everyone in the room understood the importance of an urgent call from Morgan Stone. Cecelia, Harshim, Sam, Sally, and Smohl had already excused themselves. They were searching for separate house phones that would allow them to participate in Pierre's call from Morgan.

After they all announced they were on the line, Morgan Stone declared, "Pierre, Roger Malone just called me to report the president has confirmed he is prepared to support the authorization of Nation-Independent as a legitimate American Foreign Investment Interest, provided you satisfy each of the relevant stipulations.

"Anticipating his action will be accompanied by the tightest possible scrutiny by the Anglo-American oil coalition, he has instructed me to inform you of the importance of being able to demonstrate to the federal court your conformance with all the relevant issues of the code. All this must occur before the British Parliament ratifies the placing of a naval blockade opposite the Iranian port of Abadan. He estimates that we have less than three months."

Pierre responded, "Are you sure about three months? Nation-Independent is being asked to perform in ninety days what normally takes at least six months to a year to complete?"

"It's imperative we understand we will have control over the process for only ninety days. After that, things may become much more complicated. All that we can ask is for each of you who is responsible for the execution of different segments of the solution to pull out all the stops necessary to expedite a maximum effort."

Immediately following the conversation, Pierre placed a call to his executive vice president, "It is imperative that a supporting line of credit be established in the name of Naraghi-Roth-Independent Oil in the amount of one hundred million dollars," he said. "The funds are to be used to finance Nation-Independent initial oil drilling, production, and oil delivery operations in Ahvaz."

Smohl said, "Alan, the future of the Naraghi-Roth arrangement rests on our ability to transform some of Nation's land into an active, oil-producing operation within ninety days. Nobody knows if that is enough time. Why don't you call our mutual friend, Sir Walter Parameter, at Whitehall, and see if it can be arranged for the British parliamentary approval process to be slowed down a bit to give us more time? You might consider raising the question: Doesn't the issue of legitimate title need to be resolved by the International Court before an unprovoked naval interdiction can be considered something other than an act of war?"

Smohl asked Alan, "If an English duke had been incarcerated and deprived of his legal rights, without being charged with a crime, and if that were to become public information, how do you think the British public might react?"

Harshim placed a long-distance call to his friend responsible for managing the shut-in, idle drilling rigs not then needed to support Iranian oil exploration. "It is critical you make arrangements for the first four of the twenty drilling rigs to be placed on top of the drilling pads that are scheduled to be completed within the next three weeks."

Jacques' call to the chief executive officer of Independent Oil found him chairing a board meeting. But he took the call anyway. Quickly explaining the situation, Jacques inquired if he might take advantage of the presence of the other directors to authorize whatever was required to expedite the drilling process.

Jacques was pleased when he heard his American partner say, "Tell your people we can be ready to commence drilling operations within thirty days. That is not the problem. We will require drill pipe, well casings, drill mud, pumps, valves, and piping to be delivered to the drill site before we can start. In addition, we will need to construct storage tanks and install the equipment needed to off-load oil into the tanker trucks needed to transfer it to the Abadan Port.

"Delivery times from the United States could prove to be a problem. To protect ourselves against unanticipated delays, I suggest that we send our engineers, equipped with our shopping list, to Middle Eastern oil production sites. With all the drilling activity that has been shut down, someone must have the surplus materials we will need. For the right price, we should be able to complete our scavenger hunt in time to meet Independent's proposed starting date."

In less than thirty minutes, the four men had set the wheels of progress in motion. That having been done, they were ready to resume

Madame Roth's carefully prepared dinner. The food had been reheated, the salads had been refrigerated and the white wines had been re-chilled. Out of respect to their hostess, the men made a point of enjoying the great meal, pausing on occasion to comment on its excellence. Any further discussion of business was respectfully omitted.

Chapter Fifty-Three
"Jacques and Mike to Washington, D.C."

WASHINGTON, D.C.: November 1953

Word of the failed attack on Nation by the shah's Royal Guard had been received by the White House. The president was discussing the situation in the privacy of his office with his kitchen cabinet. "Don't you find it curious the British and the shah's SAVAK have failed to react?" the president asked. "Could it be they don't wish to jeopardize their relationship with the American government?"

Roger Malone, the Fed chair, said, "If what you are suggesting is true, don't we need to pay particular attention to the validation of Nation-Independent as a protected American Foreign Investment? Until our friends fulfill the strictest definition, we won't be able to stipulate an attack by the Royal Navy as an act of war."

"That might not be so simple," said the secretary of state. "Our people in London have reported that neither the Royal Navy nor Parliament is waiting for the courts to clarify the mineral rights title question before proceeding.

"At Southampton, the boilers of His Majesty's ships are being lit. Crews are being recalled. Plans are being made for the Royal Fleet to weigh anchor as quickly as possible. It has been assumed the title question will be resolved before the fleet reaches the Persian Gulf and the pending legislation reaches the Parliament floor.

"The problem of ratification by Parliament is a bit more difficult. The adjudication of title of the mineral rights is being considered by the International Court on an expedited basis. The Roth Bank, prior to its investment in the Naraghi venture, was able to satisfy its concerns as a result of the legal process took place in the Iranian courts in 1927. The problem that remains is there is no precedent where the International Court has upheld a sovereign court ruling. The briefs are being prepared by both sides and will be submitted shortly."

Fed Chairman Malone was talking. "Mr. President, in the 1930's, when the German interest in Nation's potential oil production first arose, the American government, along with its Allied nations, declared a hands-off policy regarding Middle Eastern, oil-producing, sovereign nations. Any violation would have been regarded as an act of war.

"In a different era, and under different circumstances, our regretful involvement in Operation Ajax, if exposed for public scrutiny, could be construed as an illegal act of economic imperialism. Before we can address Nation's problem, don't we need to ask ourselves whether we want to be a party to the same action twice?

"If we were to interpret Nation's attempt to immolate the shah's Royal Guard as an effort to test its support from the United States, what kind of a message would we be sending to our international friends and our other foreign investment interests if we fail to protect Nation?

"Could we, by standing alongside Iran's Nation of Citizen Farmers, announce that the United States remains prepared to protect sovereign interests from foreign aggression? And possibly mitigate some of the confusion created by our involvement in Ajax?"

"Roger, I agree. But don't we have to assume, in this environment, the legitimacy of Nation-Independent Oil as an American Foreign Interest will be thoroughly tested? Unless something were to occur to change things, I would suggest we learn what the strictest interpretation of the congressional statutes requires. Then, let's make certain the leaders of the Naraghi-Roth-Independent organization are fully aware of all the criteria they need to satisfy, within the limited time frame they have been given."

Two flights and three days later, Jacques and Mike were disembarking at Washington National Airport. They hadn't washed, shaved, or changed clothes since their departure from Paris. They were tired, cranky, and in need of a shower, a shave, and a good night's sleep.

Unexpectedly, Chairman Malone and his detachment of security agents were waiting on the well-guarded tarmac. Familiar with the Sentinels' presidential Secret Service detail, Malone motioned for the agents to escort Mike and Jacques to the middle vehicle of the caravan of three black limousines.

Roger waited until the caravan had exited the airport before explaining, "Mike, Jacques, it appears we have an unanticipated problem. The Secret Service has received word that a Paris newspaper reporter witnessed the two of you boarding the flight to New York. We have it on reliable authority that news of your return to New York has been transmitted to Sampson, and a contract has been issued to prevent you from interfering with the Anglo-American's plan to take control of the Naraghi-Roth petroleum interests.

"Accordingly, the Secret Service has been authorized to place you under their protective custody. They have planned for you to be hidden in plain sight on the top floor of the Willard, one of Washington's most exclusive hotels. Its staff is experienced in cooperating with security agents to ensure the safety of the hotel's more important guests. You are to remain in your rooms until the president is prepared to meet with you. Secure phone lines will be provided for your use."

Arriving at the famous Washington hotel proved interesting. A four-man security detail took up positions under the awning that led from the front entrance to the street as the limousine pulled up to the curb. Upon entering the lobby, Jacques and Mike were escorted directly to a waiting vacant freight elevator car, where two more agents stood guard. Two additional agents were stationed in the corridor of the top floor, waiting to escort them to their designated two-room suite.

If the news of the possible issuance of a contract on their live hadn't attracted their full attention, the presence of eight security officers succeeded in convincing Mike and Jacques of the seriousness of their situation.

Following Malone's departure, Mike walked over to the closed, blackout curtains in their suite. After parting them just enough to peer out, he noticed two more agents, equipped with sniper weapons, lying prone on top of the building on the opposite side of the street.

Mike and Jacques didn't have any spare time to worry about what might be happening beyond the walls of their suite. Each morning, following a room-service breakfast, teams of agents would appear lugging heavy briefcases. One morning, after spreading the papers they contained on one of the room's long tables, an agent said, "We would appreciate it if you would carefully study the materials, and tell us what they might mean, or what is missing. Later, we have other matters we would like to discuss."

When one team was finished, another was waiting to proceed. The stream of focused interrogations continued well into the night. Lunch and dinner breaks were observed.

At times, when only Jacques' cooperation was needed, Mike would open the hotel room door, stand in the doorway, and absentmindedly observe the agents carefully screening guests who were arriving on the floor. When the freight elevator door opened at the far end of the hall, he watched the agent inspect each housekeeper's pass and check her identity against a list he had been provided. Next, he would inspect the piles of sheets and towels on her cart, the containers of cleaning materials, and the bins for used linens and discarded trash. Only after determining that all was in order would he motion for the two-woman teams to proceed.

Day after day, Mike watched as the housekeeping teams, starting from opposite ends of the long hall, and gradually, on a room-by-room basis, made their way toward their suite. Today, his attention was drawn to a two-person team emerging from a room two doors to the left on the opposite side of the hall. Their large cart was heavily laden; one of the women pushed it and the other pulled it as they entered the next room.

Mike noticed that they were smartly dressed in their hotel uniforms, and he was admiring their industrious efforts when he noticed the shoes of the housekeepers. Somehow, they seemed different from those he had observed on the other housekeepers. Scuff marks marred their chalk-white appearance. They looked well worn. The stack of clean linens and towels seemed to be higher, not lower, and the baskets for dirty linen and trash appeared to be empty.

After retreating into the suite, he mentioned his observation to one of the ever-present Secret Service agents. Without hesitating, the agent picked up a phone, asked for a private line, and announced "Shift Change! I repeat, Shift Change!"

Within five minutes, a van carrying the next shift change of agents pulled to a stop in full view of the front entrance of the hotel. Four agents entered the hotel.

Jacques and Mike were surprised when two of the agents -- closely resembling Jacques' and Mike's own coloring, size, and weight -- emerged from the connecting rooms. Following instructions, the agents asked Mike and Jacques to remove their outer clothing. The two men's interest was piqued when the two agents also started to undress. After exchanging clothes, the two agents moved over to the suite's game table, sat down, and started to play a game of gin.

Jacques and Mike joined the other two agents who were standing in the hall and quietly followed them as they made their way down to the service level before departing from the hotel.

Thirty minutes later, the two suspect housekeepers were preparing to enter the living-room portion of the two-bedroom suite. When their knock on the door failed to produce the proper verbal response, they used their house key to unlock the door. They announced "Housekeeping!" before pushing and pulling the heavily loaded cart into the room. Inside the room, they saw two men seated at the game table, ignoring their presence, seemingly intent on their gin game.

Following what appeared to have been a carefully rehearsed plan, the two women reached into their stack of towels and linens, withdrew their weapons, and pointed them directly at the two men. With their concentration focused on the card players, the housekeepers failed to see the two Secret Service agents who had entered from the adjoining room with their weapons drawn. Suddenly noticing their unexpected presence, the two surprised housekeepers shifted their gazes long enough for the two agents, sitting at the table, to stand up with their weapons drawn.

Faced with four weapons pointed in their direction, the two women dropped their guns and raised their hands. They were told to move the cart out into the hall and to roll it to the freight elevator. The captured maids did as instructed.

A second van was waiting at the service entrance to the garage. Unnoticed by any of the hotel guests, the housekeepers were escorted into the Secret Service van and began their journey to a secret location, beyond the reach of lawyers.

From the onset of the questioning, it was quickly determined the two women weren't regularly employed by the hotel to clean rooms. They were employed by the "Sampson" security organization.

Sampson and the Sentinels were not strangers. They had encountered each other on two previous occasions. Sampson's involvement indicated the seriousness of their confidential employer's intention to prevent any interruption of their carefully planned takeover of Iran and its oil production.

At the White House, the president and his kitchen cabinet were discussing how to take advantage of the unprovoked attack on Mike and Jacques. Roger Malone was speaking, "Mr. President, making your case with the British could become much more effective once you have had the opportunity to talk to Mike and Jacques. They are available to meet with you at your earliest convenience."

Chapter Fifty-Four
"Mike and Jacques Report"

THE OVAL OFFICE: December 1953

Three weeks had elapsed since Mike and Jacques had departed Paris for Washington. Taking advantage of the presence of existing surface, artesian-fed oil ponds, Harshim combined his familiarity of the desert with common sense in determining the locations for the initial drilling sites. Progress had been made at the drilling site. Harshim, with the benefit of his quant earth-moving equipment, had finished the construction and compacting of the first four drilling pads.

The drilling crews were pleasantly surprised to find the drill pads were ready. It was obvious to them that Sam, the engineers, and his network of distributors had located and purchased all the materials listed on Naraghi-Independent's shopping list. Open trenches, to hold the large-diameter pipes that would be needed to transport oil to storage tanks, crisscrossed each pad. Roadbeds capable of supporting the heavy, loaded tanker trucks were being excavated. Truckloads of surface aggregate, needed to construct the roadbeds, were arriving on site and being dumped into the roadbeds, where they were compacted to engineered specifications. Big trucks carrying hot asphalt were dumping their loads into a machine that applied the asphalt in smooth, even layers. Self-propelled, heavy rolling machines were standing by to apply the last of the prescribed compaction. As predicted, by the end of the third week, drilling commenced.

Plentiful supplies of oil were soon discovered within five thousand feet of the surface. The hastily built storage tanks were beginning to fill. Empty tanker trucks were waiting to be filled with oil and to transport it to Abadan. Unfortunately, they had to wait for the oil freighters to arrive in port. Without any place to store the oil, the loaded trucks were forced to wait for the next available ship.

Jacques and Mike were sitting in the president's office, delivering their most recent progress report. The president's chief of staff said, "Mr. President, as difficult as it is to believe all the progress that has been made in such a short period of time, I have received independent reports confirming that what these gentlemen are telling us is accurate.

In my opinion, these collaborative efforts suggest Nation-Independent Oil Ltd., understands the importance of fulfilling all of Congress's stipulations."

Jacques said, "While we have every confidence we can produce the stipulated oil in deliverable commercial quantities, we are concerned we may not be able to comply with the *'delivered oil'* requirement.

"From our Israeli sources, we understand that many of the ships needed to deliver our oil are prevented from reaching our port in Abadan. Are you familiar with the term 'secondary boycott'? Quite simply, it means the denial of delivery and/or acceptance is interrupting the orderly flow of goods to their intended market. Our source inside Mossad reports that the Anglo-American oil combine has threatened to exclude any ships delivering Nation-Independent Oil from future chartering considerations. Without those ships, we have only a limited access to ships to deliver our oil. And then we must be concerned about those ships being interdicted by warships of the Royal Navy. By employing secondary boycott tactics, they hope to prevent our chartered tankers from delivering our oil."

"Are you telling me the British government and the Anglo-American oil companies are attempting to introduce delaying tactics similar to the ones they used to prevent the Majlis from passing our competitive oil bidding legislation until a regime change could be accomplished?" the president asked.

"Like the rest of you, I have spent considerable time trying to figure out how the coup and regime change were able to take place without our knowledge or consent. There can only be one explanation. The power and influence of the Anglo-American oil companies, working with the British government, the CIA, and MI-6 can operate independent of the perceived authority of the American government. This situation is unacceptable and can't be allowed to occur a second time! I now think it is necessary for me to have a little chat with the British prime minister!"

The president, the secretary of state, and the chief of staff were sitting in the Oval Office when the British ambassador arrived. Never one to mince words, the president asked, "Mr. Ambassador, are you aware that private operatives, most likely employed by Sampson Security and retained by the Anglo-American oil companies, have attempted to kill or compromise my two guests -- whom you have just met -- while they were staying at the Willard Hotel?"

Without waiting for a response, the president continued, "We have also received word the British Fleet is preparing to weigh anchor in Southampton and proceed with all possible haste to the Persian Gulf. According to our sources, they have received orders to interdict Independent Oil shipping once the enabling legislation has been approved by both houses of your Parliament.

"At the same time, we have been informed that the enabling legislation has been placed on your fast-track approval program.

"As you are aware, the Anglo-American oil companies have threatened to withhold future chartering orders of shipping with any company or ships transporting Independent Oil from the port of Abadan. I assume your prime minister understands the illegality of secondary boycotts, as spelled out by International Maritime Law.

"Mr. Ambassador, it is critical your government understands the possible repercussions I am prepared to invoke unless all these efforts to obstruct are immediately canceled."

"Mr. President, in anticipation of this meeting, I took the liberty of talking to the prime minister," the ambassador responded. "He has asked me to inquire if it is your intention to interfere with our internal governmental process. We are accustomed to giving instructions to the Royal Navy and to our contracted fleet of privately owned and chartered ships without the interference of outside parties. Similarly, we are not aware of any approvals that are required before we introduce proposed legislation to Parliament."

The president responded without hesitation. "Mr. Ambassador, I would suggest you cut the bullshit and listen very carefully to what I am about to say. We have in custody the two female Sampson operatives who were assigned to capture or kill my two guests in residence at the Willard Hotel. Perhaps you might be interested to hear what they have told us?

"Second, we have received reports from three shipping companies that any opportunity for them to continue service to Anglo-American oil shipments will be suspended should they deliver Independent Oil.

"Finally, I am about to hand you a copy of a recent executive order I have signed. It reads: 'To the extent that Great Britain has violated or is attempting to violate secondary boycott laws or has committed any other crimes in international waters, I am prepared to endorse Naraghi-Roth-Independent as a valid American Foreign Investment independent of it completing all the necessary terms that are required for ratification. Once the company is protected by the United States military, any attack on it or its representatives will constitute an act of war."

The British ambassador's face turned red as he spoke. "Mr. President, are you suggesting the United States is prepared to declare war against Great Britain over a disputed interest in Iranian oil?"

"Mr. Ambassador, declaring war on a longtime ally is not the option I have in mind. You can inform your prime minister that, should the British government be identified with another act of naked imperialism, the American government is prepared to withdraw its support from the shah government and Anglo-American oil operations in Iran. At the same time, we expect to make it quite clear that we have no intention now, or at any other time, to allow third-party self-interests to take precedence over the authority of the American government!

"The question you need to ask your prime minister is this: *'Is the value of interfering with Nation and its arrangement with Independent Oil worth unraveling the current Iranian situation?'*"

Understanding the implication of the president's announcement, the British ambassador, who by now was ashen-faced, quietly said, "Thank you, Mr. President, I understand your point of view and I am prepared to relay it to the prime minister." That ended the meeting.

Following the ambassador's quick exit, Chairman Malone turned toward his two younger friends and said, "Jacques, Mike, you may have just witnessed your president make history. Do you have any questions?"

Mike asked, "Mr. President, not that we aren't grateful for your support, but why have you singled out our oil venture for special treatment? Some would question if the protection of one more oil-producing operation merits such unprecedented action. What is it that we don't understand?"

"Jacques, Mike, if it were simply a question of one more oil investment, I might have chosen a different path. My decision to present the British and the Anglo-American oil companies with a draconian ultimatum stem from my much broader concern for the preservation of a great humanitarian effort, and the authority of the American government.

"Then, there is the question of Nation. For decades, the American government and the rest of the world have watched the Naraghi and Roth families' continuing efforts to make the world a better place. It's not just these observations that have encouraged us to cooperate. The White House, members of Congress, and the press have been receiving an unprecedented volume of letters in support of Nation. You may surmise that that support has affected the votes of the friends and relatives of your Citizen Farmer families, fans of your graduate Advanced Prep ambassadors, and your many well-informed, financial contributors.

"We hope that, by responding to our global audience and by asserting our continuing interest in protecting emerging sovereign nations from external attack, the American government might regain its goodwill and remove any further discussion about Iran's regime from the front page.

"Let's not overlook how hard you worked to provide me with an alternative way to prevent the completion of Ajax. Although we may never be certain, I choose to believe that, had the American government not lost control over its covert operations, the regime change in Iran might have been prevented. I'll be damned if I will sit quietly by and allow history to repeat itself.

"Then, we must take into consideration the track record of the Sentinels. For more than ten years, the American government has watched as the Sentinels opposed different, well-organized agendas of irresponsible self-interest. Through no fault of your own, your efforts may not have stopped the unfortunate takeover of the Iranian government and its oil fields, but I will not tolerate any further efforts to compromise your Nation of Citizen Farmers and the interest of an American oil company doing business in a foreign country."

Continuing, the president said, "I hope you and your colleagues are aware your work represents an important reason why the Sentinels' efforts will undoubtedly be needed to oppose future agendas of power-hungry groups.

"Which brings me to my final point. Have you considered the consequence of converting the Sentinel program from a loosely organized effort of a few committed and dedicated individuals into a well-financed, independent organization? Properly developed, an independent organization could enhance your research abilities by developing new curricula to support what you are learning. And, most important, by recruiting and training the personnel needed to expand your current activities and, some day, to serve as your replacements. If you haven't already considered the idea, I strongly suggest you begin to think about organizing a Sentinel Institute to perpetuate what you have started."

As they stood up, preparing to leave, Jacques asked, "Mr. President, on behalf of the Naraghi and Roth families, I would like to thank you by telling you a little story. Had we failed to earn the respect and cooperation of the White House, Nation would no longer exist.

In 1932, before World War II, your government's decision to recognize the Nation of Citizen Farmers as part of the United States' hands-off Middle Eastern policy provided us with the protection, we needed to shield ourselves from Hitler's Nazi government. We referred to this process as an effective deterrent.

Now, twenty years later, due to the perceived parallel nature of our mutual best interests, you are once again making it possible for Nation to enjoy the protection of the United States. I only wish the rest of our families could be here to personally thank you."

Chapter Fifty-Five
"Re-Wrap at Versailles"

CHATEAU ROTH: April, 1954

In London, the attempt by Parliament to pass the "Blockade" legislation was tabled. In Southampton, the oil-fired furnaces of the Royal Naval fleet were extinguished. Chartered oil freighters were lining up in the Port of Abadan.

In Versailles, the excitement of achieving the long-sought "Effective Deterrent" demanded a second "Wrap Retreat." Pierre and his wife, Eliane Roth, sent invitations to Natalie Cummins, George White, two generations of Naraghis and their wives, Tom York, Smohl Cantor, Alan Kahne, Dr. Tom Burdick, Henri Demaureux, Claudia and Jacques Roth, Cecelia and Mike and Morgan Stone.

In responding, Alan Kahne requested if it would be acceptable for him to bring a mystery guest.

The arriving guests had assembled in the shade of the entry portico. They were watching as the last limousine made its way up the circular, tree-lined drive. When it pulled to a stop, Smohl was the first to step out. He was followed by Major Alan Kahne, smartly dressed in his well-pressed, Israeli military dress uniform.

For most of those assembled, this was the first time they would have the opportunity to meet the man who had provided so much assistance to them. It was only natural that they focused their attention on the shorter, slim, well-conditioned man with a well-tanned, bald head and big ears.

Stepping forward, Mike Stone greeted both men with a handshake and a tight hug. Before he could make any introductions, a well-dressed, pleasant-looking woman emerged from the limousine, stood next to Alan, and held his hand. A smiling Major Kahne said, "Mike, Smohl, I would like to introduce you to Dr. Suzanne Strauss, a professor of nuclear engineering at Israel's Weizmann Institute, who has recently become an incredibly special person in my life.

"Over the last few months, Suzanne and I have become well acquainted. We have traveled together and lived together with her two teenage daughters. Not only have we become attached, but for the first time in my life, I have learned to appreciate the importance of having a great companion, a family, and a real home."

While Mike was pleased by what he was hearing, he was wondering what kind of a message the man he knew to be David Marcus was trying to impart. Since he and Smohl were the only two who knew of Major Kahne's true identity, Mike was trying to understand why Alan would have brought a mystery guest to a highly confidential retreat.

Following the introductions, Pierre motioned for the guests to join him on the rear terrace, which was dotted by buckets filled with ice and bottles of France's very finest vintage Champagnes. The waiters were holding large trays of Beluga sorted caviar, smoked salmon, steak tartare, and the house favorite, pommes soufflées.

The eighteen guests had divided themselves into groups of two and three and were sampling hors d'oeuvres and Champagne while excitedly talking to one another. People moved seamlessly from one conversation to another.

Without trying to make their interest obvious, everyone was looking forward to speaking with Alan and the mysterious and enchanting Dr. Suzanne Strauss.

Not wishing to interrupt the moment, Madame Roth delayed her announcement of dinner for fifteen minutes. As was her custom, she motioned for Pierre to escort her to her place at the head of the table, which had been set for the eighteen guests. Place cards bearing their names had been set on the table, just above the dinner plates.

Pierre, after standing to make his traditional welcoming toast, noticed the seat between Dr. Strauss and Smohl was vacant. Directing his attention to Smohl, he said, "It would be nice if we all started together. I have prepared some special remarks that include Major Kahne. Would you mind checking on our missing guest? Please inform him we are waiting on him before we begin."

Smohl agreed to do so and left the room. Three-minutes later, Smohl reappeared and announced, "I wasn't able to locate Alan, but I ran into someone else who wishes to say hello."

David, with his red wig and bushy red eyebrows carefully attached, dressed in an expertly tailored, dark-blue business suit and an outrageous red tie, could be seen standing in the dining room entrance.

Shock, confusion, and disbelief would hardly describe the first reactions of the Sentinels upon seeing their colleague, whom they had presumed was dead. Before they could recover, David Marcus quickly made his way to where Suzanne was sitting. His first words were, "Suzanne Strauss, may I introduce Sir David Marcus?"

Stepping back to see her reaction, he was surprised when she said, "David Marcus, I recognized you when you first appeared. What do you think I have been doing since you first revealed your true identity? You have to admit, the life and times of Sir David Marcus have been well reported. It hasn't been difficult to track you and the exploits of your former life. Now that I have met your friends, I have a question: Why have you chosen to reveal David Marcus?"

But before David could answer, he was interrupted by his friends, who rushed to greet their long-lost colleague, asking questions non-stop. As the excitement began to subside, Jacques asked, "David, where the hell have you been hiding?"

"In plain sight. I am surprised you didn't recognize me when I attended Smohl's Third Alternative Conference in Tel Aviv."

"David, with your red hair, how could Cecelia, Mike, and I have failed to notice you?"

Stepping back and flashing his big smile, David said, "Maybe this might help?" Quickly, he removed his red wig and bushy eyebrows. His tanned bald head and his big ears were immediately apparent. He removed his coat, his dress shirt, his tie, and his suit pants, revealing the same Israeli military uniform he had been wearing when he arrived. Standing erect in his best military posture, he announced, "Major Kahne, reporting for duty!"

Obviously, an explanation was required. Smohl was the first to speak. "David's resurrection from his kidnapping started when Pierre, in this very house, asked for my assistance in arranging his release. Once the upper echelon of Whitehall learned the government was holding Sir David Marcus, denying him access to legal counsel even though they had not charged him with a crime, they realized that this created an enormous potential liability for the government. The problem of his illegal incarceration was quickly resolved, provided we agreed to keep his arrest a secret. It was my idea to re-invent him as a Mossad-trained, secret agent.

"You must hand it to the Mossad. They changed his appearance, trained him to be a fully conditioned Mossad agent, taught him to speak Hebrew, and provided him with access to our secret petroleum archives. Included in the files were D'Arcy's original reports. After studying those reports, David discovered that his early explorations had examined petroleum potential, not just in Iran, but elsewhere in the

Persian Gulf and its surrounding territories. Although his reports revealed the likely presence of petroleum in the Saudi Arabian states and in Iran, they failed to indicate the possible presence of enormous underground reserves of natural gas.

"Convinced of the underground presence of petroleum, the then-shah of Iran employed the geological services of Sir Edmond D'Arcy to search for Iranian oil reservoirs. Three years later, D'Arcy found it necessary to raise the cash he needed to complete his assignment. When the Naraghis offered to provide him with the needed funds in exchange for acquiring the mineral rights under Nation properties, he readily accepted. As part of the transaction, the Iranian government provided its consent, which it recorded in Iran's public records of 1921.

Smohl continued, "Changing David Marcus's appearance represented our first challenge. You would be amazed by what we were able to accomplish with ninety days of rigorous boot camp physical training. That was the easy part. Establishing Major Alan Kahne as a highly valuable oil consultant represented the more difficult challenge. Fortunately, with all the rapid changes taking place in the Middle Eastern oil community, we had no trouble arranging for him to be retained by his unsuspecting former clients. That is when we first tested the changes in his physical appearance. None of his former clients made the connection between Alan Kahne and David Marcus. When word of his excellent work began to circulate, the Anglo-American oil companies came calling."

"But there is more to the story" Mike said. "In addition to providing us with vital information, he played an important role in organizing our current arrangement with Independent Oil. It was during our Independent-Naraghi-Roth organizing conference in New York that Mr. Kahne suggested that Naraghi-Roth could achieve the effective deterrent against foreign intervention that they had been seeking by consummating an arrangement with the Independent Oil Company. At the same time, this could provide Independent Oil with a backup solution should they fail to obtain approval from the Majlis.

"After listening to Major Kahne's suggestion, I became suspicious. Unless he had been present at the Versailles strategic planning summit, how could he have known what we had discussed? Later, when Mr. Kahne and I were having a discussion in my office, he revealed his working arrangement with Smohl and provided me with that information. When I started to question him about why Smohl would be willing to divulge such confidential information, it occurred to me that Alan Kahne and David Marcus might be the same person. Since then, only Smohl and I have known of Major Alan Kahne's true identity.

"By the time Smohl invited his protégé to attend his Third Alternative organizational conference in Tel Aviv, we had decided to test if he was vulnerable to recognition by those who had previously known him as Sir David Marcus. Knowing two of the original Sentinels would be attending, we felt their reaction to Alan's presentation would be a good test. It was a risk we had to take before we could ask him to continue working for Anglo-American Iranian Oil."

Cecelia, who was having a difficult time comprehending what Mike was saying, suddenly interrupted. "I remember attending that meeting. Not once did I suspect that Alan Kahne and David Marcus were one and the same."

Turning toward David, she asked, "Your personal risk must have been immense. How did a worldly connoisseur of fine wine and beautiful women even think about becoming involved in what had to have been an extremely dangerous mission?"

"It was not so difficult," David responded. "Based on what I was able to learn during my incarceration in London, I concluded the Sentinels were involved in a profoundly serious and dangerous game. That is when I decided to become actively engaged in secretly helping you to oppose Ajax. When Smohl suggested I become a Mossad agent, I understood that, by providing the Anglo-American oil companies with information, I would be secretly working for my Sentinel colleagues.

"Let us not forget, it was my call from Tehran that focused your attention on the threat against Iran and, indirectly, against Nation. Had we anticipated that Anglo-American Oil was planning to circumvent the authority of the American president, we might have prevented Ajax from taking place. In any event, we succeeded in protecting Naraghi-Roth's Nation of Citizen Farmers. I will always be proud of what our collective energies were able to achieve."

The excitement caused by David's reappearance dominated the remaining part of the evening. The wine buckets were filled and refilled. '*Old David*' stories were being told. Suzanne was kept busy asking and answering questions. At one point, Jacques observed her standing in a corner with Kate and Natalie engrossed in what appeared to be serious conversation. He was thinking, *Will we ever learn what these three women dedicated to change are discussing?*

The next morning, over breakfast, David was asking what he should plan to do next. He paused to choose his words carefully, and then said, "Last night's experience has made me stop and reconsider my previous decision to remain Major Alan Kahne. Before coming here, I was convinced I could better serve myself and the Sentinels by continuing in my role as a Middle Eastern oil consultant.

"Naturally, I was intrigued with the idea of seeing you and receiving your affection and appreciation. Never, at any time, did I consider revealing my former self. Then, as I was being introduced to each of you as a stranger, something snapped. Seeing you standing together under the portico and later, on the rear terrace, expressing your pride over what we have accomplished, I realized how much working with you has meant to me. There was no way I could stand the idea of your not knowing I was alive and still working with you! That is when I knew I had to reveal Sir David Marcus.

"Even though my cover may be compromised, it shouldn't make a big difference. Now that the Iranian-British situation has been settled, why would my association with the Sentinels and the Mossad make a difference? If my services as a petroleum consultant are contracted, why would my different appearance discourage anyone from accepting my research results?

"More importantly, Suzanne and I have succeeded in developing a wonderful relationship, one that I am not interested in jeopardizing by pretending I'm someone who I'm not. I hope you will understand."

Chapter Fifty-Six
"Giving Birth"

THE SENTINEL INSTITUTE: APRIL, 1954

It was over the breakfast table the next morning that the subject of a Sentinel Institute was first opened for discussion. Pierre was speaking. "Now that our more immediate problems appear to be settled, Harshim and I have another item we need to discuss. Following the suggestion of the American president, we have been studying his comments regarding the organization of a Sentinel Institute.

"In our minds, the preservation of Nation and the realization of so much petroleum wealth would not have been accomplished without the Sentinels' assistance. When we coupled our achievements with your efforts to oppose major-powers' self-serving agendas of abuse, we realized how important it is to preserve the Sentinels and what you have accomplished."

Pierre then walked over to his trusted friend and partner, Harshim, put his arm around his shoulders and asked, "Would someone care to explain how a simple game of darts forty-five years ago could lead to all that we have been able to achieve by working together? As we stood on the brink of seeing our efforts come to fruition, we were forced to accept the possibility it all could be destroyed and taken away from us.

"For the last three days, I have had the privilege of participating in a most enlightening discussion with my trusted partner and our Sentinel friends. There is no doubt in our minds that, without the Sentinels' imaginative and capable assistance, all we have worked for and the lives of our citizen farmers and loyal employees would have been crushed under the heavy boot of the Anglo-American oil companies and the despotic shah government.

"You have done more than oppose bad things from happening. You have made it possible for a remarkable humanitarian effort to evolve to touch many more lives. Out of this perception, Harshim and I have concluded Naraghi-Roth would like to become a permanent friend and financial supporter of Sentinel.

"It has come to our attention that the cost of expanding the Sentinel Institute to include the curriculum required to teach water-land management and the purveyance of human services will be significant.

"I am proud to announce that Harshim and I have agreed the Naraghi-Roth partnership is prepared to match the two hundred million dollars that have already been pledged by your other 'Friends of Sentinel'."

Stunned silence marked the Sentinels' reaction. Never in their wildest imagination had they believed such generosity from any single entity might be possible. Finally, a grateful Cecelia Chang Stone stood. After taking her time to organize her thoughts, she said, "Something has changed! When I made my earlier rounds to test the interest of our Sentinel Friends, I learned they placed a high value on our ability to oppose bad things and to keep them from happening. Rarely did anyone focus their attention on the potential value of what was being threatened.

"Pierre, Harshim, if I correctly interpret your impressive expression of generosity, you are making it possible for us to focus our attention on what is being threatened and, when appropriate, to offer our continued protection and cooperation to assist them in realizing their potential.

"On behalf of all that is Sentinel, I would like to express our gratitude for all you have taught us. Without your example, we might not have been able to recognize what must be our second hand. When I think in terms of one hand washing the other, I can really become excited."

Claudine said, "Twenty years ago, when I asked for the other Sentinels' help to prevent the German industrialists from using their 'Fortunes of War' to fund a Fourth Reich, it never occurred to me that, by creating the Gold Bear Bond, we made it possible to protect and nourish the efforts of the worthy and responsible leadership."

Jacques said, "Never let it be said that searching for Sam, under the Paris Stadium, would turn out to be such a rewarding adventure. Little did Sam and I know, when we were aboard that old ship taking us from France to Cyprus, we would be learn that those families were risking all that they had to find a new life because they wanted to create a better future for their children.

"How were we to know that, by surviving our night in an Israeli observation bunker, the friendships Sam, Sarah, and I developed would allow us to help people realize those dreams? How can anyone argue that Sally's concept of Advanced Preparation hasn't made it possible for so many gifted children to push back the boundaries of their lives?"

"Wait a minute," Sam said, "Without the creative contributions of my mother Kate, the Red Queen, and my wife, Sarah, what we refer to as the Nation of Citizen Farmers, Human Services may never have come into being.

"If Kate had not envisioned the idea of her lease-to-own land concept, the Nation of Citizen Farmers may never have had the humanitarian foundation it has today.

"When Jacques and I arrived in Cyprus, we encountered the tent cities that had been set up to take care of the sick and the enfeebled. On one side of the tents, we could see people standing in long lines waiting to be admitted. On the other side, we witnessed people carrying litters filled with the bodies of the dead toward mass, unmarked graves.

"At that moment, it became indelibly clear you can't talk about groups of people without considering their health care needs. Where can you find a better public example of providing for people's health care needs than the system Kate established when she figured out how to bring UDEH Medical service to Ahvaz, and mesh it with our local emergency care hospitals?"

When Kate rose to speak, there was no question in anyone's mind that she had something important to say. "You have been quite complimentary of Sally's and my work, but I would like to remind you that none of these things would have happened if it hadn't been for the Naraghis' commitment to bring water to the desert, and the Roths' financial support.

For forty-five years, we have been learning how to harness and transport water to the desert. We have been learning how to produce the crops that feed people. We have been learning how to develop this process of land development and crop production into a successful vertically integrated agri-business empire. We have learned how to develop an international trading company to introduce our production to foreign markets. We have learned to develop, process and market petroleum products for the international market. We have developed a system of human services that improve peoples' lives.

"By funding the organization of a more complete Sentinel Institute, you are making it possible for the Sentinel Institute to teach others not only the lessons we have learned from our experiences with Naraghi-Roth, but how to protect their interests from concentrated wealth's abusive agendas.

Epilogue

Kate and Harshim Naraghi:

After discussing the goals of the pending Sentinel Institute with Cecelia and the other Sentinels, Kate saw an opportunity to leverage her knowledge by becoming involved in the Sentinel Institute teaching process. She said, "After devoting forty years of living and working in the desert world of dams, quants, irrigation districts, and humanitarian needs, I have decided that the time has arrived for Harshim and me to join in the Sentinel Institute effort and assist in organizing and teaching the curriculum required to pass along all we have learned."

To Kate's surprise, Harshim offered no resistance to her suggestion. He said, "With no more water to harness or land to irrigate, my services are no longer needed here at Ahvaz. Why shouldn't I take advantage of the institute to develop water reclamation and land management courses that can be employed in other places?

"Besides, living in Carmel could be interesting. Views of the ocean, white beaches, cypress forests, and great golf courses would represent a pleasant contrast to a lifetime of desert living. Who knows, maybe the time has come for me to take up golf?"

Sam and Sally Raphael Naraghi:

Neither Sam nor Sally was suffering any illusions. Halting the addition of land would not materially change the need for their presence and management services in Ahvaz. The demands of N-R Trading, Advanced Prep and UDEH-Nation Medical would still require their leadership. Besides, birthing and raising the next generations of Naraghis was their top priority.

Intrigued by the potential of the Sentinel Institute, Sally asked, "Why shouldn't admittance to the institute represent an exciting new alternative for some of our more adventurous Advanced Prep graduates? Perhaps I need to free up some time to meet and talk to the entrance officers at the Sentinel Institute."

Sam's view was different. "The continued growth of N-R Trading, both in geographical terms and by volume of activity, is creating opportunities for entrepreneurial, responsible leaders. What better way could there be than to include international trading and commerce in the institute's curriculum, and, at the same time, have a first bite at the more outstanding graduates? Who knows, regular visits to Carmel by the Sea might become an important way for Sally and me to expand our world beyond rural desert living."

Alan Kahne and Suzanne Strauss:

Alan, dressed in his military uniform, and Suzanne were waiting at the gate to board their flight to Tel Aviv. She sensed he had something important on his mind. Once they were seated in the plane, she asked, "Obviously, Major Kahne boarded the plane. Won't it be interesting to see who gets off -- Major Kahne or David Marcus? I want you to understand, feeling about you the way I do, that I can live with either one. It's your decision."

Their plane, flying over the Mediterranean Sea, was approaching Israel's coastline when he broke the prolonged silence.

"Give me a minute to change. David Marcus will be accompanying you to Israel.

"In thinking through my dilemma, I have come to three conclusions. First, and most important, I want to spend the rest of my life loving you, enjoying watching your girls grow up, and traveling with you.

"Second, I realize I can serve only one master. It's time for me to declare my support for Middle Eastern Oil. Following my resignation from English Oil, I devoted my time to developing Middle Eastern Oil's trust, and when the opportunity arose, to representing their interests as best I could. Now that we have witnessed what can happen when major oil companies supported by their governments attempt to become involved in the world of Middle Eastern Oil, I believe my clients will need my assistance.

"Finally, when the opportunity presents itself for us to travel, I think David Marcus can be a more charming companion."

Jacques and Claudine:

Claudine started the conversation, "Perhaps the time has come when we need to re-evaluate our Sentinel roles. First of all, when we have children, we need to ensure that they will not have to compete with our Sentinel activities for our attention. If we were to organize the

Demaureux-Roth International School of Finance at the Institute, might we be able to lock in the kind of lives we will need to lead if we are to have enough time to love and raise each of our children?

Jacques, "Claudine, I agree with everything you have just said, but I would like to add a few thoughts of my own. Effective and responsible leadership is not something you learn from a book; their achievement has to evolve by working with people of accomplishment. Don't you think we need to make ourselves available to the new students that will be attending the institute?

Smohl:

"In thinking about my future, I am convinced that I want to continue to contribute to the future of Israel. I have been informed by my government that the Israelis expect me to play a dual role – They want me to remain alert to the emergence of new ideas that will contribute to the betterment of Israel, and work to ensure that these programs are well supported by the world's philanthropic organizations. I am looking forward to this assignment. Not only will it provide me with an opportunity to work with my Sentinel friends, but I will have the opportunity to forge new relationships with exciting new groups of young people who will undoubtedly emerge. This new role will still allow me all the time I will need to devote to Suzanne, to our family, and to take advantage of traveling with my exciting new partner."

The New Sentinels Trilogy

Book 2: Big Money
Who is in Control?

In the wake of the Kennedy assassination, Sentinel Institute graduates, with the formidable Madame Cecelia by their side, embark on a daring mission to unveil an insidious plan that exploits public fear for profit, masterminded by an ancient Cartel fueled by dark money. Unearthing secrets dating back 150 years to Europe's 'Financial Elite,' the sinister Federal Reserve, and J.P. Morgan's clandestine Jekyll Island meeting, their journey unveils a financial web that transcends borders and challenges the very foundations of power.

Throughout history, concentrations of wealth and influence have pursued self-serving agendas that, if unopposed, would be achieved at the expense of the public's best interests. Who Is in Control? is the story of how the Sentinels combine their respective skills to oppose the Estate of Organized Capitalism's (EState's) efforts to promote and escalate the United States' involvement in foreign disputes that, invariably, lead to increased defense spending.

Big Money unravels the Sentinels' battle against the Estate of Organized Capitalism's plan to manipulate U.S. involvement in foreign conflicts, driving increased defense spending. Recent Sentinel graduates and Madame Cecelia unite to expose this agenda, armed with three years of doctoral research, challenging the military-industrial complex's influence on national decisions. This historical saga reveals their struggle to protect the public's best interests.

Book 3: Restoring the Dream
Making it in America

In a remarkable tale of bringing jobs back to America and championing the common people over the wealthy few, the Six Sentinels rally a resurgence akin to 'The Greatest Generation' restoring America to Superpower status.

In 1995, as American jobs flow overseas due to lower labor costs, a graduating Sentinel doctoral group unveils a groundbreaking plan: harness federal value creation to subsidize domestic job expenses. To enact vital tax legislation, the Sentinels must rally public support to challenge the entrenched power of offshore manufacturers backed by Big Money.

A historic showdown where the people's will takes on corporate interests in a battle to reshape the future of American manufacturing. The New Sentinels final mission is to rally public support by introducing a groundbreaking plan to generate federal value and subsidize domestic jobs.

Their valiant efforts culminate in a successful movie franchise, showcasing the power of entertainment to unite a nation by exposing the corruption of politics and celebrating the enduring legacy of unsung heroes.

Made in United States
North Haven, CT
26 July 2024

55489337R00157